To Mrs Mur...
Here is
story. I h...
I hope you ... ...e but I
have taken the liberty of dedicating
it to JOFF.

GODSONS

RETRIBUTION

Paul G...

by

PAUL GAIT

Grosvenor House
Publishing Limited

This book is published by
Grosvenor House Publishing Ltd
Link House
140 The Broadway, Tolworth, Surrey, KT6 7HT.
www.grosvenorhousepublishing.co.uk

A CIP record for this book
is available from the British Library

ISBN 978-1-80381-588-6
eBook ISBN 978-1-80381-589-3

Dedicated

To the memory of my childhood friend Jeff Mills
(Author of 'Hugo and the Bird' series)

Thanks

To my wife Helen, for allowing me to spend
countless hours to develop yet another story.

To family and friends for continued
support and encouragement.

To Janet for again spending many hours
proofreading my manuscript.

To my faithful international readership.

Introduction

This novel is the fifth in the Godsons series and follows on immediately from where 'Godsons – That Woman' finishes.

This novel should be read in conjunction with four previous books in the Godsons series: namely:-

'Godsons – Counting Sunsets,'
'Godsons – The Legacy,'
'Godsons – The Inheritance'
'Godsons – That Woman.'

Originally 'That Woman' was going to be the end of the Godsons series, however I felt that there was still potential for more 'adventures' for the Godsons family.

Meet the Godsons Family

If you need a refresher of the characters of the Godsons series before you start to read this novel, here they are, otherwise go to Chapter One:-

Geoffery Foster (56 when he died) – former Cheltonian. Made his millions in the building trade and through wise investments where he increased his fortune significantly. His financial success and business acumen met the strict criteria to be permitted to become a Monaco resident. Totally focused on his business ambitions he never entertained the thought of matrimony nor having children to distract him from his monetary goals.

Unfortunately, two years after an initial diagnosis of prostate cancer and despite intensive treatment, the disease progressed, and the prognosis was terminal.

He returned home to the UK and ended up in a hospice where he met Nurse Andy Spider.

During a review of his life and with no offspring to whom to leave his money, he has a guilt trip about being an absent Godfather. He persuades the nurse to help him find his three Godsons. None of whom he'd had anything to do with since their christenings.

Rather than just bequeathing the Godsons just money in his will, Geoffery sets challenges for them to improve their lives first. Unfortunately, as he is gravely ill, he needs assistance to orchestrate his plans. And he recruits Andy to help him.

Initially Andy is reluctant to get involved until Geoffery offers to buy a new Scout Hut to replace the old one, destroyed in a mysterious arson attack. The Scout Leader is suspicious about Geoffery's involvement in the blaze.

After many adventures and challenges with his Godsons and a predatory woman, Geoffery finally passes away watching his last sunset over the Cotswold Hills.

Nadine Mondegan (39) – born in Monaco (a Monégasque); Nadine was the former partner of Geoffery Foster. She broke off their relationship because she was unable to cope with the physical changes brought about during his cancer treatment. Consequently, Geoffery has 'written her out of his will.' However, as Nadine was with him when he was amassing his fortune, she contends that she's owed some of his legacy and challenges the will. She maintains that, whilst in the hospice, due to his treatment regime, Geoffery was NOT of sound mind when he wrote his final will.

Unfortunately, she is spotted and photographed in an early morning 'liaison' with Andy, the executor of the will, in a Monaco hotel by the predatory woman, Sue Williams-Screen. Consequently, when Andy's wife finds out about the 'innocent' encounter, she ends up in a slanging match with Nadine. They become sworn enemies.

Unwilling to let go of her claim into Geoffery's will, she flies to the UK to discuss her entitlement.

Andy Spider (39) – hospice nurse and Scout Leader; former reluctant aide to Geoffery Foster and Executor to Geoffery's will.

Andy is heavily involved in advising Geoffery on the best method of helping his Godsons. He counsels that the Godsons, should 'earn' their legacy, rather than just receiving a windfall. Hence improving their self-esteem.

Andy ends up administering Geoffery's will and becomes the powerhouse behind all of the Godsons activities.

Andy runs a scout troop for disadvantaged kids in a 'run down' area of the city. One of his Scouts with whom he mentors is Ben Bird, a Young Carer for his substance abuse, alcoholic mother.

Andy is married to Helen, and they have two young children, Amy, and Molly. Following Geoffery's death, Andy inherited his Mercedes and half a million pounds. Andy loves his job at the hospice and in spite of his new wealth, he continues to work 3 days a week; and is at last spending quality time with the family.

Andy's role as executor of Geoffrey's will has brought him into conflict with Sue William-Screen, the former wife of a godson. The enmity was so severe that she wished to murder him. The reason? He appears to be thwarting her plans to claim some of the legacy. A clandestine 'risqué' photograph that Sue took becomes Andy's Achilles heel.

Helen Spider (42) – Andy's long-suffering wife, is Mother to their two children Amy and Molly.

Due to the late-night incident in a hotel with Geoffery Foster's former partner Nadine, she wrongly thinks Andy is having an affair. Consequently, she hates Nadine and has publicly accused her of being a whore!

Nadine has threatened to sue Helen for slander.

Rupert Screen (39) – Godson of Geoffery Foster; (Inherited £5 million from Geoffery's will).

Rupert is Sue William Screen's ex-husband. He has suffered years of domestic abuse and physical violence during their marriage. Encouraged by Geoffery Foster, Rupert eventually worked up enough courage to walk away from his toxic marriage and divorce Sue. Completely out of character this mild-mannered man had an affair with a work colleague Joanne and they eventually marry.

Now remarried Rupert becomes a father of their pre-term baby, Jeffery.

Rupert continues to be traumatised by Sue's presence and fearful that she will re-emerge to threaten him and his family. He employs personal security team to protect his family having been let down by the police service following the kidnaping of their son Jeffrey.

Joanne Screen (39) – wife of now divorced Rupert. Worked in the same computer company as Rupert. Had an illicit affair with him, until Rupert was brave enough to leave his wife, Sue.

Joanne suffered severe spinal injuries in a road traffic collision caused by Sue. At the time Joanne was pregnant and the baby was born pre-term but was not hurt during the collision. From his inheritance, Rupert funds a trip to the USA for Joanne's specialist spinal surgery and she is just starting to walk again. She too is fearful of the spectre that is Sue Williams-Screen.

Sue Williams-Screen (41) – Originally married to Godson Rupert Screen, their marriage fails due to the level of domestic violence that she inflicts on him throughout their time together. She retained her maiden name (Williams) as part of her matrimonial surname. She vigorously resists their divorce.

She 'clashes swords' with Geoffery Foster from their very first meeting when she admits opening Rupert's letter from Geoffery about his legacy. She is upset to discover the legacy will be shared between two other Godsons. The mutual hatred intensifies, when Geoffery tries to frame her for attempted murder by getting her to assist him in a fake suicide bid to end his 'pain-filled life.'

After Geoffery dies, she is keen to get part of Rupert's share of his legacy but due to the divorce, is locked out from receiving any financial fallout.

Her hatred for Geoffery Foster continues even after his death where she violates his grave. Her volatile nature creates a clash with a gravedigger at the local burial ground. The altercation turns violent, and she murders him.

She is eventually reprehended for her various misdemeanours including causing the crash that injured Joanne and is sent to prison. However, the walls don't hold her for long. She escapes several times, kidnaps, and attempts to kill Carrie, the partner of one of the Godsons.

During one failed kidnap, the pair end up trapped in a sinking car in the flood ravaged River Severn. Carrie saves Sue's life, but the savage fight continues on to the muddy riverbank. Attempting to kill Carrie, Sue hits a fallen power line, and she is electrocuted.

But 'the devil looks after his own.' Snatched away by the flooded river, she is eventually plucked from the riverbank by a farmworker, Mike Benson.

During her recovery, Mike hides her from the law and is recruited into helping her in a series of criminal activities including kidnap and extortion. She is number one on the Police most wanted list.

Tim Springfield (38) – Godson of Geoffery Foster. (Inherited £5 million) He is a childhood meningitis double leg amputee. Initially an idle, overweight, unfit person who makes his Mother's life (Kay) a misery by blaming her for his meningitis.

Geoffery's challenge to him is to get fit and mobile enough to climb Ben Nevis. Carrie is a double leg amputee too and fitness instructor whom Geoffery Foster recruits to transform the idle sloth into an active hiker. During the training, they become romantically attached.

On receiving his legacy from the will, Tim squanders a large amount of his inheritance on gambling in Monaco.

Carrie and Tim now both avid hikers, eventually set up the 'Just Do It' walking company together with the remaining money.

To everyone's surprise, this self-centred man becomes a living liver donor for fellow Godson James (JC).

Carrie (38) – a former special forces soldier. Lost both her legs during army service and now suffers from PTSD. Employed by Geoffery Foster to get Godson Tim, a 'fellow' amputee, fit, so that he would stop wallowing in self-pity and get on with his life.

Now romantically entwined with Tim; she is a joint partner in the 'Just Do it Walking' company aimed at getting 'injured' service personnel back into normal life. Trying to protect Rupert from a beating Carrie attacks

Sue. They become instant enemies. Carrie is eventually kidnapped by Sue to kill her. But during a savage fight, they both end up trapped in a sinking car in a flood ravaged river. Carrie is injured but recovers.

Kay Springfield (57) – Tim's mother. Kay has spoilt Tim all his life. She has a guilt complex about her failure to spot the signs of his meningitis early enough. Unfortunately, the effects of the disease resulted in Tim losing both his legs. She was a former girlfriend of Geoffery Foster and had a drunken sexual encounter with him at her wedding reception when marrying someone else. As a consequence of the liaison, there were paternity questions over the identity of Tim's real father.

Unfortunately, she is in the wrong place at the wrong time and is kidnapped along with baby Jeffery and held for ransom by Sue Williams-Screen. A special police operation thwarts the ransom request and Kay is released, shocked but otherwise unharmed.

James Charles (37) – now known as **JC**; Godson of Geoffery Foster; (Inherited £5 million).Son of another former millionaire; he was orphaned due to a plane crash that killed both his parents. He 'blows' his original inheritance from his late father's estate on wild living.

He has a breakdown after his partner of five years, Sebastian, becomes infected with HIV by a new lover and dies. JC discovers his body.

Sebastian's death pushes JC into a downward spiral of despair and he ends up living as a homeless 'alchy.' on the streets of London. Coincidentally, whilst there, he meets Ben, who has run away from home.

Eventually, after many fruitless attempts by Ben to encourage him to come off the dangerous streets of the capital, Geoffery enters the debate and persuades him. JC eventually becomes 'dry' and sets up home in Cheltenham.

Unfortunately, a 'lifetime' of alcohol abuse has irreversibly damaged his liver and he becomes terminally ill. The prognosis is that he will die unless he receives a donor organ. Fortunately, he is a match with Tim, who, after a lot of persuasion, eventually agrees to donate part of his liver.

JC befriends Beth, Ben's mother, and as he is 'dry' he persuades her to get 'on the wagon' too.

JC buys a new house with his legacy, which he now shares with Beth and Ben.

Ben Bird (16) – Had a rough start to life. He was conceived through a casual sexual encounter by his naive teenager mother and a married man, Mike Benson.

Beth loves Mike but he just used her as a sex object and soon tires of her and leaves her for another teenager. As a result, Beth becomes a depressive alcoholic.

Ben and his mother are therefore a single parent family living in a council house.

Unfortunately, due to his mother's alcoholism, Ben becomes a 'Young Carer' for her at an early age looking after his mother's needs. Eventually Ben joins a Young Carers' group of children who have also been forced to take on a caring role for their parents. At the meeting he met Janie, also a young carer and they become very good friends.

Ben is one of Andy's Scouts, he is mentored by the Scout Leader, who allows him to occasionally sleep in the Scout hut due to his mother's erratic behaviour. The arrangement started after one of his Mum's casual boyfriend's threw him out of his own house in the early hours.

Worn out by his role of looking after his mother, Ben is desperate to find his father. Unfortunately, he is terribly upset when he discovers that his father is Mike Benson. Not the upstanding citizen that he was expecting to find.

Ben has several minor 'run-ins' with the law. He becomes embroiled in an incident with Sue in the Graveyard; and runs away to London; whilst there he helps JC to leave his destitute street life.

Ben is terribly upset following Geoffery's death, as the pair were quite close.

On his new mountain bike, given to him by Geoffery, Ben wins a high-profile race and dedicates the win to Geoffery's memory.

Janie (16) – Ben's girlfriend; also, a 'Young Carer' from a single parent family, due to her mother's ill health; she met Ben at a 'Young Carers' meeting. They hit it off straight away as she goes to the same school as him and shares a passion for mountain biking too and she has won some races. She has a sensible head and tries to keep Ben in check but doesn't always succeed. She took a knife off Ben to prevent him being caught in possession but was herself caught by a teacher as they entered school. She is devastated when she is temporarily expelled. She is Ben's rock

Beth Bird (33) – Ben's alcoholic Mother, made pregnant when she was a teenager by Mike Benson, a married man. She was emotionally devastated when Mike said that he wouldn't divorce his wife and marry her.

Emotionally immature and psychologically damaged by his rejection she took to drink and drugs, forgetting her responsibility to her son. Used her maiden name for Ben's surname. She had a series of boyfriends, who only used her as a sex object too.

Often in a drug induced coma she was not able to stop one boyfriend from throwing Ben out of his house in the middle of the night. Ben's crime was storing his bike in his house, whereupon the boyfriend ripped his trousers on Ben's bike.

After several trips to rehab, financed by Geoffery, she is desperately trying to keep off the alcohol and has been dry for some time now.

She and Ben now live with former alcoholic JC (one of the Godsons). They attend alcoholic support meetings.

Mike Benson (43) – Ben's absent father; a misogynistic bully. Already married to someone else when he made Beth pregnant when she was a teenager and left her shortly after. A devious, 'rough diamond.'

He lives by himself, away from his wife and kids, in a tied farm cottage. He is a farm labourer and enjoys coarse angling and poaching.

When he finds out from his own kids, who go to the same school as Ben, that Ben was associated with Geoffery Foster and had been given new bikes, Mike assumes that Ben has also been given money too. Mike badgers Ben for a share and won't believe Ben when he says he received no money, only bikes. As it's a small community, he knows all about Ben and Beth's business.

Prologue

How do the good intentions of a dying man come to create a hate filled, toxic environment? Because of man's original sin of GREED.

Once the prospect of money was mentioned, the vultures of Greed and Envy started circling menacingly.

It was with the very best of intentions that the Multimillionaire thought that he was being benevolent to his three forgotten Godsons by giving them legacies in his will.

A reminder of his neglected Godfather duties sent him on a guilt trip trying to rectify his failure to uphold his promise taken during their christenings.

But he decided it was not going to be simply a cash handout. There were conditions on their eligibility to receive their inheritances. The terms for receiving their legacies required them to make significant improvements to their lifestyles.

The conditions for the three individuals required that JC, the 'down and out' alcoholic had to become 'dry' Tim, the selfish childhood double leg amputee had to climb a mountain and Rupert, the battered husband had to find courage to walk away from his abusive marriage.

Unfortunately, the unexpected fallout of stepping away from his toxic marriage, meant that Rupert inadvertently created a malevolent cyclone of hatred that permeated all their lives.

Sue Williams-Screen was at the centre of that malevolence. Her greed was all consuming. She had no scruples in pursuing what she considered to be her entitlement of part of Geoffery's legacy.

Her greed sired a dreadful list of crimes including kidnap, extortion, murder, and attempted murder. But somehow, she was always maintained one step ahead of the police in their attempts to catch her.

Her axis of greed included the former girlfriend of the multimillionaire, who also believed that she should have been received a financial windfall in the will. But Geoffery had written the former girlfriend out of it after she'd left him at his lowest emotional point during his illness. Their breakup had ripped Geoffery's heart out.

An unlikely partnership forms when Mike rescues Sue out of the River and shelters her. And then he becomes her partner in crime, but even that evil partnership comes to a dramatic end.

And now after her latest evil act, Sue Williams-Screen was fleeing. Her attempt to shoot and kill the old man's executor, Andy, and his young prodigy Ben, had failed.

In spite of her reckless driving, the banes of her life were still in hot pursuit of her.

Andy's purpose in following her was to find her safe house and report the address to the police. However, her sketchy driving and excessive speed through the narrow Cotswold lanes was proving challenging. And then the chase suddenly ended in a spectacular fashion.

CHAPTER ONE

Sue was perturbed to see the activity across the valley. It looked like her rented 'safe house' was under siege. Had the Police rumbled her?

Unfortunately, the momentary distraction from her high- speed driving, meant that she failed to see the sharp bend in the narrow country lane in time.

Too late she spotted her error, and her heavy braking caused the MX5 to veer off the road. The skidding vehicle hit the verge sideways causing it to tumble viciously and crash through a blackthorn hedge.

'She's crashed, she's crashed,' Ben shouted, anxiously, as the car's taillights became airborne and then disappeared out of sight.

The sound of squealing tyres was replaced by a series of heavy impacts as the car collided with a tree and tumbled across the field smashing the windscreen and window glass. The noise of the crashing car echoed around the hills.

A short distance behind, Andy skidded his car to a halt in a cloud of tyre smoke. And together, with an apprehensive Ben, he quickly ran to investigate.

The pair climbed carefully through the hole in the flattened blackthorn hedge and dashed over to see what had happened to her car.

Illuminated by the bright moonlight, they saw it perched precariously on the edge of a quarry. Gouges in the grass marked the route that the out-of-control MX5 had made as it violently skipped across the field.

Missing bark on a stately oak showed evidence of an impact as the car had glanced off. The collision with the tree had sent it twisting in a series of vicious barrel rolls to land upright on the edge. Precariously balanced with its front wheels on the field, it's back wheels in mid-air, with a hundred-foot drop into a quarry underneath.

As the pair approached the damaged vehicle, they could see the car seesawing on the edge.

The wreck was prevented from sliding into the chalky bottom of the limestone quarry by a strand of barbed wire from a demolished perimeter fence.

Andy studied the situation of the stricken car. Inside they could see Sue moving around. She had been injured in the crash and was conscious but trapped by her leg.

Ben was mesmerised by the car's situation. Frightened of what he was going to see, and pleased to see that she wasn't dead.

'It looks like the devil has thrown you a lifeline again,' Andy shouted, 'You have a piece of barbed wire to thank, for stopping you going to hades.'

'Well don't just stand there, get me out,' she demanded.

'Get you out? How about if instead I released the wire and sent you to your death, you evil bitch,' Andy yelled. 'Why should we save you? You tried to shoot us remember?'

'Pity that I missed,' Sue hissed, obviously in pain.

'Well if I released the wire that would be the end of your evil ways for good then, wouldn't it?'

'Ha, you wouldn't have the balls to do anything like that.' Sue sneered. 'It wouldn't sit right in your liberal conscience, to have killed someone.'

'You're probably right,' he thought. 'As much as I hate you,' he said. 'I wouldn't do anything to kill you and lower myself to your level.'

'What can we do?' Ben asked anxiously.

'I'm tempted just to walk away and let the devil decide her fate,' Andy suggested.

'That's not the sort of person you are though Andy. You are a caring nurse,' Ben observed, nervously.

'As she's already tried and failed to kill you several times. You have a greater reason to help that wire to snap more than I do, Ben,' Andy observed.

'Him!' Sue mocked. He hasn't got the guts either.'

Incredibly, although Sue was aware of the precarious position that she was in, she nevertheless took a perverted pleasure in berating Ben.

He's just a weedy little boy. 'I should have done a better job of setting you up, so you would have really got fingered by the law,' she chuckled evilly.

'Ignore the bitch, Ben. She is talking rubbish as usual.'

'Now call me an ambulance,' Sue demanded. 'I appear to be trapped and I think my leg is broken.'

'Well, unfortunately for you, we don't have our phones. And in your position, we can't do anything about your leg either,' Andy advised.

'Well, my phone must be here somewhere,' she said feeling around in the car, unsuccessfully. 'Where the hell is it,' she ranted.

'It probably got thrown out somewhere in the field,' Andy suggested.

'I wonder if there are any phone boxes around here?' Ben pondered.

'I doubt it. Although there's lots of red telephone boxes, most rural boxes have had their phones removed,' Andy revealed.

'Just get on and do something for Chrissake,' Sue ordered. 'My leg is killing me.'

'All in good time,' Andy said firmly.

Ben studied the wire that was preventing the car going over the cliff.

'We ought to do something soon or she's going to go into the quarry,' he said, staring at the trapped woman.

'Just help me out,' Sue pleaded, as Andy inspected the crumbling edge of the cliff. 'Come on now.' Sue shouted, panicking. 'Stop messing around.'

As she writhed in pain, the car slipped a few more inches over the edge and then stopped, but rocking precariously, it's crushed bodywork groaning against the stone of the cliff edge.

Ben lay down on the grass next to the car and crawled closer.

'Be careful Ben, the car could go over any minute,' Andy said nervously watching the youngster.

'For God's sake help me,' Sue shrieked,

Ben tentatively offered his hand to her over the squashed passenger door.

'Hold my hand,' Ben said, stretching his arm towards her.

'Steady Ben. Be careful. If the car goes over, she will pull you with it.' Andy said, holding onto Ben's legs.

'I can't quite reach her hand,' Ben said desperately. 'What else can we do Andy?'

'I tell you what, I've got some rope in my car.' I'll bring the car in here and we can drag hers away from the edge.

'OK, but hurry,' Ben said dry mouthed.

'Don't do anything stupid Ben. Come away from the edge. I won't be a minute.' Andy said, dashing back to his car.

'See, I told you he didn't have the balls,' Sue ranted. 'He's left you to do it.' She leant over farther to reach Ben's outstretched hand. However, her movement unbalanced the car further and it dislodged the barb wire holding it.

Ben made a desperate grab for Sue's hand, but she was just too far away as the battered car slid over the edge of the limestone field.

Sue screamed, 'HELP ME,' as the car scraped it's death knell.

The wreck hung against the face of the quarry for a few seconds as Ben desperately moved nearer the edge and tried to reach Sue's hand.

Too late, the car slid backwards into the quarry, disappearing in a frightening cacophony of noise as it bounced against the rock walls.

Andy arrived in his car and ran back to Ben with a tow rope.

'You're too late,' Ben informed him, gutted that his rescue attempt had failed.

The noise of crashing suddenly stopped to be replaced by an explosion that echoed around the hills.

A large fireball shot up the face of the cliff, followed by a cloud of thick black smoke.

'What happened?' Andy demanded looking at the shocked youngster.

'I tried to help her, but she got agitated and unbalanced the car. It just went over,' Ben said, shocked.

'You didn't…?'

'Didn't? Didn't what?' Ben puzzled.

'Help her…over?'

'No of course not,' Ben said indignantly. 'As much as I'd loved to have shoved her over, she did this all by herself.' Ben reassured him.

'No of course you wouldn't. I'm sorry.' Andy admonished himself for the thought.

They carefully peered over the edge and saw the battered car engulfed in flames.

'And you know, I'm ashamed to say that I can't feel sorry for her,' Andy admitted.

'I feel that I should too. But I don't either,' the shocked youngster concurred.

'There's nothing we can do for her now. But we need to call the Police,' Andy said. 'Unless we find a working phone box, it will have to wait until we get back to the lodge,' he added.

'Otherwise, being down there, she might never be found.' Ben observed.

'As evil as she was, even she deserves some sort of funeral, I guess,' Andy pointed out.

CHAPTER TWO

A few miles away, across the Cotswold valley, the police raiding party lying in wait for Sue Williams-Screen to return to her rented cottage, had seen the fireball and heard the explosion. Unaware of the implications, that their vigil to catch the fugitive was now unnecessary.

However, one of the patrol vehicles from the stakeout was dispatched to go and investigate, its flashing blue light painting the hedgerows with the urgency of its task as it hurtled through the narrow lanes.

Andy and Ben were just making their way leaden footed to Andy's car as the police car arrived. It skidded to a halt in front of the damaged hedge.

Andy ran over to the patrol car as the Policeman emerged from it.

'Thank goodness you've arrived. There's been a terrible accident. A car has gone over the cliff and burst into flames,' Andy blurted as the acrid black smoke billowed up over the cliff edge.

'Was there anyone in the car?' the Policeman demanded, climbing through the hedge, and jogging quickly over to where Ben was standing.

'Yes, there is a woman. Was, a woman, Andy corrected himself.

'Who is? Who was it? Do you know?' the policeman asked.

'Yes. She is wanted by you lot,' It's Sue Williams-Screen.' Andy admitted.

'She…she tried to kill us earlier,' Ben added.

'Tried to kill you?' the Policeman repeated sceptically.

'Yes, with a shotgun. We are under the protection of armed officers,' Andy explained.

'Armed officers!'

'Yes.'

'Are they here?' the policeman said looking around.

'No, it's a long story. I'll tell you later.'

The policeman stared over the edge of the quarry and shuddered at the sight of the inferno. 'OK, well there's obviously nothing we can do for her now,' he said.

'It's horrible what's happened, isn't it?' Ben said, clearly shocked by the incident.

'Did you say her name was Williams-Screen?' the policeman checked.

'Yes,' Andy confirmed.

'That's a coincidence. I've just come from the operation to catch her. I'll call it in.' the Policeman said going to go back his patrol car.

How did you find us?' Andy asked.

The black smoke, back lit by the flames. It was like a beacon in the dark countryside,' the policeman explained.

'A beacon! Ironically signalling good news?' Andy thought. 'Thank goodness you found us. Before you go, could I borrow a phone to ring my wife please? Andy asked. 'I'm overdue and she'll be worried. I ought to let her know that I'm alright,' he explained.

'Yes, no problem,' the PC said, giving Andy his phone. 'I need to radio control to get fire and rescue to attend anyway,' the policeman explained as he hurried back to his car.

CHAPTER THREE

Andy immediately rang Helen.

After ringing out for a few minutes, she answered suspiciously.

'Hello. Who's calling?'

'Helen, it's me,' Andy said quickly.

'Andy, thank goodness you rang. I was getting worried. You're a bit late coming home from Scouts, aren't you? I tried ringing you earlier but got no reply,' Helen gabbled.

'Yes, sorry. Only I left my phone at the Scout hut.'

'Oh. Are you not at Scouts then?'

'No...we left there earlier and I...I had to borrow someone else's phone.'

'That's why I didn't recognise the number. I nearly ignored it. But where are you then?'

'Yes. Sorry. I am at...'

'What's that radio noise I can hear in the background?' Helen interrupted. 'Are you with the police? Has something happened?'

'Yes, I am...there... there... there's been an incident,' Andy explained.

'Incident! Oh my god. What sort of incident?' Helen demanded.' Not one of the Scouts?'

'No, nothing to do with the Scout Troop. It's Ben and me. But we're OK.'

'And why wouldn't you be?' Helen questioned.

'That evil woman. That Sue, tried to shoot us.' Andy explained calmly. Don't worry. 'We're not hurt.'

'Shoot you! Oh my God!' How come? I thought the police were guarding you?'

'Well, yes, they were…but it's a long story. But … don't worry. She missed us and ran off.'

'Thank the lord for that. So did the police get her?' Helen questioned.

'No, they weren't there. So, well, we…we followed her as she tried to escape.'

'What! She just tried to kill you and you followed her? Are you mad?' Helen ranted. Have you got a death wish?'

'No, of course not. But after following her for a few miles, we saw her go off the road…she crashed… Her car…it went over a cliff and burst into flames. The bitch is dead Helen. She's gone,' Andy revealed dramatically.

'Dead! Dead! Oh, that's terrible. As much as I hated the woman, I wouldn't wish anyone dead.'

'Yes, yes I know, neither would I,' Andy agreed.

'Are you sure she's…gone? What makes you think she's…dead? We've been there before, but she always turns up again.'

'Yes, I am. There was no way she could escape from that inferno.'

'Sue dead,' Helen said reflectively. 'Are you sure that you and Ben are alright? It must have been an awful shock seeing that?'

'Yes, it was. Ben is very shocked. Unfortunately, he witnessed the car going over the edge and bursting into flames as he tried to help her.'

'Oh, poor kid. He's really been through some dreadful experiences, hasn't he?'

'Yes, he has. But he's made of tough stuff. I'm sure that he'll be able to cope OK.'

'Let's hope so. Are you coming home now?' Helen asked.

'No not yet. I expect the police will want us to make statements. Then we'll go back to Foster Lodge to get my phone and do any necessary repairs in the kitchen.'

'In the kitchen?'

'Yes. That's where she tried to shoot us.'

'Oh my god,' Helen gasped at the mental image of someone trying to shoot her husband.

'I'll be home soon after I have dropped Ben at his house. So don't wait up for me,' Andy added.

'Take care,' Helen said, tearfully as he 'hung up.'

CHAPTER FOUR

'Ben, you'd better ring home too,' Andy said, passing the phone to him. 'Your folks are bound to be worried. I'll go and wait in the car.'

Ben rang his home phone number, JC answered. 'Who's calling?' he said stiffly, expecting an unwanted sales call.

'JC it's me, Ben.'

'Ben! this isn't your usual phone number,' JC observed.

'No, I guessed that you wouldn't recognise the number. I'm ringing on a policeman's phone.

'Policeman's phone ! Are you in trouble again? JC asked suspiciously.

'No,' Ben said, irritated that JC would jump to that conclusion and think that he was in bother.

'Then why a policeman's phone?' JC demanded.

'My phone's in my bedroom, on charge. I forgot to pick it up when I left for Scouts.'

'Are you sure everything's alright?' JC asked suspiciously. 'Have you been in trouble again?'

'No, I haven't,' Ben said defensively. 'Why do you always think that I have done something wrong?'

'Well, there are a lot of previous occasions aren't there?' JC reminded him.

'Yeah, but not this time. There... there's been a car crash.'

'Car crash? Oh, my days!' Are you injured?'

'No. Andy and I are OK.'

'Oh, that's a relief. So, what…what happened?'

'That evil woman, Sue Williams-Screen crashed her car over a cliff. I saw it happen. She's dead JC. She's dead.' Ben said, breaking down.

'OK Ben. Just take your time. It must have been a terrible shock,' JC said, sympathetically. 'How do you know that she's…she's dead?'

'I tried to save her JC. I nearly had her hand…but the car went over and…it crashed down into the quarry and caught fire,' Ben sobbed.

'I'm so sorry. That must have been horrific for you. What an awful thing to witness,' JC blustered, unsure how to comfort the distraught Ben. 'It must have been very traumatic.'

'I tried to save her, I really did but…' Ben repeated, and dissolved again.

'Are you able to get home? Do you want me to come and collect you?' JC asked concerned.

'No, it's OK. I'm with Andy. I'll be back after the Police have finished asking me questions. Please tell Mum I'm alright,' he concluded.

'OK, I will. Take care,' JC said hanging up.

Following the radio call from the first policeman to arrive on scene, other Police vehicles and a fire engine arrived on site and the blazing car was quickly extinguished.

After they'd made a brief statement to the police, the pair walked back to Andy's car.

'You know, I think this is near the spot where I brought Geoffery Foster just before he died,' Andy told Ben.

'Why here?'

'He wanted to see his last Sunset,' Andy, said filling up. 'The sun goes down behind that hill there,' he said, pointing.

'Well, he must be smiling down now, seeing that evil woman end like this,' Ben added.'

'Yes, he could well be. Not too dissimilar to a sunset, was it? That fireball.' Andy added.

And, with mixed emotions they drove in silence slowly back to Foster Lodge, the Scout HQ.

CHAPTER FIVE

When the pair got back to Foster lodge, the two relieved members of their protection team frantically greeted them.

'Where the hell have you two been?' they quizzed.

'Chasing after that woman,' Andy explained wearily.

'What? Chasing after that woman! You silly sods. That's our job. Why didn't you call us?'

'We didn't have time,' Andy explained. 'We had to dash out quickly in order to tail her.'

'Yes, I see the kitchen is in a bit of a state. 'So, what happened? Did she lose you? Where did she go?' they demanded.

'It's a long story. But rather than explaining twice, let's call Detective Sergeant Williams and I'll explain to him what happened.' Andy said, dialling the policeman's number on his now retrieved mobile.

The DS was quick to pick up when he saw the number.

'Andy, where are you?'

'Back at Foster Lodge. We tailed that woman and her car crashed. It caught fire. I expect you know that she's dead. So, you can call off your search,' Andy revealed flatly.

"Crashed! Fire! Dead?' the policeman repeated, clearly gobsmacked. 'What the hell were you playing at, doing our job? And why didn't you ring us earlier?' The policeman ranted tetchily.

'I've got the grid reference of the crash site if you want it,' Andy volunteered, ignoring the admonishment.' But some of your guys are already on site. We have already given them a brief statement.'

'I'll have the grid ref anyway, please. And you're sure it was her?' the DS quizzed.

'Oh yes. It was definitely her,' Andy confirmed.

'How do you know she was killed?' the policeman queried.

'She was trapped inside her car when it went over the cliff and caught fire.'

'Caught fire?'

'Yes, It was a very fierce blaze. After that fire, I would think there would be nothing left of her or of the car apart from the chassis,' Andy revealed.

'You were playing with fire yourself chasing after that one,' the policeman continued.

'Sorry, but having just been shot at, I wasn't thinking logically and, in our haste, to follow her, I'd left my phone here,' Andy explained forcibly.

'OK, wait there. We'll be with you shortly.

CHAPTER SIX

The DS made several calls and confirmed that the surveillance operation was at an end. But a forensic team were tasked to conduct a detailed examination at Sue's bolthole looking for evidence of her misdemeanours.

Within thirty minutes of his call, the DS and his colleague Detective Constable Chris Cooper arrived at the Scout hut.

Impatient from waiting, Andy and Ben were having a second cup of tea.

'I wouldn't say no to a cuppa myself,' Chris Cooper said, seeing the steaming cups.

'Kettles just boiled, help yourself,' Andy said. 'Sugar's over there,' he pointed.

'I didn't think anyone took sugar these days,' the DS observed getting himself a mug from the shelf.

'Best thing for shock,' Andy confirmed.

'If you say so,' the policeman said, sitting down. 'Look at the state of this kitchen. She really made a mess of it with that shotgun, didn't she? We ought to have forensics check things out though,' the DS suggested.

'So, what happened with your run-in with that woman?' the DC asked.

'She came into the Scout HQ with a shotgun. She was going to kill both of us, Andy explained. 'Fortunately, a passing police vehicle spooked her. She discharged one barrel at us through the kitchen door, as you can see. Fortunately, she missed. The rest of the kitchen is peppered with shot. It will need a major decoration job.' Andy said, pointing at the walls.'

'Looks like you're lucky to be alive though,' the DC suggested.

'Yes, we are. Fortunately, she ran off after firing that one barrel. So, we chased after her.'

'Idiots,' the policeman muttered under his breath.

'We had been following her for some miles at a fair speed and then suddenly she lost control. Her car crashed through a hedge.' Andy explained.

'One of the dangers of driving too fast,' the policeman observed unnecessarily.

'Anyway, we discovered that the car was teetering on the edge of a quarry, and we tried to save it from plunging over, but we were just too late,' Andy explained. 'The car went down and caught fire.'

'Still, she won't be missed,' the DC said, laconically.

But the Detective Sergeant was still angry over their undertaking. 'You bloody fools. You could have got yourself killed. This DIY policing is becoming a habit. Just as well she's gone, otherwise I might be forced to clip your wings,' the DS grumbled.

'I promise to leave it all to you guys in the future, I don't want to spoil your fun,' Andy said. 'I wouldn't want your job for all the tea in China.'

'Right Andy, I need to have a look at your motor please,' the DC said. 'Would you mind showing me where you've parked it?'

'My motor! Why?'

'Well as you're into DIY policing. I want to make sure that you aren't also judge and jury and executioner.'

'Executioner!'

'Yes. I need to be sure that you didn't also help her over the cliff. So, I'd like to inspect your car for damage.'

'What!' Andy was staggered by the DC's insinuation. 'I wouldn't dream of doing anything like that,' Andy insisted.

'Well, you've got nothing to be worried about then, have you? I just want to ensure that there is no front-end damage to the car that you were driving.'

'Well, OK,' Andy said, suspiciously. 'It's a bit unusual though, isn't it?'

'Not at all. Where there is an incident between two vehicles, it is just a check to ensure that the chase vehicle didn't cause the other vehicle to crash. In this case, with fatal consequences,' the DS explained.

'Do people do that sort of thing?' Andy asked, perplexed.

'You'd be surprised what people do to cover up their misdemeanours,' the policeman informed them. 'We had one case where someone was clubbed to death and then run over to make it look like an RTC.'

'RTC?'

'Road Traffic Collision. A car accident in other words.'

'I can assure you that there was no collision. She was way ahead of us and went off the road by herself, didn't she Ben?'

'Yes. She was driving too fast,' Ben concurred.

'God! even in death, she's still causing me grief,' Andy moaned.

The pair went outside to where Andy had parked his car. The policeman shone his torch all around the vehicle with special attention to the bumpers.

Although he hadn't done anything wrong, nevertheless Andy felt guilty and watched nervously as the DC checked for damage to his car.

'No, there's nothing here to indicate a collision,' the policeman confirmed as they returned to the Scout hut.

'No, I knew there wouldn't be,' Andy said, nevertheless relieved that the Police inspection had verified his story.

'Just checking that you didn't help her on her way,' the DS repeated. 'But in future, don't become a vigilante. Call us.'

After taking their statements, the police eventually left.

'Is it finally over?' Ben asked, looking hopefully to Andy for reassurance.

'I think so,' he confirmed, relieved. 'I think so. *That Woman* will never cause us any problems, ever again he added naively.'

CHAPTER SEVEN

It was way after two o'clock in the morning by the time Andy dropped Ben off at his home.

'You going to be alright Ben?' Andy asked, as the youngster opened the passenger door.

'Yes, I think so. But every time I close my eyes, I see her. I just can't get her face out of my mind,' Ben confessed.

'I know how you feel. It's awful, isn't it? But time will erase that memory, believe me. It will get easier, and if you need to talk about it, I am here any time you want to chat,' Andy said sincerely.

'What about you?' Ben asked.

'I'll be OK, thanks,' the Scout Leader replied.

Andy's own experience of nursing terminally ill hospice patients had provided some mental resilience for him when dealing with the finality of death.

'Thanks Andy,' Ben said, as he made his way to the front door and unlocked it. As he stepped into the hallway his mother and JC rushed to meet him and enveloped him in a 'team' hug. He was pleased to see that were still up.

Satisfied that he was safely in Andy drove off.

'Are you sure that you are alright Ben?' his mother asked frantically, looking at his pale face.

'Yes, I think so,' Ben confirmed, removing his coat.

'Are you sure? It must have been very scary,' she probed, not sure what to say.' Do you want a cup of tea? Tea is good for shock,' she rattled, making her way to the kitchen without waiting for his response.

'No, I've just…had one.' Ben said.

But Beth was already gone. She needed to cry, out of sight of her son. Relieved that he was home safe.

'Are you feeling a bit better now Ben?' JC asked. 'Naturally, when you rang earlier, you were very upset.'

'I'm slowly coming to terms with it,' Ben admitted.

'Have you given a statement to the police yet?' JC asked.

'Yes, but we've probably got to do another one in a couple of days,' Ben said wearily, collapsing on the sofa.

'Yes, because it's an extremely serious situation,' JC confirmed. 'They have to be thorough in gathering evidence. It will have to go to the coroner for an inquest. And evidence gathered shortly after the incident is vital to that process.'

'Coroner?' Ben said, surprised. 'Oh god, not another ordeal to go through, is there?'

'Yes, I'm afraid so. There's got to be an inquest because it's a sudden death,' JC amplified.

'Oh! Balls! What…what even is an inquest?' Ben queried, clearly rattled by the need for more bureaucracy.

'It's an investigation to determine the cause of death,' JC explained. 'If you are called to give evidence at the inquest, you will be expected to attend.'

'But it's obvious. She crashed her car and killed herself,' Ben said abruptly.

'Yes, on the face of it, that's what appears to have happened. But there might be other circumstances,' JC pointed out.

'Other circumstances! What you talking about. Other circumstances?' Ben said, clearly rattled.

'I've read that some gangsters stage motoring accidents after they've murdered someone in order to hide their crime, JC clarified.

'So, the cops were saying. What are you suggesting? That Andy and I killed her and...' Ben said, in a panic.

'No, not at all. I'm just explaining that that's why they have an inquest, to fully examine all the facts.'

'Oh God! This is getting worse.'

'You may be asked to give information about the person who has died or about the death. If you are giving evidence, in the witness box you will usually do so first, along with any other person who are also giving evidence.'

'You mean Andy?'

'Yes. You must give evidence under oath affirming that you will tell the truth.'

'Why? Do people lie?'

'Yes, if it suits them. You should tell the coroner's office your faith.'

'My faith. Why?'

'So that you can be given the right faith book when you swear the oath.'

'Swear the oath! What like F-ing and Blinding?' Ben queried naively.

'No, not that sort of swearing. No expletives allowed in court. It's just a term to say that you will tell the truth,' JC explained quietly.

'Anyway, I don't really have a faith, do I?'

'Yes, you do. With your scout promise. You promise to do 'Duty to god,' don't you? I suppose your faith is Christian. So, it will be the bible that you swear on.'

'It's a bit long winded though, isn't it? All this rigmarole.'

'It needs to be done because it's the law.'

'So, err…what…what happens?'

'The coroner will first ask you questions and may talk you through any written statement you've made. You may be asked questions by a legal representative if there is one.'

'Are we going to get a solicitor then?'

'Yes probably, If we need to,' JC confirmed.

'Oh! Aren't they expensive?' Ben queried.

'Yes, but don't worry about that. I'll be paying.'

'Thanks.'

'If there's a jury, jury members will also have the right to ask you any relevant questions, which may be asked through the coroner.

'Jury?'

'Yes, if the Coroner considers it's necessary, a jury will be formed to help him make a judgment.'

'So do I get to hear any other evidence, like Andy's for instance?'

'Yes. When everyone has finished asking questions, you may return to your seat and stay to listen to the rest of the hearing and any other witnesses.'

Ben's head was spinning. This was all grown-up stuff, and he didn't like getting involved with this weird 'adult' world.

Beth made her way back into the lounge with a mug of tea.

'Drink this Ben, I've put some sugar in it. It's supposed to be good for shock.'

'Thanks Mum,' the youngster said, taking the cup. 'Andy and I have already had one at the Foster Lodge too.'

'Are you sure that you're alright Ben?' Beth asked, sitting next to her son.

'I'm feeling as if I've been in a movie. It's all so unreal,' Ben admitted.

'Only to be expected,' JC added casually. 'You've been through a shocking experience, no wonder. So, what happened precisely?'

Ben relived the tale from his arrival at Foster Lodge when he walked into the standoff with Sue threatening Andy with a shotgun. And then he gave a detailed description of the white-knuckle ride as they followed Sue's car through the twisty Cotswold lanes.

'That must have been scary in itself,' JC observed.

'What…what about the crash?' Beth asked.

Ben paused before telling them the details of the crash and his rescue attempt.

'Oh, my poor baby,' Beth said, hugging him.

'That really is awful,' JC confirmed.

'Yes, it was. Now if you don't mind? I'm going to bed,' Ben said. 'I'll tell you more in the morning.'

'Okay sleep tight.' Beth said tearfully, giving her son another hug.

'I'll try,' Ben said, heading to his bedroom.

CHAPTER EIGHT

As soon as Ben got to his bedroom, he changed into his night clothes and collapsed on the bed. His head was still 'buzzing' from the evenings events and it was made worse by the thought of having to give evidence to a coroner.

When he closed his eyes, a kaleidoscope of events kept going through his mind. He tried desperately to focus on something else but failed. So, after endlessly tossing and turning, he switched his bedside light on, took his phone off charge and texted his girlfriend, Janie.

'Hi Janie. I can't sleep. Are you awake? I need to talk about something. So shocked by the accident.'

Although she was asleep, Janie's subconscious heard the sound of Ben's special text notification sound as it arrived.

Now awake, she fumbled on the bedside cabinet for her phone. Through sleep fogged eyes she examined the message and was horrified by it. 'An accident! What does he mean, an accident?' she wondered. 'Oh, my god! Is he hurt? Is he in hospital?'

Knowing what an emotionally sensitive character Ben had become, following his kidnap and several other distressing incidents, she immediately rang him.

Still with his phone in hand, Ben answered her call even before the opening bars of her special ringtone had finished.

'Jamie, sorry. I didn't want to disturb you,' Ben whispered hoarsely. 'But I couldn't sleep.

'Ben are you alright? Are you hurt?' Janie asked urgently.

'I…I'm a bit shocked A bit shocked,' he repeated.

'Why? what happened?'

'There was an accident. A car accident. Someone got killed,' he announced dramatically.

'Killed! Oh, my days.' Janie said, stunned by the news.

'I've never seen a car accident before,' Ben explained. 'Especially one that ended in someone getting killed.'

'Oh, that's terrible! I'd be upset too if that were me,' Janie sympathised. 'Do you want to talk about it? It might help,' she invited.

'I'm not sure…'

'Take your time,' she coaxed quietly.

'It was a woman that was killed,' he revealed. 'The woman was my horrible arch enemy.

'Enemy?' Janie puzzled.

'Yes. Sue Williams-Screen.'

'Sue! Williams-Screen! You're joking, right? Dead! You're sure that it's not just a nightmare that you've woken up from?

'No. It's true. I know it might sound a bit bizarre, but she had just tried to shoot Andy and I at Foster Lodge and…'

'Shoot you! Oh, my days,' Janie said, bewildered.'

She shot at us and thankfully missed. It was horrible. The noise, the smell. It was awful.'

'She…she shot at you?' Janie repeated, in a daze.

'Yes.'

'Oh my God! You could have been killed.'

'I know.

'So, I don't understand. How then was there car crash?' Janie demanded.

'She made an escape and Andy decided to follow her in his car.'

'You must have been mad chasing after her. After she tried to shoot you.'

'Yes, I know. I was scared.'

'What were you going to use as a weapon to defend yourself?' Janie quizzed.

'We didn't think of that. All we could think of, was following her.'

'Why? That was the police's job,' Janie rationalised.

'Yes, I know but the police had been unable to find her, and we had a chance of locating her hideout.'

'So, you…'

'Well, we followed her and then intended to inform the police where to find her.'

'You followed her then. So how was she killed?'

'She was just driving too fast and lost it on a bend. Then the car went over a cliff and burst into flames.'

'Oh Ben. That must have been horrible.'

'I was there when it went over the cliff. I can't get it out of my mind. It keeps rerunning every time I close my eyes,' he said, filling up.

'Oh, don't cry Ben. I wish I could come and give you a hug,' Janie said thickly, close to tears herself.

'I wish you could,' Ben said tearfully. 'Thanks for listening. Sorry I woke you. I'll try and get some sleep now. I'm exhausted.'

'OK. I'll come and see you tomorrow. Don't worry. I hope you can get some sleep. Night, night,' Janie said reluctantly hanging up.

'Night.'

CHAPTER NINE

After an age of trying to get to sleep, Ben finally succumbed to his tiredness. But his trauma ravaged mind refused to let go and played a horrifying nightmare of his experiences.

He was transported back to the site where it all happened. Suddenly a superheated blindingly bright fireball shot up the cliff, followed by a cloud of acrid black smoke. He was rooted to the spot as it came billowing towards him. He tried to hold his breath, but the fumes filled his lungs. He couldn't breathe. His chest hurt as he struggled to get air. He was going to suffocate. He was losing consciousness.

Through the smoke he saw her. Her red demonic eyes, staring at him, accusing. Penetrating his soul.

Then in a blinding flash, her hair burst into flames. She was ablaze. Her skin erupting into huge blisters as the flames licked over her body, incinerating her. He felt the heat scorch his face. Her demonic scream filled his head. His heart froze.

The fire was consuming her. He was paralysed by fear unable to move. Forced to watch the horror unfold.

He awoke with a start. His nightclothes soaked in sweat. He was panting, exhausted by his nocturnal struggles.

Once again, he reran the events in his mind endlessly and reviewed what he had done. He tossed the incident through his tired brain. Was it his fault that she had died? If only he had been quicker.

'No, that's not right,' he argued. He HAD done everything to save her. What else could he have done? Perhaps if he had been braver? No. There was no other options.

He remembered feeling the dreadful hurt after Andy's accusation. Despite all the evil things she'd done to him, it never even entered his head to kill her.

He recalled Andy and him standing together and peering over the edge, the battered car engulfed in flames, black smoke marking her funeral pyre.

Then he went on a guilt trip recalling that neither he nor Andy felt sorry for her death.

Eventually he drifted off to sleep again, still wondering if that was morally acceptable to feel no sympathy.

CHAPTER TEN

Suzette's spirits were buoyed up by the Quantas A380 seat screen showing only thirty kilometres to go.

It was Suzette's first trip to the UK, and she was beside herself with excitement of meeting her long-lost sister for the first time in the flesh.

After discovering about each other's existence, they had only spoken over the internet. They had never met and physically hugged each other.

Suddenly the soporific atmosphere in the cabin transformed into a plethora of activities. A posse of smiling flight attendants carrying rubbish bags swept through the plane, tidying up breakfast detritus and inviting passengers to 'put their trays up.'

Their tidying frenzy was, yet another indication that the twenty-four-hour flight from Sydney to Heathrow's terminal three, was finally ending.

Keen to fast track her exit from the plane, Suzette started getting her belongings together and joined the symphony of noise from the other five hundred and twenty-five passengers also getting ready to disembark.

The 'ping pong' sound on the public address alerted passengers to 'fasten their seatbelt's and Suzette quickly buckled in.

'Oh, this is so exciting,' Suzette giggled. 'In a few minutes I will be hugging my sister.'

But as the A380 approached London Heathrow the airbus pilot came on the public address and announced, *Ladies and Gentlemen, due to heavy traffic at London Heathrow, this flight has been placed in a holding pattern over central London. There will be a slight delay of about fifteen minutes before our final approach to the airport.*

'Damn,' she thought. 'Just my luck. Another delay to add to the one we had in Singapore. I hope that she's monitoring our progress, otherwise she'll be hanging around for ages. The fates are conspiring against me, delaying our reunion.' Suzette concluded pessimistically.

'However,' the pilot continued, positively. *'One of the advantages of this delay is that, if you look out of the windows, you can have an aerial view of England's capital city, at no extra charge,'* he chuckled.

As the plane slowly banked, Suzette could see, out of her window seat, the capital city in all its glory.

'Oh, how marvellous,' she thought. 'A sightseeing bonus.'

She instantly recognised the sand-coloured limestone buildings of the ancient Palaces of Westminster, home to the United Kingdom's Parliament, glowing in the afternoon sunshine.

The unmistakeable sight of the 300-foot Elizabeth Tower housing the four faced Big Ben chiming clock. An international symbol of Britishness.

Lapping around the ancient building, the muddy brown swathe of the majestic River Thames, like an ancient moat, guarding the seat of government.

The wide river's zigzag course dividing the capital as it meandered its way through the bustling city.

A multitude of bridges spanning 'old Father Thames' providing access to the city for the commuting population.

Suzette spotted the big Ferris wheel like structure of the London Eye nestling on the banks of the Thames.

'I'll add a trip on that to my wish list, when I'm settled,' she thought.

As the huge plane continued to circle the capital, she could see the imposing structure of Buckingham Palace, the centre for so many state occasions and royal hospitality.

As an avid fan of the royal family, she was delighted to see this world-famous centrepiece of Royal pomp.

Linking the palace to Trafalgar Square via Admiralty arch, she recognised the treelined Royal Mall, its long straight road steeped in processional traditions.

Surprisingly, in spite of the considerable number of buildings crammed into the capital, Suzette was astonished to see so many large areas of green. The patchwork landscape of green parks and gardens were expertly interspersed between the skyscrapers and modernistic buildings.

Finally, after circling for what seemed an age, the plane straightened up and started losing height over the Hillingdon countryside.

As the buildings appeared to rush up to meet the descending plane, Suzette's excitement and heart rate increased.

She felt the slight bump as the undercarriage was lowered and then a few minutes later heard the squeal as the tyres kissed the runway tarmac, leaving a black skid mark and a cloud of smoke, the planes signature of their arrival.

After what seemed another eternity, the A380 slowly taxied to the terminal building, and the 'bing bong' of the seatbelt light going out signalled the end of her twenty-four-hour journey.

'Thank goodness,' she thought. 'Oh god it's so exciting. I just can't wait to see her.'

Around her, there was a collective 'clicking' of seat belts being released and a hubbub as people burst into relieved conversations.

Overhead lockers were ungraciously yanked open, and passengers started grabbing their hand baggage from the yawning cubby-holes.

Reunited with their belongings they quickly joined the crocodile of people filling the gangways in their haste to disembark.

One final obstacle to their escape meant passengers waiting impatiently for the flight attendants to open the doors.

Finally, when the doors were opened 'fresh' London air gushed in and replaced the stuffy recycled and reconditioned air they had been breathing for so long.

Rather than joining the static queue of anxious passengers, Suzette dug her mobile out of her handbag and, pleased to see it had quickly logged into a network, she rang her sister's number.

Impatiently she listened as the call rang out for several minutes with no reply. Not even voicemail, which she thought was odd.

'When you're ready,' a smiling air hostess said gently, interrupting her thoughts. 'Perhaps you'd like to go to baggage reclaim.'

Suzette was surprised to see that the queue waiting to exit the plane had disappeared. She was the last to leave.

'Sorry, I was calling my sister,' she apologised. 'But I got no reply, I'll call her again in a minute,' she told the disinterested attendant.

CHAPTER ELEVEN

After disembarking, Suzette made her way to one of the four disciplined queues waiting at the busy immigration desks.

The queue shuffled slowly forward and after a thirty-minute wait she reached the head of her queue and waited by the 'do not pass' red line. Suzette waited impatiently, constantly looking at her watch, finally, after what seemed an age, she was invited to a now free immigration desk.

Suzette handed her blue Australian passport to the immigration officer, his 'dead pan' expression showed his level of boredom as he took the passport from her. With barely a movement of his head he briefly looked at her face and the passport picture.

'I'm here to meet my sister,' she gushed, excitedly.

The immigration officer made no response as he placed her open passport face down on his desk's electronic reader.

Unseen by Suzette, a red caution light immediately flashed on his terminal. Deftly, he took the passport off the scanner, pressed a reset button on his desk, and carefully laid the passport back on the reader. The retry achieved the same result.

Irritated by the possible malfunction of his reader, he rechecked the picture against Suzette's face and confirmed that they matched. However, he pressed a button marked 'escalate' and was invited to electronically 'confirm' the alarm that it generated, which he did.

Aware of the unusual delay in scanning her passport. Suzette asked, 'Is there a problem?'

'Computer problem,' the immigration officer stated, flatly. 'Wait just a minute, while we get it sorted.'

Within a few moments however, two uniformed officers were purposefully making their way through the crowds of queuing passengers.

Meanwhile, wondering what the passenger had done to merit the alert, the Immigration officer asked stoically, 'what's the purpose of your visit?'

'I'm meeting my sister for the first time ever,' she gushed, beside herself with excitement. 'I tried ringing her as soon as we landed, but got no reply,' she explained, unnecessarily.

'Perhaps she was parking the car,' the immigration officer suggested, seeing the approaching officers.

'I'm going to emigrate here to work for the NHS shortly,' Suzette continued.

The two uniformed officials arrived and positioned themselves either side of Suzette. She felt uncomfortable at their closeness.

'What's going on?' she demanded, looking from one to the other.

'If you'd like to accompany these two officers, they'd like to ask you a few questions,' the Immigration officer explained, handing her passport to one of the guards.

'Why? What's this all about?' Suzette asked nervously. 'I don't have time. I'm going to meet my sister.'

'Come this way miss,' the first guard invited. 'Don't worry, I expect it's only a computer glitch, we'll soon have you on your way.'

Disgruntled, Suzette pushed her light hand luggage away from the immigration desk, conscious that the eyes of the other passengers were staring at her.

The other guard followed closely behind and soon they entered a closed off area of the terminal.

The first guard opened a door labelled 'Immigration Interview room one.'

'You can leave your luggage out here, it's perfectly safe, he advised her.

'If you say so,' Suzette said suspiciously.' But what about my main luggage?'

'Don't worry about that. If this takes too long, we'll reclaim that for you. Having said that, I expect we'll have you on your way shortly though. We'll sort it, one way or another.'

'If you'd like to come in and take a seat,' the other officer holding her passport, invited.

'What's this all about? Is there something wrong with my passport? Can I ring my sister? She's waiting for me?' Suzette asked desperately.

'All in good time,' he said, logging onto his computer.

'What's the purpose of your visit to the UK?' he asked, studying the screen.

'I'm meeting my sister for the first time ever. We were split up when we were babies,' Suzette explained nervously. 'And I've got a work permit. So, I'm emigrating and going to work for the NHS.'

'I see,' he said gazing at the screen and putting the passport on a small scanner.

After a few minutes looking at the screen the officers exchanged glances knowingly. The other guard left the room.

'Remind me of your name again,' the first officer asked.

'My name? Why do you want to know? It's on my passport in front of you,' she said tersely.

'I just want you to tell me please,' he repeated patiently.

'It's Suzette, Suzette Brown.'

'Are you sure?'

'What do you mean am I sure? Of course I am. I've had it since I was born. What's this all about?' she demanded irritably.

'All in good time. I'm sure there is nothing to worry about. We just need to do some further checks. Have you ever used any other name?'

'No. I've always been Suzette Brown. Why do you ask?'

'There appears to be a disparity in our data. Which seems to indicate that you are using a false name.'

'False name! What false name? How do you come to that conclusion?'

'The facial recognition software indicates that you are someone else,' he explained looking directly at her.

'At the moment, the computer details do not match your passport. We will need to hand you over to the Police for further investigation.'

'What! Oh, this is all nonsense. Tell me this isn't happening,' Suzette said, exasperated. 'I know who I am and who I have been all my life. I am Suzette Brown.'

'I'm sure the Police will be able to sort it out for you,' the officer suggested.

At that moment two uniformed policewomen came into the room.

'Hello there. What have we got here?' The first WPC asked.

'We've just been looking at this lady's passport and according to the computer her name is something different. Under this other name she is on a police force wanted list,' the immigration officer announced.

'A wanted list! What wanted list? What are you talking about? 'Wanted list?" Suzette said in horror.

CHAPTER TWELVE

After a sleepless night, Ben got up at six o'clock and dressed in his cycle kit. He pulled on his favourite short sleeve lycra jersey and matching shorts over his lean body and mindful of the early hour, crept quietly downstairs.

He was surprised to see his mother already in the kitchen drinking a cup of tea.

'Oh, good morning Ben. How are you this morning?' she said, putting her cup down and giving him a hug.

'As well as anybody could be, after witnessing that horrible accident,' he said quietly.

'Yes, I can understand that,' Beth said, sympathetically, picking up her cup and peering over the top of it. Did you get any sleep at all?'

'No. I was tossing and turning all night. It all kept running through my mind.'

'Of course it would. I'm sorry. It must have been horrible for you. So, what are you going to do now?'

'D'oh! What do you think I'm going to do? dressed like this?' he said brusquely. 'Ride my bike of course!'

'Okay, no need to 'take my head off.' I was only asking. Hopefully, you'll be in a better mood when you come back?'

'Yeah whatever.'

'Do you want something to eat? I'll make you some breakfast if you like?'

'No thanks. I've got an energy bar in my back pocket,' Ben said, dismissively.

'Oh, OK then,' she said awkwardly, wondering whether to give him another hug. Instead, she stayed seated and took another sip of her tea. 'Well, go carefully.'

Ben made his way through the kitchen to the garage where his bikes were stored, his cycle shoes clip clopping over the tiled floor.

Beth owed a lot to her son, for although she was now 'dry,' she was an alcoholic. Ben had been her long-time young carer whilst she was on the roller coaster through substance abuse. The highs caused by drink, and drugs and lows where she was wallowing in the depths of despair and regret.

Beth had no partner, their one parent family, meant that even as a child Ben had to deal with the grown-up aspects of his mother's addictions. And, as a result he had built up a tough resilient nature.

Mountain biking was Ben's therapy for dealing with the stresses and strains of his chaotic 'family' life. His sanctuary was his bike. Once on his bike in the countryside, the fresh air seemed to help make his worries disappear.

Today he had another trauma to ride off and like an automaton he set off on one of his tortuous routes up and down the Cotswold hills.

He needed to ride hard to banish the disturbing movie still running in his head. Unsure of where he was going, he just rode and rode and rode, the sweat dripping off his chin, testament to his strenuous efforts.

Unfortunately, the tension was not easing. The ordeal of the previous evening wouldn't go away, like his problems usually did.

Instead, he kept seeing images of Sue's cruel face as the car disappeared down into the quarry, the intense fireball, her horrendous screams forever echoing in his mind.

Uncharacteristically he lost his focus on the technical challenges of riding his bike over the rough terrain and put his front tyre on an exposed wet root. The front wheel lost adhesion on the slanting timber and the bike slid from underneath him. Unable to unclip from his pedal in time, he fell heavily on his right leg. his foot still captive in the pedal.

As he fell, he instinctively put his hand out to save himself from 'smashing his face into the ground, but the small Cotswold stone rubble on the track pierced his gloves and dug into his hand and in pain he eased his guard.

Consequently, as his momentum carried him forward, he scraped his knee and face planted his bottom lip on the rough terrain, the peak of his helmet protecting him from more severe facial damage.

He made no attempt to stand. He just laid there prostrate, assessing himself for any significant injuries and was relieved to find that he wasn't too damaged.

Then the trauma of the previous day hit him hard. The emotion numbing effect of his adrenalin filled cycle ride was replaced by an overwhelming tide of despair. And he wept.

Ben's tough emotional shell had been breached. All the psychological resilience that he had built up from caring for his mother over the years, had gone, evaporated.

Putting on a brave face and being the 'tough guy' wasn't necessary anymore. There was no one here to judge him or from whom he had to hide his real sensitive nature.

Here, in 'his' countryside, he felt at last able to let it all out. Ben cried and howled like a baby.

Whilst lying there, the fearful episodes of trauma played in his head. He revisited the terror he felt when he'd walked in on Sue threatening to shoot Andy; then the heart stopping moment when she pointed the gun at him; their escape by the skin of their teeth when she was momentarily distracted; then the noise and smell of her blind shot through the scout hut kitchen door. Their frantic white knuckle car chase through the dark narrow Cotswold lanes following her. Then the awful realisation that she had crashed and the frightening noise of the out-of-control vehicle smashing itself to bits. He had forgotten the relief he'd felt to discover that she had survived the crash; The helplessness he felt when her car suddenly plunged into the darkness as he reached for her hand; Her scream as she realised she was going to die; The dreadful realisation that he had witnessed someone dying, burning to death.

But the worse, gut-wrenching thing was the suspicion from Andy that he had pushed her over. Andy of all people! Is that what people would believe? He felt he had put his life on the line in his failed attempt to save her, so why would everyone think he was a murderer? It was all too much.

He remained there for some time, sobbing, with the bike still on top of him. Eventually his adrenaline level ebbed and the pain of his injuries reminded him he had actually hurt himself.

He was just starting to sit up when he heard another bike approaching. Quickly he wiped his tears on the back of his glove and stood up to get his bike off the track. Immediately he recognised the arriving biker. It was Janie.

'Ben, oh thank goodness that I'd guessed right. I thought I'd find you up here somewhere,' she said, unclipping her feet from her pedals, dropping her bike, and running to him.

Ben dropped his bike too and hugged her. His tears of self-pity starting to flow again as they embraced.

'Oh Janie. I am so glad to see you,' he sobbed.

'Ben are you OK? I was so worried. After we spoke last night, I couldn't get to sleep.'

'I'm sorry, I didn't want to upset you. It was just… just all too much to take in. I needed to hear your voice,' he said hugging her tightly. 'Just to get me down. I was so hyper after what happened."

'Of course.'

'Anyway, how did you know that I was here?'

'I went round to your house and your Mum said that you were out on your bike. I just guessed that you were likely to do this route,' she said. 'Are you sure that you are alright? Looks like you've been off.'

'Yeah. A stupid tree root. I wasn't concentrating. You know,' he said rubbing his knee.

'I can see that you've been kissing the ground, too. You've got some blood and dirt on your lip,' she said, gently brushing the dirt away. 'Are you hurt anywhere else?' Janie probed. I see your eyes are a bit bloodshot. Didn't bang your head, did you?' she said, examining his face.

'No, only my lip.'

'Anywhere else?' she persisted.

'Oh, usual places, ripped my shorts, gravel rash on my hand and knee. Nothing broken.'

'What about your bike?' Janie asked, looking at his dumped mountain bike.

'I think it's ok,' he said, letting her go and walking over to inspect it.

Ben did a quick inspection and confirmed that it was OK.

'You OK to ride?' Janie asked.

'Yes. A bit stiff but nothing really. Shall we carry on round our usual route?' Ben asked, relieved to have Janie with him. 'Hopefully I won't keep thinking about the accident,' he thought.

CHAPTER THIRTEEN

It was an obvious horror for Ben and Andy who witnessed Sue's death first-hand. But the news of Sue's death in the Godsons community was met with joy and jubilation. At last, their nemesis was no longer going to blight their lives.

Carrie and Tim were opening the office of their 'Just do it' walking company. As was her normal practice, Carrie made straight for the radio and turned it on.

'You're not going to listen to that crap again, are you?' Tim moaned.

'You know that I like to listen to our area BBC Radio station, Radio Gloucestershire. It has local weather reports. Besides which, there's always Cummings County quiz with local facts that I can pass on to our clients,' Carrie explained.

'Can't we have a bit of peace and quiet for a change?'

'Look Mr Grumpy, you don't need to listen. Just go and make the coffee. It's news time now anyway.'

Tim stomped his way into the small room that held the coffee making stuff and busied himself making their refreshments.

Carrie turned the volume of the radio up and listened while she opened the post. The news had already started. ... *'There has been a fatal road crash overnight in the Cotswolds. A car has crashed into a quarry and burst into flames killing the woman driver.*

Local scout leaders witnessed the accident and tried a rescue attempt. They said the driver was going too fast down the narrow country lanes. The woman is yet to be identified formally but is thought to be someone living locally.'

'Tim did you hear that?' Carrie called.

'What?' he shouted, intent on his coffee making.

'About a car crash in the Cotswolds?'

'No, and I'm not interested either. Here's your coffee,' he said, coming into the office and handing her a steaming mug.

'Some scout people saw the crash happen. I wonder if Andy knows them?'

'Probably, the Scouting lot all seem to know each other,' Tim said, sitting down at his desk.

The phone rang.

'Bit early for business,' he suggested. However, before he could reach it, Carrie had already picked up the receiver.

'Just do it walking. How may I help?' she invited.

'Carrie. It's me, Andy.'

'Oh, hello Andy. Talk of the devil. We were just listening to the news about some scout leaders being at the scene of a crash and, like a bad penny you turn up,' she joked.

'Then you already know?' Andy suggested.

'Know! Know what?' Carrie puzzled.

'The woman that was killed, was your evil enemy. Sue Williams-Screen.'

'Sue…You've got to be joking! Never! We wouldn't be that lucky,' she refuted the revelation.

'No, it's true,' Andy confirmed.

'Dead! How do you know? Carrie demanded.

'She tried shooting Ben and I at Foster Lodge,' Andy explained.

'She what? Tried shooting you?' Carrie repeated, gobsmacked. 'Well, I suppose we shouldn't be surprised at anything that she does.'

Tim looked up from his newspaper, intrigued.

'Yes, obviously she was unsuccessful,' the Scout Leader added.

'I mean what happened exactly?' Carrie demanded.

'After she tried to shoot us, we followed her, and she crashed her car.'

'Were you racing her?' Carrie asked, suspiciously.

'No. We were keeping a respectful distance behind her then she lost it and crashed. We tried to save her, but the car went over the cliff and exploded.'

'Oh my God! I...I don't know what to say. I think I'm delighted,' she beamed.

'What are you delighted about?' Tim quizzed, hearing only Carrie's side of the conversation.

'That evil bitch, Sue Williams-Screen. Sue is dead! She crashed her car. Killed herself,' Carrie relayed happily.

'How does he know it was her?' Tim quizzed sceptically.

'Andy witnessed it.' Carrie relayed. 'There is a god after all,' she said joyfully.

Then her stoicism deserted her. Carrie started crying, tears streaming down her face.

'Andy are you a hundred percent sure, that she's not going to try and kill me again?' she sobbed.

'Yes. I'm a hundred percent. You can relax at last,' Andy reassured.

'At last. Thank God. I don't have to keep looking over my shoulder anymore,' Carrie said, breathing a great sigh of relief. 'Ever since I intervened and came to poor Rupert's aid when she was going to beat him up, she has been after me.'

'Well, you did nearly choke her to death, remember?' Tim reminded her.

'I gave her a taste of her own medicine that's all. And she didn't like it.' Carrie said recalling the frantic fight.

'The important thing is that you don't need to worry anymore. She's not going to kidnap you again or try to kill you,' Andy confirmed.

'Mmm, I wish that I could be as certain as you. The trouble is she keeps coming back from the dead. I thought she was dead when we fought in the River Severn. But she suddenly appeared again.'

'Not this time, I can assure you Carrie,' Andy reiterated. 'She's gone. Believe me.'

'I hear what you say, but she has a fearful Houdini reputation of coming back. Even when they locked her up, she escaped. Are you sure Andy, she hasn't pulled off another of her deceptions again?'

'No, not this time. Ben and I witnessed her in the car going over the cliff.'

'What's going on?' Tim quizzed his girlfriend.

'Andy says she's gone…dead,' Carrie relayed.

Tim put his arm around the sobbing Carrie. 'This news should help to get rid of some of your PTSD baggage sweetheart,' he said, uncharacteristically lovingly.

'Thank you Andy, for that wonderful news,' Tim said, taking the phone from Carrie as she blew her nose.

'My pleasure,' Andy smiled and rang off.

'Tim, we need to tell your Mum. After her kidnap ordeal with little Jeffery, Kay will be as delighted as we are,' Carrie suggested.

'Yes. I agree. Hurray! Open the champagne. Let's celebrate. At last, the wicked witch is dead.'

CHAPTER FOURTEEN

Tim rang his mother straight away and as usual she waited for the answer machine to ask the caller to leave their name.

'Hi mum, it's me, your beloved son,' he joked. 'Pick up.'

Within a few seconds, Kay picked up the handset. 'Hello Tim.'

'Mother, I have some wonderful news for you.'

'No more legacy's thank you. This last one nearly got me killed,' she said, stiffly.

'No, you're OK there. It's better than that,' Tim revealed.

'What is it? Carrie's pregnant?'

'No, definitely not. No, you can relax you're not going to be a Grandma.'

'Oh, shame. Well tell me for heaven's sake.'

'The bitch that kidnapped you and baby Jeffery,' Tim reminded her.

'Yes?'

'She's dead.'

'She's what?' Kay queried, shocked by the news.

'Dead?'

'Dead! Are you sure? I need to sit down,' Kay said, easing herself into her armchair. 'How do you know. It's not one of her disappearing tricks again, is it?'

'No. Andy was there when it happened.'

'Oh dear. He didn't kill her, did he?'

'No, she did it herself. She smashed her car up and it caught fire with her inside it.'

'Oh dear, what a terrible way to die,' Kay said. 'I might have to have a sherry to celebrate,' she beamed. 'After what she put me through. It's the least I deserve.'

'Mother!'

CHAPTER FIFTEEN

Andy continued his round of informing the Godsons community and rang Sue's former husband, Rupert. Joanne, his wife answered.

'Hello Joanne. How are you and the baby?' Andy asked.

'Oh, hello Andy. Jeffery and I are both well thanks. What can I do for you?'

'Is...is Rupert there?'

'Yes, I'll just get him for you.'

'Oh Joanne, you might like to hear what I have to say too.'

'Ok sounds intriguing.' she said, going into the garden.

After a few minutes Rupert was on the line.

'Hello Andy, unusual to hear from you. Not another old man's legacy that you've found for us, is it?' he joked.

'Not in a monetary sense, but you will be pleased to hear what I have to say. You might want to put the phone on loud speak so Joanne can hear at the same time.'

Rupert did as Andy suggested. 'Go ahead,' he confirmed.

'I have some good news for you both. Rupert, your former wife Sue, is dead.'

'Pardon!'

'The woman that brutalised you for so many years. Your ex has been killed in a car crash,' Andy revealed.

'What...killed! How...I mean?' Rupert said in surprise.

'She crashed her car, and it caught fire.' Andy continued. 'She died in the inferno.'

'Well, I...I don't know what to say. This is so unexpected. I think I should feel sorry for her. But after what she put me, us through, I can only feel a sense of relief,' Rupert admitted.

'Me too,' Joanne added and burst into tears. 'No more looking over my shoulder waiting for her to strike again and threaten us,' Joanne continued.

Rupert hugged his wife.

'Andy are you sure? This isn't just some rumour that you've heard, is it?'

'No this isn't a rumour. Yes. I am Positive.'

'Is it really over at last? Joanne sobbed.

'Yes,' Andy confirmed.

'No more nightmares. Frightened that she is going to kidnap baby Jeffery again?' Joanne sobbed. At last, we can sleep peacefully in our beds without having to have the security team here.'

'I want to believe you Andy but are you really sure? This isn't another one of her great escapes again, is it?' Rupert persisted.

'No., I'm sure. Ben and I witnessed it all.'

'Really! Oh, that must have been horrible. I'm so sorry,' Joanne sympathised.

'So, she's dead. So, what happens next?' Rupert probed.

'There will be an inquest. Ben and I will be called as witnesses. Otherwise, there's nothing any of us need to do, except be thankful that it's all over.'

'Thank you for letting us know Andy, it must have been very traumatic for both of you,' Rupert reflected.

'Yes, it was. Especially for Ben. He has not been around death like myself.'

'What do you mean?' Joanne asked.

'Well, working at the hospice, death is more or less a daily occurrence for me. Not that you ever get used to it, of course. But at least you have a coping mechanism.'

'Poor Ben,' Rupert observed.

'Yes, he will probably need some counselling,' Joanne suggested.

'It might be an idea if we all got together and talked it through too,' Rupert suggested, already feeling a deep sense of relief.

CHAPTER SIXTEEN

After Suzette had been taken away by the Police, she was detained overnight in a special accommodation block while further immigration investigations were conducted.

The following day the two immigration officers got together again in an adjoining office.

'So, what have you found?' the first officer asked.

'We've conducted a forensic analysis of her passport.'

'Did you find anything suspicious?'

'Unfortunately, not. Nothing questionable at all. Checking the hologram and the authenticity of the photo, it all looks genuine. If it's a fake, it's an exceptionally good one. No, I'd say it was legitimate,' he added.

'So, what next?'

'I've been on to our colleagues 'down under' and they tell me that there is a Suzette Brown on their database, and she is recorded as a nurse. There are no records of criminality.'

'So how does that leave us?'

'Perhaps the facial recognition is faulty?'

'Let's have a look at this other woman that the software seems to think she is then.'

The immigration guard put Suzette's passport picture and the alleged woman's picture side by side on the screen.

'No wonder! They look exactly the same!'

'Yes, you're right. Surely, they've got to be twins?'

'Well, I'll be!'

'Identical twins too by the look of it. Who'd have thought it? It's amazing, isn't it? Living thousands of miles apart, but they look exactly like each other.'

'Yes, even their hair style.'

'Right. So, we can let her in to the country, after all.'

'Before we do though, we need to get the 'cavalry' involved. It appears that she is in the dark about her sister's criminality. It's going to be a hell of a shock to her, I'd imagine.'

'I think that's a bit of an understatement. So, who issued the wanted warrant?'

'Gloucestershire Constabulary.'

'I'll give them a call.'

'In the meantime, is she still intending to meet her sister?'

'Well, that was the reason for her trip, wasn't it?'

'We'll set up a 'sting,' let the two meet and detain the sister.'

'Do you really think the sister will still be hanging around though after all this time? The perimeter security team haven't reported any suspicious activities by any individuals hanging around.'

'No but just in case she is. We'd look pretty silly if she were and we let her slip through our fingers. The warrant indicates she's a nasty piece of work, so we will need to get armed response involved.'

'If she is here, poor sister Suzette is in for short reunion!'

'Yeah. What a shame. After travelling all that way. Do we know where they were going to meet?

60

'She says she had to call her sister when she arrived, and sister would pick her up outside the terminal. But she hasn't been able to make contact with her.'

'Okay, let's stake out the area anyway. Conduct a full surveillance on her and be ready to arrest her sister.'

'I see that the charge sheet list includes attempted murder, kidnap, arson and extortion, to name but a few, so we need to be careful.'

'Nice lady!'

'Should I get Suzette to try calling her again?'

'Yes, and we can be part of the welcome party.'

'Oh! That's odd,' the first officer exclaimed, examining his computer screen.

According to this recent alert from Gloucestershire Police, they have just rescinded the wanted warrant.'

'What! Are you sure? You can't suddenly wipe away all her crimes. Does it say why?

'Yes,' the officer looked at his colleague. 'It says that the wanted suspect is deceased!'

'Deceased! Oh dear. When?'

'Yesterday by the look of it.'

'That's obviously why she wasn't answering her phone then.'

'After all that bother, it appears that Suzette's visit is going to be in vain.'

'What did you say the sister's name was?'

'I didn't but it's Williams-Screen. Sue Williams-Screen.'

'Williams-Screen! That's a strange name. What do we do now?'

'We still need to get back to Gloucestershire police to let them know we have the sister here. They might want to have words.'

CHAPTER SEVENTEEN

The call from the Heathrow Immigration Team took Gloucestershire policeman DC Chris Cooper by surprise.

'They say that they have detained someone looking like Sue Williams-Screen at immigration,' he told his colleague, DS Marcus Williams.

'What? Williams-Screen at Heathrow! 'Impossible!

'So, she's not dead then! That doesn't make sense. How come they think it's her?'

'She was picked up by facial recognition from her passport. She has just flown in from Australia.'

'Well, that's bloody nonsense. If they have her there, who was in the car?'

'Yes, whose charred remains have we got in the morgue?'

'Having said that, that Scout Leader and kid were positive it was her. So, what the hell is going on here?'

'I'll ring that Scout Leader bloke and see if he can enlighten us.'

'Good idea.'

DC Cooper rang Andy.

'Andy, Chris Cooper here.'

'Hi Chris, how can I help?'

'This might seem a bit of a strange question, but are you sure it was that Williams-Screen woman that went over the cliff?'

'Yes of course.'

'Did you have visual contact with her car all the way to the crash site?'

'Well... no. I dropped back a bit so she wouldn't see me following her. I wanted to find her bolt hole as I told you.'

'So, is it possible that it wasn't her car that went over the cliff?'

'What do you mean?' Andy puzzled. 'Someone else's car that was the same colour and model as hers?'

'Yes. That's what I'm suggesting,' the policeman explained.

'Well, I suppose so but...'No. There is no doubt in my mind. it was definitely her in the car. Although it was dark. We were eyeballing her face to face when we were trying to rescue her.'

'You're sure?' the policeman probed.

'A hundred percent. I would know that evil bitch's voice with my eyes closed, and anyway, didn't you find the shotgun that she used at the scout hut on Ben and me?'

'No, It wasn't in the wreck. The forensic guys didn't report finding it either.'

'So, she must have disposed of it somewhere when she was out of our sight then,' Andy suggested.

'Possibly.'

'Anyway, why do you ask? I thought this was all tied up,' Andy puzzled.

'Yes, so did I until we had a call from Heathrow airport to say that they had her in custody there.'

'What! You've got to be joking! I saw the fireball. There is no way that she could have got out of that inferno and got to Heathrow.'

'No. But that's the puzzle. A person resembling her has just flown in from Australia.'

'It can't be her then. It's got to be a case of mistaken identity,' Andy said, now doubting himself.

'Her identity was further verified by facial recognition,' the policeman informed him.

'Computers aren't infallible,' Andy pointed out.

'I can assure you that the immigration people don't drop clangers like that Andy. They are trained to spot people even if they are wearing disguise.'

'Well, I can't help you. But I have to say, that I'm a bit unnerved by it.'

'Yes, so am I. I'll keep you abreast of any developments.'

'Cheers.'

CHAPTER EIGHTEEN

DC Chris Cooper and DS Marcus Williams gazed at the woman through the one-way glass observation panel of the airport interview room.

Their hectic dash along the M4 to Heathrow Airport had taken barely 30 minutes in the outside lane with the blues and twos of their unmarked car parting the heavy traffic.

'Well, I'll be jiggered. If I didn't know better, I would have said that was our woman,' Chris Cooper said to the immigration officer.

'Yes likewise,' agreed his colleague. 'Well let's get this over and done with,' he continued, moving to the door.

Suzette had been sat alone and frustrated in the interview room for several hours when at last the door opened.

'Miss Brown?'

'Yes.'

'My name is Detective Sergeant Marcus Williams, and this is my colleague Detective Constable Chris Cooper.'

'Have you come to arrest me?'

'No, nothing like that. Umm... I'm terribly sorry that you've been detained for so long. But as you have probably guessed there was some confusion over your identity.'

'So I gather.'

'It was a false alarm, due to the likeness of you and your sister. It was believed that you were her and she was…shall we say of interest to us.'

'That's understandable. My DNA search showed that we are identical twins,' Suzette explained calmly.

'Yes, quite so,' the Sergeant accepted.

'So can I finally go now? My sister has been waiting for hours. She must be worried sick. Unfortunately, I couldn't raise her to let her know what was going on. I expect there is something wrong with her phone. That's why I can't get through,' Suzette reasoned. 'And I…'

'I'm afraid to tell you that's not the reason for her not answering,' Chris Cooper interrupted quietly.

'What do you mean? Why would you know the reason?' Suzette asked apprehensively. 'Is there something wrong? Is she in prison? Is she in…'

'I'm sorry…to inform you…unfortunately… there is no other way of telling you this.'

'What do you mean? Telling me what?' Suzette demanded fearfully.

'I'm sorry to inform you that you won't be able to contact your sister.'

Suzette's heart sank.

'Unfortunately, your sister was involved in a fatal road traffic collision. I'm sorry to tell you that your sister did not survive it and died at the scene. She is dead,' the detective, revealed sympathetically.

'Dead! What do you mean dead? I only spoke to her…well just before I left Sydney,' Suzette blurted in disbelief. 'You must be mistaken. Yes. Just like your facial recognition cock up. You must be wrong. Please tell me you're wrong. There must be a chance that its wrong. Please.' Suzette sank to her knees, her grief overwhelming her.

'I'm afraid not,' the Detective Sergeant added. 'She was involved in a road traffic accident, and she was trapped inside the crashed car which unfortunately caught fire. I'm so sorry.'

'No. No it can't be true,' Suzette squealed. 'How do you know it was her in the car? It could be mistaken identity.'

'To the best of our knowledge it was her. No, I don't think it is a case of mistaken identity,' he added. 'There were witnesses. She was escaping after a shooting incident.'

'A shooting incident!' the distraught woman said in horror. 'Why would anyone be shooting at her?'

'This might come as a shock to you,' he revealed. 'But I'm sorry to say that… in fact she was the shooter. Not the victim.'

'What! No that's not possible. My sister a gunman! You must be joking? Are you sure that we are talking about the same person?'

'I'm sorry to have to tell you that your sister has been on a crime watch for some time. She has been involved in a series of unlawful activities.'

'Oh, my days!'

'At the time of the accident she was a fugitive and subject to a county wide person hunt,' the policeman continued. 'Which is why you were mistakenly detained and the reason that we are here.'

'No, no. You must be mistaken! Please say that you have got it wrong,' Suzette pleaded, wringing her hands. 'It took me so long to find her…and now you're telling me not only that she's dead, but she was a horrible person too.'

'Sorry. There was no other way of telling you. I am sorry for your loss.'

'I so desperately wanted to see her in person; to hug her; to give my sister, my sister… a…a kiss.'

The policeman looked away, disturbed by her distress.

'And now you're telling me that my dream has gone,' Suzette sobbed.

The officer cleared his throat, trying to think of something to say.

'Can I see her? You'll need a formal identification, won't you?' the distressed woman asked.

'No, I'm sorry. She was involved in a fire after the crash. She was severely burnt.'

'Oh God. That's awful. So, all this has been the waste of time. Coming here.'

'So, it seems. I'm terribly sorry….sorry for your… your loss,' the DS said quietly.

'There will be an inquest to reveal what actually happened, if that's of any comfort to you,' Chris Cooper added.'

'No, nothing will help,' she wailed. 'I just want my sister.'

'Umm…what plans have you got for accommodation while you're here?' the DS asked, after a respectful pause.

'I haven't got any. Sue was making all the plans. I think we were going to be travelling,' Suzette explained.

'Well, I presume you would want to go to the inquest? Would you?' the policeman asked.

'Yes, I think I should, don't you?'

'Well, if it's of any help, we can take you back with us to Gloucester and you can book into a hotel there until you decide what you're going to do.'

'Thanks. At the moment, I don't know what to do. My head is spinning. It's all just too much,' Suzette replied.

'Don't worry. We understand. If you come back with us, we can also arrange for you to go to the crash site, to pay your respects. Perhaps put some flowers there if you like?'

'Yes…yes. That's truly kind. Yes please. I don't know what I'm doing. My world has been turned upside down. Please help,' she sobbed.

CHAPTER NINETEEN

The policemen arranged for the airport staff to look after the distraught woman, while they went and cleared their proposed actions with their boss. Having explained the situation to the Inspector they got a 'green light' to proceed, and they returned to the interview room.

'Are you feeling better now?' Chris Cooper asked, anxious about Suzette's 'meltdown.'

'Yes, I think so,' she confirmed. 'But it was such a shock. Not only to learn about her...her death. But all those horrible things that you say she had been accused of.'

'I can appreciate that,' the policeman said, compassionately. 'Not the best of news, was it?'

'A double whammy,' the Sergeant observed.

'It was awful. But I'm starting to come to terms with it, thanks.'

'Good. Pleased to hear,' Chris Cooper said, sympathetically.

The trio made their way back to the unmarked police car and started their journey back to Gloucester.

'Well, why don't you tell us a little about yourself and, if it's not too painful, how you discovered about your sister,' the DC suggested.

'Well. If you really want me to. Where to start?' Suzette pondered. 'Well, my father, Bruce… (the policemen flashed an amused smile to each other both thinking all Australians were called Bruce)…was an Australian soldier stationed here with the British army.' Suzette explained.

'He met and married my mother, a local girl called Clair. I gather, at the time, it was believed that she was unable to have children. Consequently, they adopted me when I was six months old.'

'Oh, so did you know that you were adopted?

'No. I didn't. Not until much later,' Suzette revealed. 'In those days, like all cases of adoption, my adoptive parents were unaware of my birth family's history.'

'That's right, I gather there was a taboo about revealing adopted children's backgrounds then. It was all hushed up and 'brushed under the carpet,' Marcus Williams agreed.

'Well, shortly after adopting me, my adoptive Dad's army service came to an end, and we went back to Queensland Australia to live with my dad's father.'

'Queensland. Wonderful place I hear.'

'Yes, my dad's father, Digger, had a large cattle ranch there.'

'So, your Grandfather was a farmer?'

'Well, yes. But strangely enough, I never thought of him being my grandfather. He was a strong minded, tough individual. He didn't fit the typical granddad image of pipe and slippers. He was gruff and distant with me. It wasn't until later that I found out why.'

'I suppose he needed to be tough to survive in the harsh conditions on the outback farm,' Chris Cooper suggested.

'It was a beef cattle farm, in the middle of nowhere, three hundred miles Southwest of Brisbane. We used to get brumbies there too.'

'Brumbies?' Chris Cooper wondered.

'Yeah, they're wild horses that roam the countryside,' Suzette explained.

'Probably like the Exmoor ponies,' the other policeman suggested. 'Sorry, carry on with your story.'

'Thanks. Well shortly after they returned from the UK to the farm, amazingly my adoptive mother became pregnant. She had a baby boy, whom they called Barry.'

'Change of air perhaps,' Marcus suggested. 'So, you had a brother?'

'Yeah, a pain in the ass brother,' she said disparagingly. 'Unfortunately, shortly after, Grandad Digger was killed during a round-up. His horse slipped, threw him off and then rolled on him.'

'Ouch. Not a good way to die,' the policeman observed.

'No, it was terrible. But following the tragedy, Bruce, my father, inherited the farm.'

'Silver lining to the tragedy then?'

'Yes, I suppose you can say that. As we kids grew up, we helped on the ranch, rode horses, and were involved in 'round ups'. The herds of cattle were enormous.'

'That must have been hard work?'

'Yes, it was. Hot and dusty too,' Suzette added. 'As a kid, It was a bit daunting. I was frightened to start with. But as I grew up, I loved the whole experience of it.'

'I bet. My daughter loves riding and wants a pony,' Marcus Williams added. 'But she's probably not anything like the standard of your horsemanship.'

'Tragedy was never far away from my life,' Suzette revealed. 'My father Bruce, died suddenly.'

'Oh dear! Heart attack was it?'

'Yes. We were all devastated. And much to my annoyance, although I was the eldest of us two kids, when the will was read, Bruce had bypassed me and left the farm to my brother Barry.'

'Yeah, I think I'd be miffed as well, if that happened to me,' Chris concurred.

'So now in charge of the farm Barry bossed me around. Which, as you can imagine, I did not like. But I gave him as good as I got.'

'Good for you,' the DC concurred.

'Eventually, I got fed up with the hassle from my domineering brother and we had a blinding row, and I moved out. I left the farm and moved to Brisbane.'

CHAPTER TWENTY

'Moved to Brisbane! Bold move for a country girl, wasn't it? Chris Cooper suggested. 'Suzette, you must have been overwhelmed by the busy city crowds?'

'Quite the opposite, I enjoyed the buzz of the city. I was away from the hot dusty, smelly farm. No, I was in my element.'

'What did you do?'

'Having worked long hours on the farm, I wasn't work shy, so I did waitressing while I trained as a nurse. Then, when I was qualified, I went to work in the local hospital,' Suzette explained.

'Hence your intention to work for the NHS here in the UK?' the DC concluded.

'Yes, that's right. It was at the hospital that I found out from my work colleagues, about DNA testing and tracing family lines.' Suzette revealed.

'I quite fancied the idea of tracing my family genes too. But I've never got round to doing it,' Chris Cooper volunteered.

'Anyway, I quite liked the idea of doing a family tree and was keen to trace our family history. Obviously, I needed to get my mother involved in the DNA modelling. So, on my day off I went back to the farm to persuade her and my brother to take part in the exercise.'

'But, to my surprise, my attempt to get them involved led to some dramatic arguments. My adoptive mother flatly refused. And didn't want anything to do with it.'

'At this stage you didn't know that you were adopted?' Chris Cooper probed.

'No that's right.'

'I can see why she'd be reluctant, if they'd never told you that you were adopted,' Marcus added sympathetically.

'I was angry about her refusal and brought up how unfair it was that as the eldest child I had not inherited the farm.'

'Understandable.'

'Unfortunately, I obviously touched a raw nerve, and my adoptive Mother blew her top and blurted it out. 'Get this into your thick skull, she said, you have no claim to the ranch. You are not even my child.'

Wow! That must have hit you like a bomb going off?"

'Yes. I was devastated. Eventually, things calmed down and she revealed that I had been adopted from an English orphanage.'

'Shit!'

'Oh heavens! What a way to find out.'

'In spite of the secrecy about adopted children, I was told that I was born to a woman in 'unfortunate' circumstances,' Suzette revealed. 'My birth mother was unmarried and had twins.'

'Oh dear. Not a good start to your life,' Chris Cooper observed.

'No, it wasn't. I was told, that to avoid a scandal, her family forced her to put them into an orphanage.

'How awful. Poor woman,' Chris Cooper observed.

'You can imagine how distraught I was with that news. I was, in my own eyes, a reject. A family reject.'

'A reject! Oh, that's a terrible way of self-judgement,' the policeman remarked.

'Bizarrely I had felt close to my adoptive mother and our family - even to my domineering brother up to that point. Then it all made sense. I knew then why the farm ownership had bypassed me.'

'So, what did you do?'

'I left the farm in tears, vowing never to go back. I was psychologically destroyed; I didn't know who I was anymore.'

'Understandable,' Chris Cooper sympathised.

'However, when I recovered from the shock, I decided to try hard to find my real family. So, I submitted my DNA to a company that advertised worldwide DNA matching.'

'Any luck?'

'Yes. I was amazed when, within a couple of weeks, I got a report with a positive match,' she relayed enthusiastically.

'That must have been exciting,' Chris agreed.

'Unfortunately though, they didn't find my birth mother or father. But excitingly they found an identical match to my own DNA.'

'Identical! What were the chances of that?'

'Well, I did some research and found out that DNA is inherited from parents; Only certain parts of siblings DNA match exactly; but Identical twins have exactly the same DNA. The report indicated that I had a sister with matching DNA. I was one of a pair. A twin!' Suzette revealed excitedly.

'You must have been elated?' The DC suggested.

'Yes, I was. I was not a reject after all. I had a blood relative.'

'Amazing. Did they tell you, her name?'

'Well, yes... eventually. As we all now know it was the lady called Sue Williams-Screen. She was Sue and I was Suzette. How spooky was that? I guess my mother had named us.'

'How come her DNA was available? Was she looking to find her family history too?'

'No. She told me that her DNA had been picked up by the matching site due to a hacking attack on the UK Home Office computers.'

'A hacking attack! You got to be joking,' the DS said in disbelief.

CHAPTER TWENTY-ONE

'Yes, I heard about the hacking attack. There was a serious breach of security,' Chris Cooper confirmed. 'Foreign hackers got past the firewall security system of the Home Office's computer farm.'

'What happened?' Marcus asked.

'Apparently the Home Office refuted allegations that they were being blackmailed and denied that they been the target of a hacking attack.'

'As expected,' the DS observed.

'Obviously, they refused to pay, so consequently, the hackers called the Home Office's bluff and released a small amount of data on the dark web. This proved that they had indeed breached the firewall,' Chris Cooper revealed.

'Unfortunately, the press blew the Home Office's denial out of the water and uncovered the security breach. Questions were asked in the house.'

'Yes, that's right. Sue's DNA was amongst the data illegally published, I later found out,' Suzette added.

'She was obviously up to no good even in those days, if her DNA was recorded on the database,' Chris Cooper thought.

'Whatever, I didn't care how it had been obtained. I had a sister,' Suzette said sadly. I was so excited by the

DNA match, that I started searching the internet for this woman. Eventually I discovered an 'old' Facebook page that she'd set up when she was first married to a man called Rupert.'

'Yes, we know all about him and their difficult relationship,' Chris Cooper thought, exchanging a knowing glance with his colleague.

'Anyway, after many failed attempts, I managed to initiate a discussion with a highly sceptical Sue. She was convinced I was a scammer, because, like me, she was unaware that she had a sister. Especially an identical twin.'

'And when you know all about her past crimes, you'll probably wish you hadn't too,' the policeman thought.

'As Sue's belief grew about the reality of our relationship, we swapped photographs with each other and were amazed at our likenesses. Spookily we even had the same hair style.'

'Yeah, well you certainly look like her that's for sure. Hence the confusion at the airport,' Marcus added.

'We started having regular FaceTime sessions. But as I was fed up with life in Brisbane, I told Sue that I had applied for a work visa in England, I gather there is a shortage of nurses in the NHS.'

'Yes, that's very true,' Chris Cooper confirmed.

'Initially she was reluctant to meet me but, I eventually persuaded her,' Suzette continued.

'No wonder she was reluctant, for unknown to Suzette, at the time, Sue was deep into her vicious campaign against the Godsons community. And was dodging our attempts to capture her,' Marcus thought.

'As you know, we finally planned to meet at Heathrow airport. I was so excited,' she said.

'Not exactly the ending that you were hoping for then, is it?' Chris observed.

'No. It's all been a nightmare,' Suzette sobbed.

'Just give yourself time to get over the shock and then review your plans. When did you plan to start work here?' Marcus probed.

'I'm not sure if I want to stay here anymore. One of the main reasons now no longer exists,' Suzette confessed. 'I will stay for the inquest and decide after that.'

CHAPTER TWENTY-TWO

However, in reality, Suzette had 'burnt her bridges' in Queensland.

For after the heated family row and revelation that she was adopted, she said that she was emigrating to the UK to start a new life anyway.

Unhelpfully, Barry derided her plans and said that she wouldn't be able to stick it.

Frustrated by his negative comments and the disastrous turn of events, she'd stormed out.

Consequently, returning early was not an option. 'She was going to be stubborn and stick to her plans, just to spite him.' Suzette concluded.

'Yes, you need to give yourself time,' Chris Cooper agreed.

'In the meantime, I suggest that you keep a low profile and avoid any newspaper people catching up with you,' Marcus added.

'Why? Why would the newspaper people be even interested in me?' Suzette puzzled.

'Unfortunately, before she died, your sister was the subject of a large publicity exercise trying to track her down. Her photograph was displayed everywhere, and all police patrols were actively looking for her. Although we have now cancelled the person hunt, there might be some delay in the removal of the notices. So, well-meaning people might occasionally target you.'

'Oh, heavens. She really wasn't a nice person at all, was she?' Suzette observed. 'She obviously upset a lot of people.'

'That's an understatement,' Chris Cooper thought. 'Kidnap, assault, multiple cases of attempted murder, arson; 'to name just a few, is a lot of 'upset.'

'Unfortunately, your physical likeness to her is bound to attract a lot of attention. So, we'll have to give you some sort of disguise if you are going to stay in a local hotel,' Marcus suggested.

'Disguise?' Suzette exclaimed. 'What sort of disguise?'

'On the other hand, perhaps we put her up in a safe house?' the other policeman suggested.

'If we do that, what about meals and provisioning?'

'Yes, there is that,' Chris accepted.

'Look, I don't want any special favours. At this moment all I want to do is go to bed. I am completely exhausted,' Suzette said filling up.

'OK, we'll take you to a hotel where we know the manager. He owes us a few favours. He will make sure that there is no press intrusion,' the other policeman continued.

'OK thanks. I can't think straight anymore,' Suzette confessed tearfully.

'We'll make arrangements for a police liaison person to keep an eye on you too and we'll try and protect you as much as we can from press intrusion.'

'Would you like to...to place some flowers for your sister?' Chris Cooper asked sympathetically.

'Yes please.'

'OK we'll arrange something for you for tomorrow?'

'Yes, that will be OK. So long as I can get some sleep. I'm exhausted.'

Finally, alone in her hotel room Suzette 'crashed out on the bed, her head in a whirl. A combination of jet lag, shock and fear sapping her strength.

But before she gave way to her exhaustion, she retrieved her mobile out of her handbag. Through misty eyes she looked at the last text message Sue had sent.

'I have been fighting to get my legally entitled share of my former husband (Rupert's) legacy. I have at last succeeded and will meet you on your arrival at Heathrow airport (Outside the terminal three building). We can go on a luxury trip to celebrate our sisterhood. I am excited by the prospect of meeting you in person and giving you a big hug. I am so looking forward to it. LOL XXX'

Suzette sobbed. Tears cascaded down her face, wetting the bed sheets.

What Suzette didn't know was that the 'legally entitled' money would have come from a ransom from kidnapping Rupert and Joanne's baby Jeffery and their babysitter, Tim's Mother Kay.

But the scheme had failed disastrously. There was no money.

CHAPTER TWENTY-THREE

Completely drained by the traumatic events of the day, blessed sleep eventually came to Suzette, but even then, nightmares stalked her tired brain, and she awoke to find her bedclothes in a twisted heap on the floor.

Heeding the policemen's recommendation of keeping a low profile, she had requested room service to bring a breakfast tray to her room.

After a small bowl of cereals and a glass of orange juice, she fought the aching tiredness and jet lag to get herself motivated with a refreshing shower.

As she showered, waves of self-pity crashed over her, the warm water mixing with her tears and washing them away.

She admonished herself for being so emotional. 'Come on Suzette, get a grip,' she chided herself. 'Perhaps I should have waited a couple of days before I agreed to visit the crash site. It would have given me a bit more time to get my head together.'

However, at the agreed time Suzette was collected from her hotel room by a kindly matronly looking person.

'Hello dear. You must be Suzette. My name is Jenny from Police liaison. I'm so sorry to hear about your tragedy. Do you still want to go and pay your respects?'

'Yes, please,' Suzette said, taking a deep breath to galvanise herself.

As they drove to the crash site, Jenny kept up a light, one-way conversation with an apprehensive Suzette.

Enroute, they collected a bunch of flowers from a florist that Jenny recommended.

Despite the driver's endeavours to draw her out, Suzette was noticeably quiet, becoming increasingly emotional as they drove up through the meandering Cotswold country lanes.

Finally, the Police driver pulled off the narrow lane onto a small layby and stopped the car.

'This is it,' Jenny told Suzette quietly. 'Take your time. Do it when you're ready. There is no rush.'

The pair got out of the car and studied the hole in the hedge where Sue's out of control MX5 had punched its way through.

Reverentially they looked at the flattened branches and violated undergrowth waymarking Sue's final journey and stepped into the field.

They looked at the deep gouges carved in the grass by the crashing car. A tell-tale signature across the field leading to the car's final resting place before it's trip into the quarry.

As they walked across the field Suzette gently ran her finger around the edges of the missing bark in the tree scarred and wounded by the buckling bodywork.

They crunched their way along a path of glass fragments, like a deathly confetti trail, which waymarked the way to the scene of the final fatal act.

Police blue and white incident tape fluttered in the breeze as the pair walked toward the edge of the field.

'The forensic team have spent some hours examining the sites,' Jenny informed Suzette.

'Sites?' Suzette queried.

'Yes, the one up here. And the cars final resting place at the bottom of the quarry.'

Suzette shuddered at the mention of the final resting place.

'Unfortunately, the quarry is not safe for us to enter I'm informed. So, are you happy to lay your tribute up here?'

'Is it OK to go through the tape perimeter though?'

'Yes. They will have captured every little bit of evidence you can be sure of that,' Jenny said, trying to reassure Suzette.

As they walked further, they could see damage to the edge of the field.

'This is obviously where the car had balanced before it finally disappeared into the void,' Jenny thought. 'Taking it's trapped passenger to a fiery death into the quarry below.'

Suzette was overwhelmed. She knelt and laid her bouquet of flowers near to the edge, her gaze drawn to the blackened limestone quarry walls, her tears falling onto the delicate petals of the floral memorial for a sister that she never got to know. Sobbing over lost opportunities of what might have been.

'You OK?' the Police liaison person asked quietly, putting a sympathetic hand on Suzette's shoulder.

'Yes. I just need a few minutes to myself,' Suzette explained thickly.

'Ok, I'll wait in the car. Take your time,' the driver said gently, leaving Suzette with her grief.

CHAPTER TWENTY-FOUR

After she'd recovered from the initial shock of losing the sister that she never knew, Suzette decided to try and track down their birth parents while she was waiting for the inquest.

She logged in to the hotel internet to find some background about tracing relatives and quickly found a site.

Excited, she read the details on the website on a page entitled: *Find birth relatives if you were adopted.*

The page revealed exactly what she needed to do to start the process.

The fee is £15 - instructions on how to pay are on form CR part 1

When an adopted child turns 18 years old, they have a legal right to request information about their birth family, so may make direct contact.

*You can add yourself to the **Adoption Contact Register** if you're eighteen or over and your birth or adoption was registered with the General Register Office.*

You need to fill in form CR part 1 to add yourself to the register.

You can also use this form if you are an adopted person looking for other adopted siblings.

'Oh great, if only I'd known this existed before, perhaps it would have been easier to find Sue in the first place,' she thought. 'But it's too late now.' And she dismissed the thought.

'I'm going to fill out a form on the Adoption Contact Register and see where that gets me, at least it's a start,' she said to herself, scrolling down the screen.

'Right so I have to read the guidance notes on how to complete the form first.

So, I need:-

original birth name – I don't know that. I wonder if mum in Australia has got it.

date of birth – Yes, I know that, at least I know when I celebrate my birthday.

the full name(s) of your birth mother (and birth father if known) – Oh dear, here's the stumbling block. How do I find that?'

Frustrated at not being able to complete the form, she accepted that her search was going to be unsuccessful.

But surely as she was born here in England, there must be some clues to her background and information about her parents. The trouble was, finding that trail.

CHAPTER TWENTY-FIVE

Suzette had been at the hotel for three weeks keeping a low profile as the police had suggested.

The only good news that she'd had was that the coroner had brought forward the date of the inquest, so at least she could move on and finally make funeral arrangements.

The anticipation of the inquest was getting to Suzette, her head was pounding. She needed fresh air. The hotel's stuffy air conditioning wasn't helping, so she decided to go for a walk in the local park.

It was dark as she left the hotel, but she felt safe. This was gentle England after all. Not the crime ridden streets of New York,' she reasoned. 'And, in any case, if anyone approached her, she was tough enough to see them off. Just as she had with the randy wranglers with their wandering hands on the ranch back home.'

As she walked through the park, she couldn't stop thinking about her sister's alleged crimes. Surely, she had been wrongfully accused. Was there another reason behind her reputation?'

Suddenly the peace was shattered. A noise broke into her thoughts. Shouting, she could hear distressed shouting. A woman shouting for help.

Suzette ran along the meandering concrete path, to the source of the noise. She discovered an elderly lady desperately hanging on to the strap of her handbag. The woman was in a 'tug of war' with a hooded character who was trying to grab it off her.

'Let that go,' Suzette shouted, as she ran towards the melee.

'Ha, what you going to do about it?' the thug said, yanking on the strap and causing its owner to fall heavily.

As the woman hit the tarmac path, she immediately let out a cry of pain, but much to the frustration of her attacker, she still held on to the strap of her handbag.

Suzette ran at the assailant and rugby tackled him, sending him sprawling on to his back.

Shocked by the unexpected assault, the yob let go of the handbag strap, desperately putting his hands down to soften his fall as Suzette's momentum knocked him off his feet. The pair crashed to the pavement with Suzette on top, still encircling his waist.

A mouthful of expletives from the shocked mugger filled the air, as Suzette fought to stay on top of the struggling figure.

Now, sat on his chest, attempting to pin his arms down, she caught the unmistakeable smell of cannabis exuding from the assailant.

'Not so brave now, are we?' she shouted in his face.

In response, the yob brought his knee up and catapulted Suzette off him.

Free from Suzette's restraint, the yob quickly scrambled to his feet and ran off shouting, 'If I ever see you again, I will cut you,' he threatened.

Slowly Suzette picked herself up, assessing her injuries. She had grazed her hands and knees as she landed spreadeagled on the path.

'Not if I see you first, you bastard,' she shouted.

Breathing heavily from her exertions, Suzette knelt and turned her attention to the prostrate woman. 'Are you OK?' she asked gently.

'My hip. Oh, my hip. I think I've broken my hip,' the woman,' groaned.

'OK, don't worry. I'm a nurse. We'll soon have you sorted,' Suzette explained calmly, reaching for her mobile.

Through the excruciating pain, Kay opened her eyes. Lit by the light of Suzette's mobile, she saw her good Samaritan's face for the first time. She was stunned by what she saw. The shock of seeing that hateful face again was too much. She screamed and passed out.

CHAPTER TWENTY-SIX

Tim had received the dreaded phone call from the police.

'Mr Springfield?'

'Yes.'

'I'm sorry to be the bearer of bad news, but your mother is in hospital,' the policewoman advised him.

'In hospital! Why what's happened?' Tim demanded.

'Unfortunately, she was subjected to a mugging attempt,' the officer informed him.

'Is she alright?' Tim asked, concerned.

'We don't have any more information at the moment. She is currently being treated for her injuries in hospital.'

'What hospital?

'Gloucester.'

'OK thanks. I...I'll go and...' Tim ended the call before finishing the sentence and quickly relayed the information to Carrie.

The pair rushed to the hospital and quizzed the A & E receptionist. She checked her computer screen.

'And may I ask your relationship first?'

'I'm her son. The police called me.'

'She is in bay four. Just along the corridor,' the receptionist directed.

'Do we know what she's being treated for?'

'A suspected broken hip, I believe,' the receptionist informed them.

Following her directions, they found Kay lying on a trolley in a curtained off cubicle.

'Oh, my days, Kay are you alright?' Carrie asked the distraught woman, cradling her hand sympathetically.

'It was awful. A man tried to grab my handbag and a…a woman came to my rescue. That woman…that woman that you told me I would never see again, it was her…it was that horrible Williams-Screen,' Kay shouted angrily.

'Don't be so daft Mum. Williams-Screen is dead. You must have imagined it.'

'I tell you. She is not dead,' Kay insisted fearfully. 'She tackled the mugger.'

'Look Mum. It's not possible. Andy and Ben saw her crash,' Tim said impatiently. 'It might have been someone who looked like her.

'Then they must be mistaken,' Kay said passionately. 'I definitely saw her. I'd know that awful face anywhere. I thought she was going to kill me for not carrying out her orders about the ransom money.'

'But she didn't, did she?' Tim argued. 'Besides, you're safe here in hospital. So, get that crazy thought out of your head.'

'You think I'm going gaga, don't you?' Kay challenged.

'No of course not. No crazier than you were before,' he joked, trying to lighten the conversation.

'Timothy!' Carrie rebuked.

'It was a joke,' he replied defensively.' Anyway, what were you doing in the park at that time of night?'

'I had a reunion with a few of my former working colleagues and I was taking a shortcut to get to the bus stop. I've done it lots of times before.'

'Yes, but unfortunately, tonight you were in the wrong place at the wrong time,' Tim pointed out.

'It's a pity that I wasn't with you,' Carrie added.

'No, with her special forces background the guy wouldn't have got anyway near you to even grab your bag,' Tim observed.

'Don't worry Kay. You aren't going daft. The trauma of your kidnapping and ransom drama that you experienced recently causes strange psychological illusions. I know from my army days,' Carrie revealed.

'Yes Mum,' Carrie is often having episodes and seeing phantom events.' Tim interjected.

'I can fully understand what you're going through Kay.' Carrie said, empathetically.

'Yes, remember Carrie was nearly killed by that woman during one of her attacks. Thank goodness it failed,' Tim added.

'But I tell you it WAS her. She WAS there. As large as life. As god is my witness.' Kay insisted. 'The only odd thing was, that unlike her usual vicious self, she was actually being kind to me,' Kay added. 'She tackled the robber and knocked him over.'

'Well that definitely wasn't her then,' Tim said adamantly. 'She didn't have an ounce of kindness in her body. Unless she's come back as an angel to pay for all her wickedness,' Tim added, flippantly.

'It might have been the shock of the attack and the pain that caused you to hallucinate and think it was her,' Carrie suggested. 'Perhaps your mind linked the past trauma with what was happening to you then?'

'Just because you're his partner, you don't have to stick up for him,' Kay charged. 'After she's sorted the mugger out, she came and asked me if I was OK. The last thing that I remember was that hateful face and... oh yes and she...she spoke funny...and then I don't remember anything else because I passed out.'

'Look, you've been through an awful ordeal being kidnapped with baby Jeffery. You're probably suffering from post-traumatic stress. You will get better, it will fade believe me,' Carrie encouraged.

'We'll find out soon anyway,' Tim added. 'The Police said that it was an Australian woman who reported the incident. Apparently, she was with you until the ambulance people arrived.' Tim advised her. 'Perhaps it was her that you saw. She is due to give a statement and will try to identify the mugger from their photo gallery.'

'Then you'll see if I'm imagining things,' Kay said stubbornly.

'Look Mum, along with the others, I'm going to Sue Williams-Screen's inquest tomorrow. An inquest is held when people die. So, the woman can't be alive, can she?'

'Don't talk down to me like that Tim. I am not mad,' Kay huffed irritably.

'Yes, I'm going too,' Carrie intervened quickly.

'I thought you couldn't stand the woman Carrie. Especially after you had that punch up with her, all those years ago, when you intervened to stop her beating up Rupert!'

'No, you're right I couldn't stand her,' Carrie confirmed. 'We had a lot of battles over the years. She was a right bitch.

'So why are you going then?' Kay demanded.

'We're going to support Andy and Ben.' Tim revealed, squeezing Carrie's hand.

CHAPTER TWENTY-SEVEN

Andy stopped mid stride. His heart skipped a beat. Surely, he was dreaming. For ten feet in front of him, Sue Williams-Screen was walking into the coroner's court...walking to her own inquest!

'How was that possible? She is dead!' he reasoned. 'He had been there when the car went over the edge and caught fire.

The police had found what was left of her in the burnt-out wreck. But positive confirmation had not occurred because she was so severely burnt. And no dental records could be found to collaborate her identity.

So, did she escape after all? It was dark,' he reasoned. 'There were no streetlights, only the light from the moon. Did we get it wrong? Were we chasing the wrong car? After all, the police didn't find the shotgun. Surely that's the only explanation if it wasn't her in the car. Otherwise, how could she be coming to her own inquest?

Andy felt lightheaded, unable to process the evidence of his own eyes.

'I must get to Ben to warn him. Otherwise, it will blow his mind.'

But it was too late. Ben was just ahead of him and had already seen the woman. He too was horror struck.

'Oh my god! She's come back to haunt me,' he'd panicked.

A sense of foreboding overwhelmed him. For as shocked as he was about the manner of her death and his failed efforts to grab her hand, he had felt relief that her terrible presence was gone forever. And now, horror of horrors, she was back.

This was the woman who had kidnapped him and attempted to kill him.

Rooted to the spot, staring at her, he reran the events of that terrible moment of her death through his mind.

Despite her vicious animosity to him, he had put his life on the line and tried to help her even as her car balanced precariously on the cliff edge.

Unfortunately, as she panicked, the car overbalanced, and he failed to reach her hand in time. The woman and the car had gone over.

He experienced mixed emotions at the disaster. Guilt about the uplifting of his spirits and shock at her end. He was horrified at her death but at the same time relief that she wouldn't be hurting him anymore.

But now, she had come back to haunt him for his lack of sympathy.

His heart froze, his stomach tensed in sheer fright. He was overwhelmed by this spectre and in blind panic, ran out of the court entrance and into the car park.

Fearfully, crouching on the ground, behind a Nissan X-Trail, he hugged his knees to make himself as small as possible. He was frightened that she had spotted him and would come after him.

Andy saw him run and chased after him. And after a brief search found the frightened youngster, sitting behind the car, trembling with fear.

'Oh, thank God, I found you,' Andy said, looking at the terrified teenager.

'She's still alive Andy,' Ben said in shock. 'She's come back to haunt me.'

'No, there must be some mistake,' Andy said, trying to sound calm. 'She was definitely in the car when it went over wasn't she?

Yes of course she was,' Ben confirmed weakly.

'Although, I didn't actually see when the car went over,' Andy added. 'Obviously, she was, wasn't she?'

'I tried to give her a hand, but the car went over and crashed and...we saw it together. It just burst into flames,' Ben recounted.

'Yes, it did,' Andy confirmed.

'You said it was all over Andy. You lied to me. It'll never be over. She will always haunt me,' Ben whimpered.

'I don't understand. There has got to be another explanation,' Andy suggested. 'Perhaps it's a relative. Someone that looks like her. Yes, that's it,' Andy said, thinking it through. 'A relative!'

Just at that moment Chris Cooper arrived and parked his car in a reserved space. Spotting them in their conspiratorial huddle he went over.

'Having a quick fag break?' he asked flippantly.

'No. We don't smoke,' Andy replied, missing the joke.

'I keep meaning to give it up myself,' he said. 'Just to give you a 'heads up' so that it doesn't come as a shock, but that Williams-Screen woman has an identical twin. So don't be surprised if you see her. You're not seeing ghosts.'

'Too late with that bit of news, we've just seen her,' Andy divulged. We thought we were going mad. Didn't we Ben?' I knew that there had to be a logical explanation.' Andy said quickly.

'Sorry about that, I suppose you should have been told earlier,' the policeman admitted. 'She has recently arrived here from Australia. Obviously, she's come to the inquest today.'

'I'm not going into the court if she's going to be there,' Ben stipulated.

'You must. You have no choice. The court has ordered that you attend to provide evidence,' the policeman advised him.

'I don't care,' Ben said firmly.

CHAPTER TWENTY-EIGHT

JC joined the group in the carpark.

'Sorry I'm late. Couldn't find a parking space in here. So I parked up the road. Is there a problem?' he enquired, seeing Ben sat on the floor.

'Hi JC. Yes, Ben is saying he won't go into the Coroners court to give his evidence.' Andy informed the Godson.

'Why? What's changed Ben? He was OK when I dropped him off,' JC queried.

'She's in there,' Ben blurted.

'She! Who's in there?' JC queried. 'Who are you talking about?'

'Sue's sister,' Andy explained. 'She is an identical twin to that woman.'

'Yes, it's quite spooky to see her,' the Policeman admitted. 'Sorry Ben, but if you don't attend, It's likely I shall be ordered to arrest you for failing to assist the coroner in the execution of his duties.'

'God, that's not fair. I haven't done anything wrong,' Ben moaned.

'Unfortunately, that's the law. We can't change that. Come on fella. The apprehension is often worse than the event,' the policeman encouraged.

Finally, Ben capitulated, and they made their way to the main glass fronted entrance.

Outside the courtroom door a small group had gathered, including Suzette, her solicitor, and her Police family liaison officer.

Ben's heart was in his mouth as they approached. He stood directly behind Andy to try and hide. Unfortunately, the police liaison officer pointed him out to Suzette, much to Ben's great discomfort.

Suddenly Suzette broke away from the group and made her way towards Ben. As Suzette approached him, Ben's blood turned to ice, and he wanted to run away.

G'day, I believe you're Ben? You're the one who saw my sister last,' she said.

'Yeah...yes,' Ben muttered, trying to avoid eye contact, his saliva dry mouth making speaking difficult. Frightened at what would come next.

'You saw my sister go to...go to her death?' she said tearfully.

'Y...yes,' he stammered.

'It must have been horrible for you,' she said quietly, dabbing her eyes.

Ben was taken aback with her calm words, expecting a tirade of abuse from her as her sister would have done.

'I...I... I tried to save her. Honest. But I couldn't grab her hand in time,' he explained all in a rush.

'In the circumstances, I expect you did your best,' Suzette suggested, sympathetically.

'We were just too late to save her. I'm sorry.' At which point, Ben broke down.

Quite unexpectedly, Suzette moved to him and gave him a hug.

Ben was gobsmacked. He just stood there and accepted the embrace without responding.

'It's OK to cry,' she said; her own tears wetting Ben's hair. 'I gather she wasn't very kind to you. But in spite of that, you still tried to save her. That must have taken a great deal of courage. Thank you Ben, for trying. Bless you.'

Suzette's likeness to Sue confused Ben's senses. He had been fearful of that woman for years, but now this lookalike was showing genuine sincerity, which her sister would have never done.

'Umm, that's umm, OK. I...I'm sorry that I ....that she...she died,' Ben stuttered.

'I'm sure that you did your best,' Suzette repeated and smiled compassionately.

At that point, the doors of the court were opened, and people started going in and taking their places.

'Right, let's get this over and done with,' Suzette said, giving Ben a final hug and leaving him.

Ben shot a 'what just happened' look at Andy and entered the court room with the others.

Tim, Carrie, and Rupert arrived just in time to see Suzette leaving Ben and heading into court.

'Oh my god! Am I seeing things?' Carrie gasped and stopped in her tracks, horrified. 'It's her. How the hell! I told you she would do her disappearing act and reappear again didn't I? You didn't believe me, did you?' Carrie said, thunderstruck, grabbing Tim's arm. 'I don't want to stay. Can we go home?' she begged.

'Don't be so daft. It can't be her. Unless Andy and Ben got it very wrong,' Tim said rationally.

'She wouldn't be coming to her own inquest. That doesn't make sense,' Rupert pointed out.

'No. It's got to be a look-a-like. 'This must be the woman who came to Mum's rescue when she was being mugged,' Tim acknowledged. 'Perhaps Mother isn't going batty after all.'

'If it isn't that horrible woman, she's a frighteningly spitting image of her though.'

Their deliberations were cut short by a court official. 'We're just about to start,' he informed them. 'Please hurry and take your seats, 'the clerk directed and steered them into some vacant chairs.

CHAPTER TWENTY-NINE

'Please stand,' the court was ordered.

The voice of the court clerk broke into Ben's thoughts as the coroner entered.

The Coroner duly took his seat, and the attendees were invited to sit.

The coroner addressed the court.

'Today's inquest is the investigation into the death of Sue Williams-Screen.

In calling this inquest I have to advise you that where there has been destruction of a body by fire as Coroner, I am required to apply to the Secretary of State for permission to hold this inquest....'

Although she already knew the manner of Sue's death, Suzette gasped as the coroner explained the legal process to the court.

His declaration suddenly brought home to Suzette the painful reality of the manner and horror of Sue's death. There was no denying it, her sister was really dead.

'...I have been directed to proceed; and have to provide evidence to the Secretary of State that a death has actually occurred.

The post-mortem of the deceased revealed that she died of severe burns.

Her body was incinerated in an inferno following her car going off the road and crashing down into a quarry.

As a result, identification has proved difficult. She was not able to be identified by her dental records, as is often the case when severe fire is involved. However due to her previous criminality, the body was identified through her DNA.'

Her sister gasped and dabbed at her eyes. The cruel irony of this particular DNA match was not lost on Suzette.

'At the time of the accident she was being pursued by another car following an earlier shooting incident.

This inquest will only focus on the cause of her death. The shooting incident is currently part of a criminal investigation by the police,' the coroner explained.

'I'd like to call Mr Andy Spider to the witness box to give his evidence.

CHAPTER THIRTY

Giving Ben a strained smile as he squeezed past, Andy walked quickly to the witness box as directed by the court official.

The coroner's officer asked Andy his oath preference for swearing to tell the truth. Due to his Scout promise, of duty to God and to the King. Andy chose the bible and duly made his declaration.

Satisfied with the oath promise, the coroner consulted his notes and spoke to Andy. 'Prior to the accident, I understand that you were chasing Sue Williams-Screen's car at high speed?'

'Well yes and no. To be strictly accurate, we were tailing her, not chasing,' Andy clarified.

'So, as you had a grandstand seat, so to speak, in your view why did she crash her car?' the coroner probed.

'She was driving too fast and lost control on a sharp bend in the narrow lane.'

'And remind me why you were chasing...tailing' her?'

'Because she had earlier attempted to kill us with a double-barrelled shotgun at the Scout HQ.'

'Us! Who is us?'

'Ben and myself.'

'Ben Bird?'

'Yes.'

'Is there any corroborating evidence to support your claim of the shooting incident?'

'Yes, there is. A shotgun hole blasted in the kitchen door at the Scout Headquarters. And the kitchen peppered with shot.

I imagine that the police forensic people will also verify that too. And I believe Ben will confirm it in his evidence as he was with me at the time.'

'If that was the case, rather than tailing her why didn't you ring the police immediately from the scout hut and report the shooting incident?' the coroner probed.

'There wasn't time to call them. After shooting at us, she was escaping, so I decided to follow her, to find out where her hideaway was. 'I knew that she had been evading the police for some time,' Andy explained.

'If it was a double barrel shotgun, can you think why she didn't discharge the second barrel?

'I think it was because of a police car with blues and twos going past the hut spooked her.'

'It sounds like that coincidence possibly saved your life then?'

'Yes. We were incredibly lucky,' Andy confirmed.

'So, you wanted to chase after her?'

'Tail her, not chase. Yes, I wanted to find out where she was going,' Andy repeated, annoyed at having to emphasise that he wasn't chasing her car.

'If you had a companion in the car with you, why didn't he call the police as you drove after her?'

'Because, I had foolishly left my mobile in the Scout hut.'

'And the boy's mobile? It's unusual to hear of a teenager disconnected from his phone for any length of time. Why didn't he use that?'

'He didn't have it with him.'

'Inconvenient. Why was that?'

'It was on charge at his home.'

'I see. Just when it was really wanted,' the coroner observed, further studying the paperwork on his desk. 'At the time of her attempt on your life, weren't you protected by two armed police?'

'Yes.'

'That's curious. So why didn't they intervene?'

'They were on a meal break.'

'On a meal break?' the coroner said, with incredulity. 'Both of them?

'Yes.'

'They were supposed to be protecting you.'

'Yes Sir. But to be fair, they had been guarding me all day and they'd left for a few minutes to pop to the shops. Unfortunately, that was when the woman appeared.'

'Bad timing.'

'Yes, it was. Whether she had been staking me out or whether it was an unfortunate coincidence, I don't know,' Andy observed.

'Whatever it was, it was unlucky timing,' the coroner agreed. 'It could have led to dire consequences.'

'Yes, well, we were fortunate I guess,' Andy reflected.

'As a side note, I will be asking questions to the chief constable about this lapse in your protection.'

'It wasn't their fault though. She was just lucky to find the chink in our protection. Her mythical protector, the devil, was continuing to look after her,' Andy said vehemently.

Suzette was horror struck to hear Andy's revelation that her sister was indeed the shooter, although the police had mentioned it previously. She was becoming increasingly depressed about the disclosures.

The coroner shuffled papers on his desk. 'Now we have the background to the reasons for the high-speed pursuit, I have to establish the causal link between the death, and the manner and the standard of driving. This, I believe, is a crucial factor in this case.'

'Sir. Excuse my ignorance, but what does that mean?' Andy puzzled.

'It means, did you cause the accident? Irrespective about the earlier shooting, was there any evidence that showed the victim's car was pushed off the road by another vehicle?'

Suzette tensed; she had not given this aspect of the accident any thought until now. Did Andy's car crash into her? Was Sue pushed over the cliff and murdered?

'It was nothing to do with us.' Andy pleaded defensively. 'She had crashed her car a few minutes before we even arrived on the scene.'

'Yes, I can see from the police report that an inspection of your car immediately after, showed no suspicious damage to suggest you were involved in the accident.'

'No Sir, that's correct. We weren't.' Andy said firmly.

'So, on arrival at the scene of the accident what did you see?'

'Her car had gone through a hedge, across a field and was balancing precariously on the edge of a drop into a quarry. The woman was trapped inside.'

'What did you do?'

'I could see that the car was in a precarious situation. Some barbed wire from a broken fence was entangled in a tyre. I decided that I needed to do something quickly to stop the car from going over. So, I ran and got my car,' Andy explained.

'For what purpose?'

'I was intending to tow her car away from the edge by attaching a tow rope between our two cars.'

'Please continue.'

'In the meantime, Ben volunteered to stay with the woman and calm her down. In her agitated state she was causing the car to slide further over the edge.'

'Were you there when the car actually went over the cliff?' the coroner asked.

'Well, no... I was just on my way back in my car with the tow rope and...

'Is it possible that you accidently nudged her car over as you approached it?'

'No, it had already gone over.'

'So, you weren't there at the point where the car and driver went over the cliff edge?' the coroner repeated.

'Well, no but...just immediately after.'

'So, the car could have been pushed over the cliff without your knowledge?'

'Well...yes, I suppose... but of course it wasn't. We were trying to save the woman.'

Suzette was shocked. She hadn't even considered that scenario. Had the young lad, whom she'd thanked and empathised with earlier actually deliberately pushed the car over and killed her sister?

'But you can't definitively, categorically say that it wasn't helped on its way?' the coroner probed.

'Well...No but...' Andy was wrong footed by the line of questioning. He had assumed that the facts spoke for themselves. She had lost control of the car and had crashed. It was her own fault that she'd ended up on the edge of a cliff. Despite what she had done to them, they had desperately tried to save her, but it had been too late.

'It is suggested that there was animosity between the boy and the woman?' the coroner revealed, examining his notes.

'Yes, quite understandably.' She had kidnapped him and tried to burn him alive. Then she'd tried to shoot him. Wouldn't you have some animosity?' Andy became animated. 'Yet, in spite of that, he still tried to save her.'

'She is not on trial here,' the coroner reminded him. 'We are only trying to establish the circumstances of the death of Sue Williams-Screen. Any criminal investigations required will be done on another occasion in a court of law."

'Yes, sorry.'

'Thank you, no further questions.'

Andy stepped out of the witness box feeling drained and uneasy. The coroner had introduced doubt in his mind as to Ben's actions.

As Andy took his seat next to Ben, Suzette stared at Ben in a new light, 'So, it was not just simply an accident, that I was led to believe. Was there a conspiracy against her sister after all?' she wondered.

CHAPTER THIRTY-ONE

'Ben Bird can you please come to the witness box.' The coroner asked softening his voice.

Ben self-consciously walked the short distance to the witness box as invited.

Suzette stared at him intensely.

'Before I start questioning you, let me explain how we conduct the session. The inquest is an inquisitorial process rather than an adversarial one. So, what that means is that it is my duty to tease out the actual details of the victim's death. Do you understand?

'Yes Sir.' Ben shuddered at the finality of the word death. This was all grown-up stuff, and he didn't want to be there.

'Are you Ben Bird?'

'Yes Sir.'

'Please read the oath from the card,' the clerk directed.

I do solemnly, sincerely, and truly declare and affirm that the evidence I shall give shall be the truth the whole truth and nothing but the truth.

'Remember that it is a criminal offence to lie under oath. Are you OK with that?' the Coroner asked.

'Yes Sir.'

'Do you concur with Mr Andy Spider's account of the accident?'

'Yes Sir.'

'We have heard Mr Spider say that the car was balanced precariously on the edge of the drop into the quarry.'

'Yes Sir.'

'And he left to get his car and was on his way back in it with a tow rope.'

'Yes Sir.'

'So, you were alone with the victim?'

'Yes Sir.'

'You were the last person to see her alive,' the coroner observed.

'Yes Sir,' Ben gulped as he suddenly realised the enormity of the role he'd played.

'I expect that you were frightened. In shock, after being shot at and seeing the car crash?'

'Yes Sir. It was all a bit of a blur.'

'I'm sorry that I have to ask you this. But did you push the car over the cliff?'

Ben was horrified at the accusation. 'No Sir. I tried to save her,' he said defensively.

'Perhaps your actions accidentally caused the car to go over the cliff?'

'No Sir,' Ben said, fearful of the way the questioning was going.

'Now there are many reasons for the car to suddenly plunge over the edge, and nobody could blame you, if you helped it go; Especially after all the terrible things that she had subjected you to.'

Ben couldn't believe his ears. He was being accused of killing the woman. Fear gripped his belly, his mouth dried.

'No, I didn't.' Ben said in panic. 'I was reaching out to grab her hand, when...when it went down. I still hear her scream as she fell into the quarry. I have nightmares about the fireball.'

Suzette winced at Ben's elaboration of the inferno. Her sisters funeral pyre.

Discussing the incident in detail caused Ben to relive the disaster in his mind. The mental image of the night flashed before his eyes, and he was now clearly distressed. He was shaking. His knuckles white from holding tightly on to the top of the witness box. All the while Sue's face stared at him from her lookalike sister.

Concerned with Ben's obviously distressed state, the coroner apologised. 'I'm sorry to have pressed you. I appreciate how terrible it must have been to relive the incident. But I must reveal the facts for the family and to establish if there is any criminality involved. Do you understand?'

'Yes, Sir.'

You may step down.'

'Thank you, Sir.'

As Ben walked back to his seat, out of the corner of his eye he saw Sue's twin leering at him. Through his questioning, the coroner had planted a seed of doubt in her mind. Had this young man actually deliberately killed her sister?

Her eyes lost their earlier compassion. She gave him a steely look. A look that Ben had seen many times from her sister before and it made his blood run cold.

The scenes of crime officer was called and gave evidence about their findings. She confirmed that the skid marks on the road, the hole in the hedge, the damage to the grass as the car rolled to the edge of the quarry were consistent with a car crash. She also confirmed the damage to a barb wire fence which would have played some part in the accident.

Much to Suzette's dread, she also explained about their examination of the burnt-out car and the position of the deceased inside.

Suzette couldn't hold the tears back any longer.

Seeing Suzette so distraught the Coroner called for a ten-minute break.

CHAPTER THIRTY-TWO

Away from the court and having finally composed herself, Suzette asked her solicitor to request that the coroner consider giving a verdict of unlawful killing.

'Now I've heard all that evidence. It's obvious the people who saw her last, hated her and wanted her dead.' 'I want you to get the coroner to investigate further.' Suzette directed.

'For what reason?' he asked.

'They are lying about those last moments. I believe that no verdict can be reached on the balance of probabilities,' Suzette suggested.

'OK, I'll give it a try,' the Solicitor finally agreed.

The court duly reconvened and the Coroner took his place.

Suzette's solicitor cleared his throat. 'Sir, if I may. I would like you to adjourn the inquest.'

'On what grounds?' the coroner demanded.

'I think there is sufficient doubt about the circumstances of the accident that requires further investigation by the Police.'

'And on what do you base that?' the coroner challenged.

'According to rule 25 (4) of the coroners (Inquests) Rules 2013, it requires a coroner to adjourn an inquest and notify the Director of Public Prosecutions, if during the course of the inquest, it appears to the coroner that the death of the deceased is likely to have been due to a homicide offence and that a person may be charged in relation to the offence,' the solicitor explained.

'Yes, I am fully aware of the process, thank you,' the coroner sparked, irritably. 'So, you are suggesting there is possible homicide associated with this death?' the coroner suggested.

'Yes Sir. Based on what we have just heard and the precedent that cases where a death appears not to be suspicious at first, but evidence is subsequently found to give grounds for suspicion of homicide,' the Solicitor elaborated.

'I will consider your proposal and give my decision after the lunch break,' the coroner explained. 'In the meantime, I will adjourn the session for one hour thirty for lunch.

The court stood, as the coroner duly left.

Andy and Ben looked at each other anxiously.

'Does that mean they don't believe us,' Ben asked, concerned.

'I'm sure it's just one of those legalistic things that us ordinary folk don't understand. We haven't done anything wrong, so don't worry,' Andy counselled.

The other Godsons quickly made their way to Ben and Andy.

'Oh, that's a bummer,' Tim said. 'I bet that bloody woman is at the back of this. She's as bad as her sister. A shit stirrer.'

'What's she hoping to achieve with a possible delay?' Carrie wondered.

'Look, let's go for a bite to eat before the coroner announces his verdict.' I'm sure he will see sense,' added JC. 'Don't worry Ben. It will be alright.'

Neither Ben nor Andy had an appetite, so didn't join the others at the local café. Instead, they just walked around the 'block' until it was time to return.

The coroner duly returned after the lunch break, and when everyone was seated, he informed the court of his judgement.

Ben had sweaty palms and butterflies as he waited.

'In view of your objection, I agree to adjourn the inquest. I will make appropriate arrangements for the police to further investigate the circumstances, with the aim of determining if Sue Williams-Screen died as a result of an Unlawful killing,' he announced.

Suzette pumped her fist in a victory salute and patted her solicitor on the shoulder. 'Well done,' she said, smiling. 'They aren't going to get away with whitewashing Sue's death. Lookout for a fight,' she added firmly.

After the Coroner had ruled, the court emptied quickly.

Out in the court vestibule Suzette approached Andy.

'So, you are the famous Andy that my sister told me about.'

'I'm sorry for your loss,' Andy said nervously. 'But if the Police are going to be investigating, I don't think it's wise for you to be talking to me,' he said walking away from her.

'No matter what she'd done, she didn't deserve to die like that. You killed my sister,' Suzette shouted as Andy moved away.

Alerted by the disturbance, a journalist introduced herself to Suzette.

'Hello, I'm from the local newspaper. May I ask your involvement in the inquest?'

'Yes, It's my sister. She was killed in the accident,' Suzette explained.

'I'm terribly sorry for your loss. By your accent you're not from round here,' the reporter observed.

'No, I'm from Australia. I came over here to meet my sister. We are identical twins. We were separated at birth, and she died the day before I arrived here. It would have been the first time meeting each other,' Suzette said tearfully.

'Oh, dear how sad. Let me buy you a coffee,' the reporter said, realising the prospect of a juicy story.

CHAPTER THIRTY-THREE

Janie was unable to attend the inquest and unusually Ben hadn't texted her with the result either, as he said he would.

'It must be over by now,' she thought. 'It's been over three hours.'

Janie tried unsuccessfully to reach Ben but kept getting his answer phone.

'I'll pop round. Perhaps he's forgotten to take it off silent,' she concluded.

She cycled over to JCs' four-bedroom house, where Ben and Beth were living.

After getting no reply from her knock on the front door, she wandered around the side of the house and was delighted to find Ben sitting on the grass at the bottom of the large garden.

By Ben's side was his rehomed rescue dog. The animal was looking concerned at his young master. But as soon as she saw Janie, the dog ran to her, its tail wagging a welcome.

'Hello Rusty,' she said, stroking the old Labrador. 'Are you looking after Ben? Are you?' she intoned. 'Ben, you're still alive then,' she said testily, making her way towards him. 'Why didn't you text me after the Inquest? I was worried.'

No reply.

'You look like a sack of potatoes. Why are you slumped against the side of the annex?' she demanded.

Then she stopped, horrified at seeing a half full bottle of wine in his hand. 'Ben what are you doing?' she demanded, angrily.

'I'm...having... having a drink, he said, swigging from the bottle. 'Nothing wrong with that ish there?' he slurred.

'Oh, my days, you're drunk!'

'No. Not drunk. I'm happy, relaxed, chilled. Now I understand why JC and my mother drank. It helps blunt the anxiety, the pain. It blurs the memory. Helps you forget.'

Janie crouched next to him and stared at her boyfriend. 'You can't be serious! After what you've been through with your mother, with JC and their alcoholic problems.'

'They don't believe me,' Ben slurred, ignoring her observation.

'Who doesn't believe you?' Janie demanded.

'In that court. They didn't believe that I never pushed her over. I tried to save her,' he contended. 'I did, I did,' he said, tearfully, touching her arm.

'I know. I believe you. Andy believes you too,' she confirmed.

'They think I deliberately pushed her over and that I killed her. I didn't, I swear it.'

'Oh Ben, you don't need to convince me,' Janie coaxed, sitting next to him, and putting her arm around his shoulders. 'The evidence shows that it was an accident caused by a road traffic collision; So, stop beating yourself up about it.'

'Yes, initially that's what they thought. But they adjourned it didn't they? They could charge me with unlawful killing. Manslaughter even. I could go to jail.'

'No, you won't. Now get that silly thought out of your head. Look, I know you and I know the truth and drinking isn't going to help persuade them either.'

'I can't stop thinking about it. I'm my mother's son. A hopeless drunk. What can you expect.' Ben moaned. 'I shall end up just like her.'

'No, you won't! Now stop this self-pity nonsense. Give me that bottle.' Janie demanded and snatched the bottle off him. She immediately poured the contents on to the grass. 'There now. It's gone,' she said angrily. 'Let it be the last one too,' she continued crossly.

'You should have seen her sister give me an evil look,' Ben said, staring at the wine-coloured grass. 'Did I tell you her sister is that woman's twin. She's identical.'

'No! Really?' An identical twin! That must have been spooky.'

'Yes, it was. I nearly shit myself when I first saw her. I thought that woman had come back to haunt me.'

'I didn't know that she had family,' Janie observed. 'Oh dear. I'm so sorry.'

'The trouble is, It's never going to end, is it? Her sister will be after me for ever. And the police too. What have I got to look forward too? Nothing!' he blurted tearfully.

'Ben, you've got your whole life ahead of you. And... you've got me. I will stand by you. You've had a tough time recently. But now she's gone, it's going to be a lot better.'

'You think so?' Ben asked, needing Janie's reassurance. 'Her solicitor was a horrible man. He was the one who asked for the inquest to be put on hold.'

'I expect that he was only doing his job. Probably following orders,' Janie explained.

'Why are you saying that?' Ben demanded crossly.

'What?'

'You're defending him. You think I'm guilty too, don't you?' Ben said, tearfully.

'No of course not. You're not thinking straight. It's the booze talking,' Janie suggested.

'No! The booze is helping me think,' Ben rationalised.' 'It's all a big conspiracy. It always has been.'

'Ben, for heaven's sake, stop it,' Janie pleaded.

'The son of a drunk can't possibly be any good,' he continued. 'Why, even my father didn't want to know me until he saw me as an asset and kidnapped me for money.'

'Stop it Ben, you're scaring me.'

'They think I'm a low life. Well, I'll show them,' Ben said angrily, toppling over as he attempted to stand.

'Just sit still or you'll hurt yourself,' she soothed. 'Nobody thinks you're bad. Everybody loves you. You are a brave, brave person.'

'What do you mean brave?'

'Well, look what you did to rescue your dad in that blazing barn. You didn't need to do that, did you?'

'I suppose not. But that's another thing, I'm my father's bastard son. Born out of wedlock. What else would you expect of me. Right from when I was born, I was a loser. Always have been.'

'No, now stop it,' she rebuked. 'You're not a loser. That's the booze talking again. It's making you depressed. That's what it does.'

'No, I feel happy. I could take on the world,' Ben said, rolling his sleeves up ready to take on an imaginary opponent.

And at that moment he passed out.

'Oh Ben, you silly boy. I love you to bits but not like this. I need to get help.'

CHAPTER THIRTY-FOUR

Despite the police suggestion that Suzette kept a low profile, she was persuaded by the reporter from the inquest to give her an exclusive.

Consequently, the journalist made capital of the tragic story and took a photograph of a distraught looking Suzette. It became front page news.

'*Australian twin greeted with tragic news.*

Aussie Suzette Brown travelled from the other side of the world to meet a twin sister that she'd never met. Tragically her sister was killed, before they got to meet when her car caught fire following a car crash. The tragedy happened at the exact time when Suzette was flying to the UK to meet her.

Sue Williams-Screen was wanted by the police for several major crimes and was being chased by one of her victims when her car crashed. The coroner has ordered an investigation with a charge of Unlawful killing being considered. The two people who were chasing the unfortunate woman are thought to be the centre of the investigation.

A sixteen-year-old teenager, who cannot be named for legal reasons, and Scout Leader Andy Spider were first on the scene and attempted a rescue. Inexplicably the car toppled over the cliff and exploded in a ball of flames. The teenager had, allegedly been badly treated by Sue Williams–Screen and there was some antagonism between the two.

The twin sister of the deceased, Suzette Brown, is seeking justice for her lost sister. She is urging an investigation to seek further evidence into the circumstances of the crash and her death. The coroner has adjourned the inquest.'

From inside his remand prison, Ben's estranged and violent father, Mike, subsequently read the newspaper story about Sue's sister. He was taken aback by the picture.

'Oh, God, she's the splitting image of Sue,' he mused. 'I wonder if there's anything in this for me, I'm sure that I could tell her a thing or two about her deranged sister.'

Mike had a personal interest in the report, not only because his alienated son Ben, was the 16-year-old featured in the article, but also that he was on remand for his own crime of aiding and abetting Sue Williams-Screen.

His destiny had been sealed, right from the first chance meeting with Sue. He was 'innocently' poaching salmon on the banks of the River Severn; when he spotted her unconscious, half drowned body, floating in the flooded river.

After rescuing and resuscitating her, she persuaded him to hide her from 'foreign agents' who were pursuing her. So, taken in by her lies, he gullibly took her home to his tied cottage.

In truth, he later found out, she was the assailant of a failed kidnap and attempted murder which had gone horribly wrong. Her pursuers were the police, not enemy agents.

Mike was a bit of a 'jack the lad' character anyway and was often in trouble with the law. Therefore, it was easy for Sue to draw him into her own criminal activities, including extortion and kidnap.

Unfortunately for their relationship, after a few more failed schemes, she eventually decided that Mike was more of a liability than a help.

She blamed him for the failure of Ben's kidnap extortion scheme and tried to dispose of him and Ben in an arson attack.

Her sadistic plan had been to burn them alive and get rid of the 'evidence' in a farm fire. But thanks to Ben's bravery, Mike escaped with his life but suffered full thickness burns to his arm.

However, Mike's problems were only just beginning, for after his stay in the specialist burns hospital receiving treatment for his severely burnt arm, the law caught up with him. He was arrested and remanded in custody, awaiting trial.

Subconsciously, as he read the inquest article, he rubbed his heavily bandaged arm, for which he was still receiving daily treatment at the local hospital.

The irony of Sue's own fiery death in the car crash was not lost on him, and he laughed at her demise.

'The devil has called her home,' he reflected vengefully.

'So, she has a sister, has she?' he thought. 'She obviously looks like Sue, but I wonder what her temperament is like,' he pondered. 'I'm sure that as I've spent a lot of time with her sister, I could provide some evidence for her. I wonder if she'd be interested in meeting me?'

Despite Sue's disdain of him, Mike was no fool and had a shrewd brain for making a 'fast buck.' He thought by associating with Suzette, he could make some money out of it.

Using his contacts inside the prison, Mike found out who Suzette's solicitor was and eventually, after cutting through the 'red tape,' contacted her.

'I have some evidence that might help prove a conspiracy against Sue Williams-Screen,' he told the lawyer.

For having heard his late 'partner in crime' go on and on about the conflicts with the inheritors of Geoffery Fosters' fortune, he felt he was going to be able to provide some useful background for her case.

'Such as?' the solicitor probed. 'How do I know that you're not just a chancer,' the lawyer challenged.

'Let me think, what she used to say,' he told the solicitor. 'Oh yes, she was particularly wound up about being falsely accused of attempting to kill the millionaire, Geoffery Foster. From then on relationships with Foster, Andy Spider and the Godsons, the beneficiaries of the millionaires will, had got worse and worse,' he informed her brief.

'Yes, then there were the issues about seeking half of her former husband's legacy. In reality, Sue had been in a constant battle with the Godson's families and that Scout Leader bloke, Andy Spider,' he recalled.

Furthermore, Mike knew locations where Sue was likely to have stored evidence.

The solicitor was pleased to hear his story and advised his client, Suzette, to meet with Mike.

CHAPTER THIRTY-FIVE

Following Mike's contact with her solicitor, Suzette visited Mike in prison.

She was uneasy about meeting with someone that she had never met or even talked to before. It could all be just one big ruse by a conman having read about her in the newspaper.

Worse still, she was going into the austere building with its strict security measures. Cameras were everywhere and uniformed guards watched her suspiciously as she headed for her meeting with this stranger.

She had never considered herself to be a snob, for as a nurse she dealt with all manner of people, poor, rich, addicts, homeless, vagrants, but she felt apprehensive at mixing with 'rough' looking visitors in the prison.

She was further dismayed by the security screening that she had to undertake. The scrutiny, included being 'patted' down, opening her mouth for an inspection to detect concealed sachets, apparently a method of passing drugs on during a kiss, emptying her handbag, removing her shoes, and going through an airport style metal detector.

Consequently, she was ill at ease as she arrived in the visitor's room to be directed to a table where Mike was already sitting.

Immediately she was wrong footed. His swarthy appearance and wild hair made him look like a tramp. He was not the person that she'd imagined with whom her sister would have kept company.

'Hello,' Mike said, standing. 'You must be Suzette. I'd know you anywhere. God, you do look just like your sister. It's quite spooky.'

'Yes, as I now know, we did look the same. G'day. So, you must be Mike?' She said extending her hand for a handshake.

'Yes, that's me.'

Immediately the warder in charge bellowed, 'No touching.'

Suzette quickly withdrew her hand. 'Gee, I was only being polite,' she muttered, embarrassed at being shouted at.

'They don't like visitors touching in here. People pass on drugs, weapons, and phones,' he advised her.

'Oh. I'm sorry,' she said, quickly sitting down.'

'No problem. Now about your sister...'Mike started to say.

'I didn't know that I had a sister until recently,' Suzette interrupted nervously. 'It's all very unnerving,'

'Well, I spent a lot of time with...' he continued.

Suzette interrupted again. She was so focused on trying to find what to say to this stranger, that she wasn't listening. 'It was a shock when I saw her photograph. It was like looking in a mirror,' Suzette giggled nervously.

'Jesus stop wittering,' he thought. 'She is just like her sister; I can't get a word in edgeways.'

Yes, you're the perfect likeness to her for sure,' Mike quickly reiterated. 'Except this woman didn't have the cruel penetrating evil eyes of her sister,' he thought.

'Sadly, I never got to meet her in person,' Suzette shuffled nervously. 'Although we talked over the internet. We were due to meet at Heathrow, but...but sadly she died the evening before,' she explained nervously.

'I'm sorry about your...a...your a... loss,' Mike said, unconvincingly.

Although in reality, he was secretly pleased that she was dead. Especially when he recalled how 'the bitch' had brutally attacked him and even attempted to kill him.

'Thank you.' Suzette said quietly.

'Sue and me were good friends,' he lied. 'After I rescued her from the river, we became quite close,' he said, exaggerating the reality of their relationship. In truth, she barely tolerated him.

'The river?' Suzette said in surprise.

'Yes, I saved her life. She was on a secret mission and enemy agents were after her. They beat her up and threw her in the flooded river to drown,' he relayed, repeating the false story that Sue had sold him. 'But I saved her life,' he repeated. 'Rescued her off the riverbank I did and hid her in my house.'

'A secret mission! An agent!'

'Yeah, that's what she told me.'

That's amazing. I knew she was going to be someone special. Thank you,' she gushed.

Suzette latched on to this first bit of positive news. An agent! Perhaps there was more to Sue's life than she knew. Perhaps she had been assassinated after all. By the same enemy agents that threw her into the river. Perhaps Andy was an enemy agent. Her imagination went wild.

'Although I only knew her briefly, I think she was a nice person,' Suzette said, hoping that he would confirm her early views of her sister.

'Umm, well yes... you can say that,' Mike lied, thinking instead of the pure evil that Sue exuded.

'So why did you want to see me?' Suzette probed.

'I understand that the coroner has delayed the inquest while the possibility of 'unlawful killing is investigated?' he added.

'Yes, that's right. I'm sure those people that were with her after her car crashed had something to do with her death,' Suzette revealed.

'Yes, you might be right. Don't forget she was a secret agent. So having failed with the river attempt... eh!'

'Really? I suppose you could be right,' Suzette agreed, absorbing anything that would negate the hurtful stories about her twin.

'Well, I know for a fact that the boy and his Scout Leader, that Andy, were very unfriendly to your sister.'

'Interesting!' Suzette sat up, now giving the 'tramp' her full attention.

'I wouldn't be at all surprised that they 'tail ended her' and pushed her over the edge to her death,' Mike revealed conspiratorially.

Mike revelled in creating the false rumour. His lack of moral fibre meant that, despite Ben's heroics in saving his estranged father's life in the farm fire, Mike had no conscience about making trouble for his own son.

'The police reckoned that there was no evidence on his car to suggest that' Suzette said.

'The police! Ha! They are probably in it as well. You can't trust them as far as you can throw them,' Mike ranted.

'Why do you say that?' she probed sceptically.

'Because I have seen that lot abusing your sister,' he exaggerated. 'I'm prepared to say so in court too. If you want me to?'

'So why would you do that?' she asked suspiciously.

'Because I want to see them get their comeuppance,' Mike said, vehemently.

'Really?'

'Yes. I'd obviously need some expenses too,' he continued.

'I thought that you wouldn't be doing it simply out of the kindness of your heart,' she remarked sceptically. The warning lights of a scam were just starting to flash in her head.

'To be fair. I am now broke. I had to fund your sister for a long time while I was hiding her see.

'Why?'

'Well, she lost everything in the river, didn't she? She said she was going to pay me back, but obviously now…that ain't going to happen. So, I'm out of pocket,' Mike said, laying it on thickly.

'That was very generous of you,' Suzette acknowledged. 'Well, I'm sorry, you're out of luck. I haven't got any money. So, you can forget that idea of trying to fleece me,' she said, firmly.

'Oh, that's a bummer,' Mike said, disappointed that his anticipated meal ticket had failed at the first hurdle.

'Anyway, to state the obvious, you're in prison. How can you help me?'

'Oh! You haven't found out about Sue's legacy yet then?'

'Legacy!' Suzette recalled Sue's final message. '*I have at last succeeded in getting my share of my former husband, Rupert's legacy. I will meet you on your arrival at Heathrow airport. We can go on a luxury trip to celebrate our sisterhood.'*

'She confided her plans with me about getting a legacy from her ex-husband when I helped her,' Mike revealed.

'What sort of legacy are we talking about?' Suzette said acting innocently, already aware of it from Sue's message. The prospect of getting her hands on an unexpected windfall wouldn't erase the pain of losing Sue but it would add another dimension to her trip to the UK.

'I've got some significant information,' he continued.

'What information?' Suzette demanded quietly.

'How to get Sue's legacy from her ex-husband.'

'I assumed that she had actually got it. Are you saying that she hadn't?'

'Yes. She was still trying to get her hands on it.' In reality it was another of her failed schemes involving a kidnap and ransom.

'Oh, don't say this is going to involve a court battle. The only winners of those are the lawyers,' she said dismissively.

'No. No court battles.'

'Then how?'

'I'll tell you. But first, you must promise to help me escape,' Mike whispered conspiratorially leaning towards her.

'Stop leaning over the table,' an eagle-eyed Prison Warder shouted.

Mike casually sat back into his chair, having sowed the seeds.

'Help you escape! You must be joking,' Suzette said quietly, amazed at the audacity of someone that she had only just met.

'No, I'm not. I'm deadly serious. If you help me to escape, I will tell you…show you, how to get your legacy. It's a considerable sum of money,' Mike said, smugly.

'How do I know that there is a legacy? This could be a con,' she challenged, calling his bluff.

'Yes, it could be. But it could also be true. Can you afford to take a chance and miss out on a possible fortune?'

'No, I'm not sure about this,' Suzette said, hesitatingly, studying his body language to assess the validity of his proposal.

'So, the deal is this. When you help me to get out, I agree to help you prove that your sister was 'unlawfully killed.'

'And I'll end up in jail for helping you to escape. No thanks.'

'It's simple. We share the money and leave the country. No jail.'

'Forget the money for a minute. How are you going to provide evidence to the court if you are a fugitive?' Suzette probed.

'I'll write an affidavit and get your solicitor to witness it,' Mike said, quickly.

'Mmm…I'm not sure.'

'Deal?' he pressured, smiling.

'I'll think about it.' Suzette said firmly, standing. The enormity of what he was asking her to do was mind numbing. It was all starting to overwhelm her. 'I must go,' she said leaving him.

'Cheerio. Don't take too long,' he said loudly as she left. A big grin spread across his face. 'Got you,' he thought.

Her head was 'buzzing' as she made her way to the exit, passing security checks all the way.

At last, she was in fresh air. She was trying to make sense of it, to weigh up all the facts.

Of all of the people that she'd met, he was the only one who had good things to say about her sister. And besides, despite his swarthy appearance, she found Mike quite likeable. He was a kindred spirit, she thought. Someone on her side in this strange, new land.

CHAPTER THIRTY-SIX

Suzette returned to her rented house and made herself a cup of tea.

'Why is life so difficult?' she asked herself, as she slumped on the sofa.

Her visit to the prison had emotionally drained her.

She thought of what might have been with her planned meeting with Sue. It was going to be a joyful happy reunion but now, the wheels had come off. She was involved in a complication that she could never have envisaged.

Cruelly, fate had dashed all her hopes and dreams for an exciting future with her sister. The magic of seeing her had vanished just like the smoke of Sue's funeral pyre. Even worse, the dreadful news that Sue was branded as an evil criminal was a 'twist of the knife' in her grief. But Mike had given her hope explaining that Sue was misunderstood because, if it was true, of her secret shadowy life as an agent.

Although her adoptive family weren't that emotionally close to her anymore, Suzette nevertheless felt helpless in a 'foreign' land without being able to turn to them for their support.

It was bad enough trying to cope alone with the trauma of Sue's death. Now she needed her friends to talk through her problems. She felt isolated.

'Although those policemen were quite friendly, especially that Chris,' she thought. 'Perhaps I could give them a call. No that's no good. What am I thinking, I will be doing a criminal act helping Mike to escape.'

Mike's approach to Suzette came like a 'bolt out of the blue. His suggestion that Sue was an agent and that she might have been deliberately assassinated, added to her anguish. It was a devastating thought.

She comforted herself by the fact that at least this Mike, a complete stranger, was offering to help her. He obviously knew Sue, so it wasn't a con.

Initially she wasn't sure, but putting Sue's killers in the dock was what she really wanted. The legacy was an unexpected bonus. But it might tip the balance and persuade her to help him.

On the other hand, in order to help him to escape, she would become a criminal...But only if she were caught!

The ramifications could be profoundly serious. She would be jailed, deported. Her nursing career would be at an end. No, he was asking too much.

But if she wasn't caught? That would be OK, wouldn't it?

What were her commitments to Sue? Was it her duty to clear her sister's name at any cost and to bring her killers to justice?

'Think it through,' she encouraged herself. Her head was spinning.

'So, you help him to escape and then what?' She said to herself. 'Where will you go? How do you know that he won't hurt you, rape or even kill you once he is out?

Will he keep his part of the bargain and provide the evidence?

'Are you going to have to stay together to ensure that he does come up with his part of the bargain. How long is that likely to take?'

'What should I do? What should I do?' she muttered to herself. It was going round and round in her head. She couldn't think straight anymore.

Suzette decided that she needed to see him again to help her make her decision. Was it the right thing to do? She didn't know.

But If she were going to help him, they would need to make some detailed plans for his escape.

CHAPTER THIRTY-SEVEN

Walking through town, Suzette saw Ben and Janie out on their bikes. They were larking around and giggling. This incensed her. 'How can they be so disrespectful to the memory of my sister. I am not having fun, why should they?' she thought to herself.

Therefore, fuelled by the misconception that Ben and Andy had deliberately killed her sister, and against her better judgement, Mike's persuasive argument won the day and Suzette finally decided to help him escape.

A week after her first visit, Suzette took an anxious taxi ride to the prison and took a card from the driver to call him for a return journey.

She was less wound up this time with the security procedures as she was subjected to them. Now that she knew what to expect and what Mike looked like she was more relaxed.

Mike was sat at the table as before and stood as she entered. Anxiously she sat down opposite him.

'So have you made your mind up?' he asked, forgoing the niceties.

'It depends. What are you going to do for me in return,' she said firmly.

'I will help you get justice for your sister,' he promised. 'Helping me is the key to getting those who killed your sister banged up.'

'How will you do that?' she demanded. 'How do I know that it's not all a con?'

'I have documented evidence that will prove that they hated her and intended to harm her. It's strong stuff, it will condemn them, I assure you,' he lied.

'Well, I'm still not sure,' Suzette muttered.

'All the time those people are enjoying life and your poor sister is...'

'Oh...OK then. I will do it.' Suzette blurted. 'I might regret it but, it's for my sister.'

Mike was taken aback, he never thought she would fall for it.

'OK, well thanks...You won't regret it,' he said positively.

'I hope not,' Suzette said, unconvincingly.

'I...I've been thinking a lot about this,' Mike revealed. 'I go to the hospital outpatient clinic every day to get my arm professionally dressed at a specialist burns unit.'

'Yeah, I meant to ask you about that. What have you done to your arm?'

'It was severely burnt in a fire and needs regular dressing,' he replied, holding back on the details of her sisters involvement in setting fire to the barn in the first place.

'You poor thing. It was obviously very severe if you are having daily dressing,' Suzette said knowledgably from her nursing background.

'Yes it was. They told me that I was lucky not to lose my arm altogether,' he added. 'Another few minutes and the deep tissue burn would have been game over for my arm.'

What he didn't say was that it was Ben's fast actions in plunging his arm in the horse trough that stopped the irreparable harm from occurring.

The wound was a constant reminder of the evil Sue and the lengths that she would go to, to get her way.

'I go to the hospital in a prison van every day at the same time, he informed her.

'So, are you handcuffed to the warden? Suzette asked.

'No. The prison guard is quite happy to keep a relaxed relationship with me. They don't consider me to be an escape risk,' Mike revealed. 'So, my guard leaves me in the treatment room and goes for a coffee in the restaurant for about twenty minutes,' he continued.

'My dressing usually only takes five minutes, because they don't like prisoners in the room, so they 'fast track' me through. After the warden has finished his coffee, we rendezvous in the waiting room.' The time gap in between me being treated and his arrival is my opportunity to escape,' he smiled.

'How long is that?'

'It varies, but it can be ten to twenty minutes some days.'

'OK, so where do I fit in?'

'I want you to hire a car and wait for me in the hospital carpark. I'll slip away while the warden is finishing his coffee and we'll make a get-away.'

'When do you want to do it?' Suzette asked, nervously.

'The day after tomorrow. OK? That will give you time to sort out hiring a car.'

'I suppose.'

During the wait for the taxi to return to pick her up, Suzette was regretting her decision to go ahead with the plan but kept reminding herself it was for Sue. 'Retribution for Sue,' she muttered. 'For my sister.'

CHAPTER THIRTY-EIGHT

With mounting apprehension, Suzette sat in the hospital carpark and watched the prison van arrive, dead on time as Mike had predicted.

Her mind was plagued by so many self-doubts that she nearly abandoned the idea and drove off without him.

But, against her better judgement and charmed by his smooth talking, she had finally decided to stay.

Although Mike was a bit of a 'rough diamond,' but he certainly had the 'gift of the gab.' He had the ability to charm gullible young women into his lecherous tentacles in what he jokingly called his 'penis flytrap;' A trap that many had fallen into, including Ben's mother in her young teenage years.

Suzette had done a thorough job sussing out the logistics of the escape plan. Including going to a charity shop to buy a baseball cap and a large overcoat for Mike. She toyed with the idea of disguising herself with dark glasses and a hat but thought it was too Hollywood. So, she went in normal clothes but wore a wig.

Suzette watched Mike and his prison guard leave the van and head for the entrance. She waited the agreed ten minutes after they'd gone into the building before leaving the car. Quickly she made her way to the parking machine with her ticket, produced automatically on entry. She had previously checked the 'pay on exit' machine and got change in the correct denomination.

Now it was happening for real. Butterflies filled her stomach as she waited. Nervously checking her watch, she stood, money in hand by the pay point. All the while conspicuously watching the hospital exit door, waiting for him to emerge.

He'd told her that normally, his prioritised treatment only took five minutes while they changed the dressings and to add an additional five minutes, walking to and from the treatment room.

But the ten minutes came and went. Still, he hadn't emerged. She waited apprehensively, wondering if things had gone wrong. The clock ticked on, 'thirty, thirty-five, forty minutes.'

As each minute passed, she was getting increasingly anxious. Had they rumbled his escape plans? Was he unable to leave? 'Oh, come on Mike, for heaven's sake,' she muttered, under her breath.

'Is there a problem with the machine?' a man asked seeing her inactivity.

'No, no. Sorry I'm waiting for someone. Please go ahead, the machine is not out of order.'

'Embarrassed, she waved on several other puzzled drivers who were waiting to pay for their own tickets.

To her relief, after forty-five minutes, Mike finally emerged from the entrance. He quickly spotted her. She breathed a sigh of relief. He was alone.

She immediately fed the ticket into the slot, noting the amount to pay shown on the screen. And with fumbling fingers, she fed in coins to the correct value. After an age of the mechanism clicking and whirling, the paid ticket eventually spewed out.

She quickly snatched the validated ticket from the device. Her shaking hands reflecting her nervousness.

Looking furtively around, Mike trotted over to her.

'Where's the car?' he asked urgently.

'Over there,' she pointed.

Together, they made their way rapidly across the carpark. weaving through the lines of parked cars. Expecting at any moment to hear, a shout from the prison guard for him to stop.

'This is the one,' she told Mike, indicating, a bluebird blue two door ford focus.

He tried the door handle; it didn't budge.

'It's locked,' he ranted. 'Come on for Chrissake, the guard will be out shortly.'

'I know...I know. I'm looking for the key fob,' she bleated.

'Well come on then. Open the frigging thing for Chrissake.'

Suzette fumbled in her handbag and retrieved the key fob. Quickly she pressed the open symbol. And was relieved to hear the 'clunk' as the door solenoids released.

'Have you got me a disguise?' he grunted, peering inside.

'Yes, there's a hat and coat on the passenger seat,' she told him.

Mike yanked the passenger door open and reached inside, quickly putting on the coat and baseball cap.

Hurriedly they scrambled into the car and slammed the doors.

'Quick. He'll be out soon looking for me,' Mike urged.

'Why were you so late?' she demanded, starting the engine, and fishing the parking ticket out of her handbag, she put it on the dashboard.

'They were short staffed, so it took longer dressing my arm today than usual,' he told her,' Come on hurry up,' he urged. 'Although the warden has gone for a second cup of coffee, he'll be looking for me soon. Let's get going,'

'Alright, alright. Keep your shirt on,' she shouted. 'I'm doing it.'

Anxiously, Suzette manoeuvred out of the parking place and drove quickly to the barrier, winding down her window as they arrived.

Taking the parking ticket from the dashboard, she offered it to the card reader and attempted to insert the ticket into the slot. But in her nervous haste she missed the slot and dropped it on the floor.

'Damn,' she muttered, as she opened her door and got out.

An impatient driver behind her beeped his horn at the slight delay.

Already 'wound up' by her guilt and mad at herself for her clumsiness, she picked up the ticket and stormed back to the car with the impatient driver.

'WHAT'S YOUR PROBLEM COBBER?' she shouted angrily.

The driver's courage deserted him seeing her furious face, and he quickly wound up his window.

Suzette stormed back to the card reader, inserted the ticket and was relieved to see the single arm barrier go up. Quickly she got back into the car and much to Mike's relief drove out on to the road.

'Thank god for that,' he uttered. 'I thought you were going to pan him one for a moment.' 'You are quite like your sister after all with that evil temper,' he thought.'

'It was close. I hate car horn jockeys,' she said, her face white with anger. 'Have you decided where we're going?' she demanded.

'I'm still not sure.'

'Oh, that's a great help. So, we're going to drive around all day?' she said flippantly.

'Well, unfortunately, your sister burnt down my place,' he said subconsciously rubbing his bandaged arm. 'So, we can't go there. Didn't you say you've just rented a house? What about there?' he suggested.

'No. I don't think that's an option. The neighbours are a bit nosey. It's a quiet cul de sac,' she explained. 'And if anyone is outside, they are bound to ask who you are. And I will have to say that you're my partner.'

'Well, what's wrong with that?' he smirked. 'I could gladly be your partner,' he said, putting his hand on her thigh.

Suzette looked across at him wondering how the hell she had allowed herself to get into this situation but, already frightened by his presence. She allowed his hand to remain, reminding herself that she needed his help to clear her sisters name.

'We've been driving for twenty minutes around the town, now, have you decided where we're going yet?' she quizzed,

'I'm thinking. Don't nag woman,' Mike spat.

Suzette was concentrating on the road signs, whilst trying to ignore his hand on her thigh.

'At the moment we're not being followed by a prison van or police car,' she said, continually checking in her rear-view mirror.

'No, but I expect they will have started looking for me now,' Mike said, glancing over to her. 'And I forgot about the number plate cameras too. Hopefully, they didn't clock us leaving the car park.'

'Make your mind up where do you want to go? I want to get rid of the car.' Suzette said nervously.

'Alright, stop here. I should only be a minute,' Mike directed, gesticulating for her to pull over.

'What here in town? Shouldn't we get as far away as possible from the hospital?

'Yes, but I want to get something. I won't be long,' he added, pulling down his baseball cap.

Suzette pulled up in a parking place by the kerb and Mike got out.

'Hurry, I don't want to be hanging around here,' she implored, glancing in the rear-view mirror again for any signs of surveillance.

Mike disappeared onto the crowded pavement. He too wanted to get away as far as possible from the car, which he assumed would have been clocked by the carpark CCTV.

He knew that once his escape had been discovered, the car's number plate would be quickly dialled into the ANPR numberplate recognition camera network. And the police would quickly track it down. So, if he stayed with the car, his dash for freedom would be short lived.

Suzette didn't matter. He had used her as intended. She was disposable, like so many other women that he had treated badly before.

CHAPTER THIRTY-NINE

After his second cup of coffee and a delicious custard slice, the prison officer was further delayed going back to get Mike. An unexpected meeting with a retired prison colleague in the restaurant added more delay as they gossiped.

Eventually, the warden glanced at his watch. 'Blimey is that the time? I must go. I've got one downstairs waiting for me,' he finally said.

'Cheers.'

'Cheers.'

On his return to their rendezvous point, to his annoyance, Mike wasn't there.

The prison officer went back to the burns clinic that Mike attended and was told he'd left much earlier.

He then asked several members of staff if they'd seen his prisoner and they concurred that Mike had left earlier.

The prison officer was annoyed. He wandered around the hospital grounds looking for Mike, getting increasingly angry and apprehensive that Mike had actually legged it.

'Bugger,' he muttered. 'I hope he hasn't escaped, otherwise I'm in for it. I wonder if hospital security can see him on their cameras?'

With mounting apprehension, the warden went to the hospital security office to see if any of the bank of

CCTV monitors showed Mike. Hoping that he was still wandering around the premises, somewhere.

Giving the hospital security woman a description of Mike, the pair scanned all the monitors to see if they could find him.

After a few minutes, having no joy with live cameras, the prison officer asked to look at recent archived recordings.

And eventually, after scrolling through the multitude of screens, they saw Mike getting into a car.

'There. That's him,' he said, pointing at the screen.

The prison officer was furious. 'The bastard. He's escaping. Just goes to show that you can't trust these cons. Now I'm in for it,' he ranted. 'I should have known better. I'd better let the Governor know. Shit,' he moaned.

'I presume they'll get the Police to track him down?' the security woman asked.

'Yes. The sooner the better before he gets too far,' the guard confirmed.

'I can try and get the number plate of the car if that's any help,' the security officer offered.

'Yes, if you could, the police might be able to pick the car up on their Automatic Number Plate Recognition cameras.'

While the warden rang the prison and confessed to losing his prisoner, the security person was trawling through recordings from various cameras.

'Any joy?' the warden asked hopefully.

'No, sorry. Only the colour and model of the car, some stupid ass parked directly behind his car at the barrier, so I can't see the number plate at the moment. But the driver is a woman. Ooops, looks like there was nearly a confrontation there. So, you've got a witness if you need one,' the woman suggested.

'So, he wasn't driving?' the prison officer queried.

'No. it's a woman. He's got an accomplice. She's the driver.'

'What about the other cameras,' the Prison officer suggested, ignoring her observation.

'We'll give it a try,' she said, deftly switching through the various archived records. 'It was a Ford Focus, and the colour was bluebird blue, wasn't it?' she said recalling the image they'd seen earlier.

'If you say so,' the guard acknowledged.

By piecing together footage from other CCTV camera's they were finally able to get an image that showed the number plate.

'Right, here's the registration,' the Security woman said, giving him a written note. 'Best of luck.'

Immediately the officer phoned through the information to the controller of the ANPR cameras. The database of 'vehicles of interest' was instantly updated. All police patrol vehicles received an automatic download and details about the escaped prisoner which was annotated to the vehicle's data.

Mike had effectively sacrificed Suzette to the police. He had already sussed out the ANPR camera situation. He figured that they would spend time looking for the car and not trawling for him through the towns facial recognition cameras.

He had guessed correctly. For within ten minutes of leaving an increasingly anxious Suzette alone in the car, a passing patrol car's ANPR camera captured the registration number and 'pinged' it.

Now alerted to the wanted vehicle, the police driver immediately parked nearby and called for assistance.

'*Control from echo two zero, wanted escaped prisoner's car identified. Before I make an arrest, please send support.*'

Within a few minutes Suzette's car was hemmed in by three police cars. Her heart sank. Her worse nightmare had come true.

She was ordered out of the car and immediately arrested.

'Where's your passenger?' the arresting officer demanded, pulling her arms behind her back, and putting on a pair of handcuffs.

'I don't know,' Suzette said, miserably.

I have to warn you that aiding and abetting a prisoner to escape is a serious matter. You will make it easier on yourself if you tell me where he's gone,' the policeman encouraged.

'I'm sorry. I genuinely don't know where he's gone. He asked me to wait here and now I think he's abandoned me. I have been conned,' Suzette said, filling up.

'OK Miss. If you'd like to get in the back of my patrol car,' he said guiding her to the open door. 'We'll get you down to the police station and they can interview you there.'

'Oh, this is such a mess,' Suzette sobbed, getting into the patrol car.

'Single female occupant arrested. No sign of the escaped prisoner.' The patrol policeman radioed his control. 'Suggest you get the street camera operators to see if they can see any suspicious characters around town. Can you arrange for the facial recognition database to be updated with his mugshot and we'll look around here to see if we can spot him here too?'

'Yes, will do, leave it to us. We'll inform the local radio station too, You never know, one of the people he has upset might like the opportunity of dobbing him in.'

'Good thinking. Victim's revenge, I like it.'

CHAPTER FORTY

Helen and Andy heard about Mike's escape on the car radio as they were going shopping.

The escape became the local radio news main story.

Police are looking for an escaped prisoner in the Stroud area. The man was receiving hospital treatment for arm injuries when he slipped away from his prison escort. He was on remand following a series of crimes including kidnap. He is not thought to be dangerous, but members of the public are advised not to approach him but should ring 999.

An Australian woman accomplice has been arrested for helping the prisoner to escape.

'I wonder what that's all about,' Helen wondered. 'They could have provided a bit more detail about the prisoner. How do they expect members of the public to know who they are talking about?

'Another poorly reported story,' Andy observed. 'The prison people really need to tighten up their act, though. That evil bitch Sue, managed to escape from prison too,' Andy replied, parking the car. 'Why would an Australian woman be mixed up with an escaped prisoner?

'Perhaps it's part of a drug smuggling ring or something?'

'Yeah perhaps. Right, let's get this shopping done.'

When they got back to the car and had loaded the shopping into the boot, Andy switched on the ignition and the local radio news came on carrying an update about the escaped prisoner.

'*The Police have asked us to update our earlier news item about the escaped prisoner. Mike Benson escaped from his escourt at the hospital whilst having medical treatment.*

'Did she just say Mike Benson?' Helen queried, 'Ben's father.'

'Yes. Oh dear. More stress for Ben,' Andy suggested.

'*He was helped by an Australian woman accomplice,*'

'God, you don't think it was Sue's twin sister, do you?'

'Too much of a coincidence if it wasn't, don't you think? So, evil does run in the family.'

Mike Benson is five feet ten and of swarthy appearance. He has long curly black hair. He has a heavily bandaged left arm which needs regular treatment. Hospitals and Pharmacies have been alerted if he seeks treatment options. He is not thought to be dangerous. But members of the public should not approach him and are encouraged to ring 999 immediately.

'We must warn Ben,' Andy said, urgently.

'Yes, let's call him straight away.' Helen suggested.

Andy took his mobile out of his pocket and looked at the screen. 'Oh damn, it's flat. I forgot to charge it. Have you got yours?' he asked his wife.

'No. You know that I seldom carry it around with me.'

'Can we pop round to Ben's house on the way home?' Andy asked, desperately.

156

'No. Not unless you want a tub of melted ice cream sploshing around. I need to get my shopping in the freezer. It shouldn't take long, and you can ring Ben from home.'

'OK. Let's go.'

CHAPTER FORTY-ONE

Ben was at home feeling sorry for himself when he heard the car arrive; He immediately recognised it. He knew it was the police. The detectives had been to his house before.

'Now what do they want?' he grumped. 'Haven't I got enough going on with this bleeding inquest,' he muttered.

But before he could tell JC not to open the door, he heard it open, and JC had stepped out to greet the two policemen.

'How do you do. We've come to talk to Ben please,' the DS said.

"Not wishing to be rude to you guys, but unless you've got a warrant or something, I think he's had enough and you should leave him alone,' JC warned.

The two policemen looked at each other, before Chris Cooper spoke.

'OK, I hear what you say. But we've actually come to warn you and Ben,' the detective said calmly.

'Warn us! Warn us! Why? What are we supposed to have done now?' JC said defensively, irritated by the perceived threat.

'You haven't done anything wrong. Not that we know of anyway. But we've just heard that Ben's father, Mike Benson, has escaped the clutches of the prison service and is on the loose.'

Ben was eavesdropping on the conversation, straining to hear the distant discussion. And two words that he heard drove a dagger through his heart. 'MIKE' and 'ESCAPED.'

'How the hell has he escaped? JC demanded. 'He was supposed to be behind bars while on remand.'

'Yes, I know. We're as pissed off as everyone else that he's out. It sounds like he did a runner while his guard was having a coffee break.'

'A coffee break?'

'Yes. I gather that they had an arrangement that while Mike was having his arm dressed at the clinic, the guard went off for a coffee,'

'You're joking. What sort of prison service are they running?'

'Makes you wonder, doesn't it? The guard trusted his prisoner to wait for him after his treatment. He had complied before, but not on this occasion.'

'I wouldn't trust Mike Benson as far as I could throw him. Keep a promise! I mean how naive can you get?'

'Having arrested him several times over the years, I agree.' Chris Cooper added.

'How did he slip away?' JC demanded.

'He had an accomplice. A woman, who drove him from the hospital. We've just heard that they've caught her though.'

'But not him?' JC queried.

'No, not yet. But she is being held at the police station.'

'Do you know who this woman is?

'No. We haven't been involved yet,' the DS explained.

'That doesn't surprise me about his accomplice being a woman. He is always using one woman or another,' JC revealed.

'He's obviously got something that attracts the women,' the DS suggested.

'Yes, He's got a bit of a reputation for manipulating women for his own perverted needs, according to Ben's mum,' JC explained.

'Yeah, that ties up with what we know of him. He's a misogynist. A bit of an unsavoury character,' the DC added.

'Ben will be gutted when he hears,' JC suggested.'

'Yes, well we thought we ought to let him know as soon as possible,' the policeman explained.

'Thanks, I'll pass on the 'good' news to him. I'm sure he'll be 'delighted',' JC said, sarcastically.

'Understandably. But not of our making, I'm pleased to say,' the DC said.

'Do we get a police guard?' JC asked. 'Surely Ben should be included in your witness protection scheme?'

'I'll see what we can arrange. Although he's not considered to be a dangerous threat to the boy. Ben is his son, after all.

'Doesn't make any difference if he's his son or not. The man's an animal. He is completely unscrupulous. As you know, he's already kidnapped him once.'

'Yes, Well I appreciate your concerns, I'll see what we can do. In the meantime, if he turns up, make a 999 call and we'll be out here like a shot.'

'OK thanks.'

'Right, we'll go and see what this getaway driver has got to say for herself.'

'Thanks.'

The policemen departed leaving JC to figure out what he was going to tell Ben.

CHAPTER FORTY-TWO

JC strode back into the house still trying to find the right words to inform Ben of his father's escape.

He found Ben in the lounge, sat on the floor rocking back and forth, cradling his knees. The dog, ever attentive by his side, watching his master with sad eyes.

'You don't need to say anything. I heard,' Ben muttered hoarsely. 'My Dad's on the loose, isn't he?'

'Yes. But he's not going to come here, is he? Unless he's going to thank you for saving his life,' JC said, flippantly.

'Yeah, you're right. HIM, say thanks! That's never going to happen, is it?' Ben agreed.

'No, that would be expecting too much. The man doesn't have a decent bone in his body,' JC added.

'What should I do if he turns up?' Ben wondered.

'Ring the police straight away.' JC advised.

'But I'm his son. I shouldn't grass on him,' Ben said, perplexed. 'Perhaps I should help him?'

'Help him? Help him to do what? Continue committing more crimes? Look Ben, I know that it's difficult. But you have to divorce yourself from feeling sorry for the man. He's made his bed...'

'Yes but...'

'You've got enough on your mind without concerning yourself about him. You probably saved his life, and definitely his arm by your quick thinking. You owe him nothing. Quite the opposite in fact,' JC counselled.

Ben's mobile burst into life. 'It's Andy.' Ben said, looking at the screen display. 'I wonder if he knows... Hi Andy.'

'Hi Ben, how you feeling now?' Andy asked, compassionately.

'OK. As well as can be expected, you know.'

'Good. Ummm. Unfortunately, I have some unwelcome news for...'

'Yes, I know. Mike's escaped,' Ben gushed, interrupting the Scout Leader.

'Oh, you do know. Are you OK with that,' Andy probed.

'Oh yes, I'm over the moon,' Ben said, flippantly. I can't do a lot about it though can I? The police have just been here to warn me. They're going to look at providing me with some protection while he's still on the loose. How did you know about it?'

'We heard it on the local radio news about an escaped prisoner. We couldn't believe our ears when they gave the details. Are you sure that you're OK?'

'I have never been so happy,' Ben said, jokily. They're accusing me of murder and now my evil father is on the warpath. He wants to stop me giving evidence against him. Yes, I'm great. What do you expect?' Ben ranted and threw his phone down miserably.

JC was shocked at Ben's reaction, as the teenager resumed his agitated state of hugging his knees and rocking back and forth.

The dog sensed Ben's distress, went to him, and licked his face. Ben, comforted by the dogs attention, put his arm around the dog and hugged her.

Hearing the sound of the phone being discarded, Andy was concerned that something had happened to Ben. 'Ben, Ben are you alright? Ben!' he shouted.

JC picked up the phone.

'Andy, it's JC. Ben's OK. Understandably he's feeling a bit tense at the moment. Don't worry we'll look after him.'

'Thanks.'

CHAPTER FORTY-THREE

Andy rang the others to tell them about Mike's escape.

Tim answered the 'Just Do It' walking company phone.

'Just do it walking,' he answered woodenly.

'Tim.'

'Oh, hello Andy. More shocking news?' he said, suspiciously.

'Yes, I'm afraid so. How did you guess?'

'That's the only time that you ever call. What is it this time? Flood? Famine?' Fire? Tim asked, frivolously.

'Ben's dad, Mike, has escaped from his prison guard. He's on the loose.'

'Escaped? You got to be joking. Well, he'd better not come here, or he'll get what for,' Tim said angrily. 'What the hell's the matter with the police?'

'Prison guards this time,' Andy interrupted.

'Yeah well, whoever let him escape. We saw their professionalism in failing to detain criminals with letting that evil bitch Sue escape, didn't we? Remember? The prison people let her out and she nearly killed my Carrie,' Tim said furiously.

'Yes, I know, it's terrible, isn't it? Well, all I'm saying is be careful. Ring the police if he turns up.'

'Thanks Andy. Appreciate your warning. And do us a favour. The next time you call, bring us some good news,' Tim joked.

'If there's any good news around, I'd be delighted to be the bearer.' Andy confirmed and hung up.

'Who was that?' Carrie asked.

'That nurse chap Andy. The harbinger of doom,' Tim groaned.

'What's up this time?' Carrie queried.

'That woman's oppo has slipped his guard and he is on the loose.'

'What! Ben's dad?' Carrie said in disbelief.

'That's the bloke.'

'Poor Ben. He's really going through it isn't he?' Carrie said, sympathetically. 'I remember the terrors that I went through at the hands of the evil bitch Sue, after she had escaped from custody.'

'He'd better not come here, that's all,' Tim said picking up a baseball bat from under his desk and slapping it against his palm.

'We'd better let Mum know,' Tim said. 'Just in case he pays her a visit.'

'I'll pop around and see her rather than phoning her. She might need some reassurance,' Carrie suggested. 'After all, she has been through a terrible ordeal. With that mugging and her hip operation too.'

'Yeah, good idea,' Tim observed. 'Do you want me to come?'

'No. One of us should stay for the delivery of that hiking stuff. I'll manage it. Your Mum likes me. And I could do with some fresh air,' Carrie said.

'OK,' Tim agreed, giving her a quick hug. 'Take care.'

'Love you,' she smiled as she headed for the door.

CHAPTER FORTY-FOUR

Andy rang Rupert next.

Joanne answered. 'Hello Andy, I recognise your number these days. What can I do for you today?'

'Sorry Joanne, but have you heard the news about a prisoner escape?'

'Prisoner escape! No.'

'Then it's more bad news, I'm afraid.'

'Go on,' she invited.

'Mike Benson, Ben's dad has gone on the run,' Andy informed her.

'Oh god no!' Joanne's blood turned to ice. She immediately went to see baby Jeffery.

'Joanne are you still there?' Andy asked, concerned by the silence.

'Yes...yes, I'm here. I've just checked, the baby is OK. Rupert is out at the moment. I'll lock the door and ring him on his mobile,' she said anxiously.

'I'm sorry to be the bearer of shocking news. Don't worry I'm sure he'll be too busy evading the police to bother any of us.'

'Yeah, I'm sure you're right,' she said, unconvincingly, feeling weak kneed.

'I'm sure that there is nothing to worry about,' Andy said gently. 'Ring Rupert as soon as I hang up. Take Care. Bye'

'Bye.'

After Andy had hung up, Joanne immediately rang Ruppert, and after two rings he answered.

'Joanne what is it? I'm about to tee off.'

'Well, you can put your clubs back in the car and come home here, straight away,' she said forcefully.

'Why? What's the matter? Is it the baby?' Rupert said in alarm. 'What's wrong?'

'That woman's accomplice is on the loose. Rupert, I'm scared.'

'Who do you mean, on the loose?'

'Mike Benson, Ben's dad. I just had a call from Andy.'

'Oh my god. Not again. OK, I'll be straight home.'

Joanne could hear him apologising to his golfing colleagues as he hurried back to the car. 'Joanne you still there? Should we call the police, get our protection team together? I'm on my way. Don't worry.' Rupert said, hurrying back to his car.

It was fortunate that there were no mobile speed camera's operating that day, otherwise Rupert would have lost his licence twice over.

'What do we do now?' Helen asked.

Andy racked his brains to think of anything else that he needed to do while Mike was on the loose.

'I don't think that he's likely to bother us. Just wait and hope the police get him soon and keep him locked up and throw away the key,' Andy suggested.

CHAPTER FORTY-FIVE

After Suzette had dropped Mike off, he had made his way to a mate's house. Hoping his mate would put him up whilst he hid from the police, Then he was going to get some money, before leaving the country for Spain. Unfortunately, to his annoyance the house appeared to be deserted.

'Sod,' he cursed. 'Now what do I do?'

Despite getting Suzette's mobile phone number, Mike had no intention of getting involved with her again. She was his sacrificial lamb. He had duped and discarded her like so many other women with whom he'd had dealings.

And besides Suzette's facial similarity to her sister was spooky and it made him feel uneasy. He had to keep reminding himself that it wasn't her and wasn't going to be 'scythed' down by Sue's withering vitriol.

Still thinking of a plan 'B,' he was rushing through the arcade when he saw Beth, Ben's mother. He watched her for a few moments and his devious mind churned out a new plan. '*Hide in plain sight*,' Sue used to tell him. '*The police don't look under their noses.*'

'Now there's a thought,' he whispered to himself. 'I wonder if the gullible cow still fancies me. Worth a try I suppose.'

He immediately crossed over to her and stood in front of the shocked woman. At first Beth didn't recognise him with his baseball cap pulled right down over his eyes and thought that she was going to be mugged. Then he spoke and she recognised him straight away.

'Hello my darling. How are you my sweet? So good to see you,' he gushed, embracing her.

Although she was stunned to see him, her heart gave a flutter, and she spontaneously returned the embrace.

'Oh...h... hello Mike. What a surprise to see you,' she uttered.

'Yes, so lovely to see you, as always,' he lied.

'So lovely to see you too,' she mimicked, completely lost for words. She was spellbound by his presence and beside herself. Her heart going ninety to the dozen.

Mike's glib chat up lines, did as they always used to do. Made her weak at the knees. She lacked so much self-belief and felt that she wasn't worthy of his interest. So, when he spoke to her, she was transported to another planet. There was no one else there to divert his attention from her. He was talking just to HER and her alone.

Finally, she reluctantly pulled away from his embrace, trying desperately to regain her sense of loyalty to her son.

'S...Sorry to hear about your arm,' she stuttered.

'Oh, it's nothing,' he said, feigning modesty. And OUR boy...OUR Ben saved my life. I am so proud of OUR brave boy,' he lied.

OUR Ben! It was the first time that she had ever heard Mike say anything that recognised Ben as his son.

'Yes so I heard. I was very proud of him too. He's a good boy,' Beth added, feeling that she had to outbid Mike in the pride stakes.

But Mike's sudden unexpected appearance, sent her head spinning. His presence gave her mixed emotions.

On the one hand she was overjoyed and doey-eyed to see him.

On the other hand, she knew that she should be distancing herself from him. And condemning him for what he'd done by kidnapping Ben and endangering his life.

But as usual, where it came to Mike, her heart was ruling her head and she was putty in his hands, again.

'I'm not sure that I should be speaking to you anyway,' she said, reengaging her sensible head. 'After what you did to Ben. And getting involved with that woman,' she added.

Mike bowed his head and made himself look pathetic. 'Beth, you're right of course,' he whined. 'You know I've been set up, don't you? I've been framed. It was that horrible Sue that tried to kill our boy and then she tried to kill me. Look at my arm for the proof.'

'Is...Is that right?' she queried naively. With all of her heart, Beth wanted to believe him. After all these years, she surprised herself. She was still lovestruck over him. He had dominated her young impressionable mind as a teenager and now....

Her teenage crush whilst he was in his twenties, and she only sixteen, had left her pregnant. When he found out, he immediately ditched her for another wide-eyed fifteen-year-old. And told Beth to 'get out of his life.'

She thought that she would never get over his rejection, her heart was broken.

She had not coped well when it ended. Her lack of self-confidence had driven her into a downward spiral of dark despair.

She took to alcohol and drugs to ease her emotional pain and soon became a desperate alcoholic.

The miracle was that Ben was born healthy in spite of her substance abuse. However, the knock-on effect was that Ben had to become her young carer at an early age and look after her when she was 'spaced out.'

But those alcoholic days were a thing of the past, she had been dry for some time now having moved away from the bad influence of some of her boozy friends.

'The last I'd heard about you was that you were in prison. Have you been released,' she queried, bluntly.

'Yes, compassionate leave because of my arm,' he fibbed. 'I've just found my freedom again.'

'You mean you've escaped?' she surmised.

'In a way, yes,' he admitted.

'I knew it. You haven't changed, have you? You're still a chancer.'

'Yes, well I just need to hide somewhere for a short time, while the police are looking for me, so I can get to the evidence in order to clear my name.'

'Evidence to clear your...but I thought you were...'

'Guilty? Yes, that's the problem. Everyone thinks I'm guilty. Because I have a criminal past, I don't stand a chance of getting a fair trial. I've been set up. I just need time to prove it though. Please help me,' he pleaded and touched her hand, salaciously.

Subconsciously she sandwiched his hand between hers in a warm gesture of acquiescence. She was already mentally making excuses for him.

'Well...yes...of course. But... I... I don't know where you could go,' she explained.

'Could you…could you put me up somewhere? I know that you live in a big house with a lot of outbuildings.'

'No…no, I'm sorry. I can't, sorry,' she said removing her hands and stepping away from him. 'It's completely out of the question.'

'If they put me back inside, I'll never be able to clear my name. I just need some time that's all,' he grovelled. '…and then I'll give myself up,' he lied.

'I…I don't know. It's not even my house and in any case, I don't know how we would hide you.'

'It's a big house. There's bound to be somewhere, surely?' he persisted.

'No, it's not practical. Anyway, it's JC's house and Ben lives there too. Obviously, Ben hates you after the way you treated him.'

'I know and I'm ashamed of myself. But I'll make it up to him. I promise. But I can't do that unless I can talk to him. At the right time of course.'

'Well, I don't…know.' Beth said, her resolve weakening.

'It would have to be our secret until I had my evidence to show him that it was that bitch Sue, which caused all his grief,' Mike added, conspiratorially.

'Oh, I'm not sure,' she said, trying to think of a discreet way of turning him down without upsetting him.

'She hasn't changed,' Mike thought. 'She's still the pathetic excuse for a woman that I shagged.'

'What about a shed or something that I can rough it in,' he volunteered, frustrated that he couldn't persuade her.

'Well, um… there is a bit of a rundown granny annex at the bottom of the garden that nobody uses…but…I'm not sure,' she revealed, her stoic resolve collapsing around her.

'That will do, thanks.'

'But I...I didn't say yes,' she protested.

'If it's run down. I'm sure you can make sure that it's good enough for me to live in....it's only for a short time of course. You're good like that,' he flattered.

'Well...I probably could but...'

'I'm sure you could get food and stuff in there, to make my stay comfortable, can't you?' he demanded.

'I'm really not sure...'

'Now, look. I need to get out of town because the cameras are everywhere, and they will pick us both up. You could then be in trouble too.'

'No...I can't help,' she protested, nervously looking around.

'Look Beth, I know I treated you badly in the past and I'm sorry about that. Perhaps...perhaps I can... make it up to you somehow.' Mike grabbed her hand and pulled her to him, kissing her hair.

Beth's blood pressure went off the scale, she nearly passed out at his touch.

'Oh, OK...OK,' she relented.

'I shall be forever grateful,' he gushed, hugging her tightly.

'Assuming the building is usable, how do I get you in there?' she asked finally capitulating.

'That's my girl,' he said, tightening the hug.

'I tell you what, there's an alley at the bottom of the garden,' she explained, thinking on her feet.

'Right.'

'There's a six-foot-high panel fence around the garden. You can leap over the fence, and hopefully no one will see you.'

'My arm might make that difficult, but I'll try it. Thanks. How soon can I get in?' he probed.

'Well, I need to get home from here. But I can't do anything if JC and Ben are there,' she explained.

'Look, the longer that I'm out here, the greater the chance of me being caught,' he said, adding pressure on the reluctant woman.

'Ok...OK...mmm... say a couple of hours,' she suggested, glimpsing at her watch. 'Let's say three o'clock.'

'What's the address? Write it down for me.'

Beth took a little notepad out of her handbag and wrote down the address.

'Remember use the alley at the back of the houses,' she added.

'Right. That's great. In the meantime, have you got any money? I could get a coffee and a bite to eat while I wait.'

Immediately Beth dug into her handbag and retrieved her purse.

'How much do you want?' she asked naively.

'As much as you can afford. I'll get some groceries too while you're sorting out the hide for me.'

Beth had a flashback of when he was 'courting' her all those years ago. She provided him with money then, to satisfy his gambling habits. Naively she thought, that by bankrolling him, that would ensure that he'd stay with her.

However, eventually, when she gave up work to have Ben, the money wasn't forthcoming and that didn't make her attractive to him anymore. Consequently, Mike found another young girl to keep him in the manner to which she had kept him.

She shook her head to banish the memories of the hurt and foolishly handed him all the notes from her purse.

Mike brazenly counted it. 'Fifty quid! Is that all you've got?'

'Yes, sorry.'

'Have you got a card? Can't you get some more? I will need to buy some clothes.'

Surprising herself, Beth said 'No. I am restricted in the amount of money that I can withdraw,' she explained.

What she didn't say was that the restriction was an agreement between her and JC to help her from falling off the wagon again and buying lots of alcohol.

Beth was proud of her achievement at being 'dry' for two years. She attended regular weekly meetings of fellow addicts to provide a mutual support network when the craving was strong.

'Oh well, this will have to do then,' he said, dismissively. 'I'll see you at three.'

He gave her another hug and disappeared into the crowds.

Beth made her way home, kicking herself for falling under Mike's spell again. She was lovestruck. Her heart ruling her head. But love is blind to logical thinking. She realised that she had made a terrible mistake.

'I feel disloyal to my son,' she thought. 'Perhaps I can help them to improve their relationship by talking to each other and mending fences.

I can just imagine them on a photograph together, Mike and Ben, like a real Father and Son.

However, as much as she wished it would happen, she concluded that it was a utopian dream, never likely to come to fruition.

CHAPTER FORTY-SIX

The two policemen arrived back at the Police station and made arrangements to interview Suzette.

She was sat in an interview room feeling deeply sorry for herself as they entered.

'Oh, hello again Suzette. Well, you've been busy since we picked you up from Heathrow, haven't you?' the detective constable observed.

'We really weren't expecting to see you again, especially under these circumstances,' Marcus Williams added. 'We didn't think that after bringing you here, you'd end up with a criminal record.'

'Right Miss. What have you got to say for yourself?' Chris Cooper demanded, sitting opposite her.

'I'm very sorry. No, it wasn't my intention to get involved with anything like this. It...it just happened,' Suzette sobbed.

'So why did you? What were you thinking of? Helping a prisoner to escape from custody.'

'I'm sorry to have caused you work, especially after your kindness and thoughtfulness. But I'm trying to get evidence to prove there was a conspiracy against my sister and that someone had a motive to kill her,' Suzette explained sorrowfully.

'Really? Do you want to explain why helping Mike Benson to escape will do that?' Marcus Williams continued.

'No comment.'

'Now don't start that nonsense. No comment won't help you sorting out this mess. Pretty soon you'll be on the next flight back to Australia, unless you cooperate,' Chris Cooper said firmly.'

'I...I want to clear my sisters name and put those murderers in prison,' she said welling up.

'How? By helping a prisoner to escape?' Chris Cooper puzzled. 'That's a strange way of going about it,'

'And what's this about murderers?' Marcus Williams queried.

'He offered to help me clear my sisters name. He said he had evidence that would show those...those people were out to get Sue and fit her up. To murder her.'

'Right, so where is Mike Benson now?' Chris Cooper demanded.

'I don't know,' Suzette snivelled.

'Where did he go to after you dropped him off?'

'I don't know. He was supposed to come back to the car after he got something,' she explained.

'What something was that?' the DS probed.

'I don't know. He didn't say. I thought it might be the evidence that he'd promised me that he would get for me.'

'You don't know a lot do you?' Chris Cooper pointed out. 'So, why didn't he come back to you?'

'I don't know. Perhaps, because he saw the police cars surround me.'

'Knowing what a lowlife he is, it was more likely that he'd used you and thrown you to the lions,' Marcus Williams surmised. 'Wise up! He'd set you up. Conned you.'

'No, he was definitely going to get some evidence. He told me,' she sobbed, now realising that they might be right. She had been used. It was a trick.

'Alright, I think we've heard enough. We don't think there is any point in holding you in custody. We will recommend that you are released on police bail.'

'Police bail!' Suzette said in surprise. 'What does that mean?

'Police bail is where, having interviewed you, we release you back into the community. But we will insist that you hand in your passport so that you can't skip back home. Do you understand?' Chris Cooper explained.

'Oh, thank you. Thank you so much,' she sobbed.

'And for heaven's sake, don't have any more dealings with him. If he tries to get in touch with you, ring me straight away,' the detective constable said, giving her his card.' Is that a deal?'

'Yes. Thank you.'

'If you do get involved with him again, you <u>will</u> go to prison for sure. Now I know that you've had a hell of a time with the loss of your sister and hearing the manner of her death at the inquest. Just keep your head down,' Marcus Williams advised.

'Come with us while we sort the paperwork out,' Chris invited.

'Thank you.'

'Where are you staying?'

'I've rented a house because of my sister's inquest. I don't know how long that I shall be here.'

'OK. I'll take you home,' Chris Cooper advised her. 'Much to his colleagues surprise. 'We don't want you getting into any more trouble, do we?'

CHAPTER FORTY-SEVEN

After the unfortunate meeting with Mike, Beth caught the bus home from town and rushed to sort out the Granny annex.

She had only gone into the annex once before and wasn't sure what state it was going to be in. 'Oh God, what have I done promising him he could stay here?' What was I thinking of? Where even is the key?

She couldn't believe that she'd allowed herself to be persuaded to help Mike hide from the police.

Although now a woman, just like before as a teenager, she was still 'putty' in his hands.

The tension of her decision caused a massive headache; her mind was a whirl. What had she allowed herself to get involved with?

One thing at least was in her favour, JC had taken Ben out for a drive to give him a change of scenery and some fresh air. Hopefully, a respite from the thoughts of the inquest. So, fortunately, apart from a confused dog, she had the run of the house to herself.

Beth's first challenge was to find the annex door key. Normally all keys were kept in a special drawer in a kitchen unit. But she didn't know what the key even looked like.

However, after frantically shuffling through a multitude of keys, she eventually grabbed several and rushed down the garden, accompanied by the dog who was winding her way around her legs, demanding some fuss dropping her ball at Beth's feet.

'I'm sorry Rusty, I haven't got time to play with your ball. I have a job to do,' she said, frantically trying key after key in the lock. hoping to identify one with appropriate markings on it. Finally, much to her relief, one slid into the unused lock. But in spite of her efforts, it didn't turn. So she tried another key which looked the same,

'No that doesn't turn either. Damn it,' she cursed. 'Now what shall I do? Perhaps the lock is seized up. I know, Ben has got some of that clever releasing oil, WD40, that he uses on his bikes. I'll use some of that.'

She then rushed back to the house and got a can of the lubricant. Shadowed again by the confused dog, she then rushed back to the annex.

Beth liberally sprayed the WD40 into the lock and tried the keys again, although stiff, after several attempts, while working the keys back and forth, the lock finally clicked. She pushed the door handle down, but the door refused to move.

She put her shoulder against it and it reluctantly creaked open. She picked up the WD and sprayed the hinges, working the door open and closed for the lubricant to get into the bearing surfaces.

Satisfied that the door was usable, she stepped gingerly into the small entrance hall. It smelt musty. The interior was dark. Blinds on the windows were only partially open.

Tugging gently on one of the blind's strings, she opened it. She was pleased to see that, considering that it had not been used for several years, the interior of the small annex was in surprisingly good condition apart from large cobwebs everywhere and a thin layer of dust.

She quickly visited all the rooms, a single bedroom, with a bed and small wardrobe; a toilet with a bath; a small lounge/diner with an armchair, small table and two wooden chairs arranged around the table.

The place was like the Marie Celeste. Someone had obviously walked out and left everything of their home in place.

'Perhaps someone left and didn't return as expected. Perhaps they died while they were out shopping,' she thought gloomily. 'At least I don't have to furnish it to make it habitable.'

She dashed back to the house got the vacuum cleaner and her cleaning kit and ran back and tackled the challenges of the annex.

Fortunately, the electricity was still connected and providing power to the building, so she was able to use her vacuum.

'I wonder if the water is still on?' she wondered, turning on one of the taps.

After a bit of effort and more WD, the cold tap turned and with some gurgling noises in the pipes water eventually flowed into the sink. 'Thank goodness for that.'

She tried the electric cooker and was pleased to see that it worked too.

'What would I have done if there was no electricity or water,' she thought.

Keeping an eye open for JC and Ben's return, she did a thorough clean of the annex.

After an hour of hectic activity, she locked the door and went for a cup of tea in the house, exhausted by her efforts.

As she drank her tea, she reviewed her decision. 'I suppose it's not too late to tell Mike to sod off. I haven't done anything wrong yet.'

'If I do, what if he turns violent? How would I cope with that? No, I'm going to have to see it through now and hope he gets caught soon.'

'If I'm going to provide him with food. How am I going to do that?' she pondered. 'How am I going to shop without JC and Ben knowing what I'm doing? Oh, God. I wish that I hadn't said I'd help.'

'What time did I tell him to be here?' she said to herself glancing at her watch. 'Oh god is it that time already?'

Suddenly the dog started barking and dashed off down to the annex.

Beth followed quickly after the dog. As she made her way down the garden, she could hear someone shouting, 'Get off you mangy mutt.'

'Oh, you're here already,' she said, flatly, seeing Mike there.

'Yes, of course. This was the time you said. Will you shut that bleedin dog up before I do...permanently,' he said, glaring at the barking dog.

Beth unlocked the annex door and seized the dog's collar. She led the still barking dog back to the house. 'You be a good girl,' she said, giving the dog a treat and shutting her into the kitchen.

On her return to the annex Mike was just emerging from it.

'Thank god you got rid of that frigging dog,' he moaned. 'Is this it? It's a bit of a shithole, isn't it?' he said disparagingly.

'Sorry, it's the best I could do. You don't have to stay. You can go if you want,' she said, hoping that he would, and she wouldn't be incriminated.

'And I nearly got the wrong house, you silly mare,' he said cruelly. 'How was I supposed to know which was your house? From the back with a six-foot fence in the way, it's impossible to see.'

'Sorry.'

'And I nearly broke my bleedin neck getting over that effing fence. I hurt my bad arm too. You do realise don't you, that you're going to have to dress my burns?'

'No. No sorry, that wasn't part of the deal, and besides, I don't have any medical stuff here. I thought you'd be going back to the hospital to have it dressed,' she replied meekly.

'Don't be stupid. I see that you still don't have any more brain cells than when you were born. If I do that I'll be caught. Won't I you pillock?'

Beth sagged under his verbal onslaught. All pretence of him being a thoughtful individual had disappeared. He hadn't changed. He was still the horrible vindictive person that she fell in love with. She was his helpless victim again. She gave him a key and scurried back to the house sobbing.

CHAPTER FORTY-EIGHT

Following completion of the necessary paperwork, Suzette had been released on police bail and Chris Cooper had taken her home.

'I'll take you to a takeaway en route if you like. You must be starving,' he offered.

'No thanks. I'm not hungry,' she explained. 'I just want a shower and my bed.'

'OK, but don't forget to eat,' he reminded her. 'It's been a traumatic day for you, and you need to keep hydrated as well.

'Yes, it has. It's nice of you to think about me but don't worry, I'm not hungry or thirsty.'

The journey was completed in silence.

'My house is down here in the cul de sac,' she said. 'This is it,' she confirmed, as he pulled up outside her house. Thanks for the lift,' she said, getting out of the car.

The policeman switched the engine off and got out too. 'If you don't mind, I'd better check if he's inside your house.' the detective suggested.

'No, he's not. Well, it's unlikely,' she corrected herself. 'I don't think he knows where I live.'

Chris Cooper hesitated, unsure whether to insist. 'OK but keep away from him. Hear me?'

'Thanks for bringing me home and being so understanding.' Suzette said, walking up to her front door.

'It's my pleasure. A pity that it's not under different circumstances,' he suggested.

'Yes,' she said, embarrassed by the obvious chat-up line.

'I'm sorry that you've had such a bad start to your visit to the UK. Hopefully, it will get better from now on. Don't forget if he gets in touch, give me a bell, or even if you just want to talk. You've got my card, haven't you?'

'Yes, thanks.'

'Cheerio then,' the policeman said, thinking it would be nice to take her out for a meal sometime.'

The next-door neighbours curtains twitched as the owner watched the policeman drive away. She returned to her chair as the car left the cul de sac.

'Well, I hope we're not going to have an endless stream of men coming to her door, otherwise I shall be on to her landlord,' the old woman moaned to her husband. 'We don't want that sort of thing going on round here, disturbing the peace and quiet of the neighbourhood.'

'No dear.'

Suzette went in and locked the door. She looked around to make sure that she didn't have any uninvited visitors. Satisfied that she was by herself, she ran upstairs, undressed, went into the bathroom, and had a long refreshing shower. As the warm water cascaded over her body, she imagined the tensions of the day washing away, pooling at her feet. After ten minutes, she reluctantly turned off the water and vigorously dried herself with a large soft bath towel. She dressed in her pink pyjamas and lay down on the bed.

Her mind was still active from the catalogue of the recent events. She just relaxed there, gazing at the ceiling, trying to get control of the whirlwind of chaos in her mind. She felt like a ragdoll, swept into a tornado of uncontrolled mayhem.

Her saving grace was that the two detectives had been sympathetic to her misdemeanour. They presented Suzette's crime as an out of character lapse. 'Helping Mike escape, occurred when she was under great stress, following the discovery of the horrendous death of her sister,' they'd said. 'Her judgement was further clouded while she was being manipulated by a forceful individual.'

But, irrespective of the warning that the policemen had given her about getting involved with Mike, she was still hoping that he would contact her. She needed the evidence that he said he had to clear her sister's name.

CHAPTER FORTY-NINE

Mike eventually came to terms with living in the annex and stopped moaning about it. But, true to his egotistical personality, he didn't offer any gratitude to Beth for hiding and feeding him. Instead, he demanded that she got him a mobile phone.

'Well, where's yours?' she asked. 'You used to be glued to it.'

'It's obviously with my personal belongings in the prison, you idiot. Come on you can buy me one.'

'I thought you wanted to keep a low profile. Why do you need it?' she asked.

'I need a phone to make my arrangements to leave here. So, it's in your best interests to get me one. The sooner the better,' Mike demanded. 'I just want to get out of the country and go to the Costa del Sol.

'The Costa del Crime, more likely,' Beth thought.

'Why?' she asked naively.

'Obviously, I need to contact my mates,' he berated. 'As soon as I get the money that's owed to me, I'll pay you back,' he lied.

From their early years together, Beth could fill a catalogue with his false promises. He knew that she was gullible, and she knew that she was going to be the paymaster.

'Make sure that it's a burner phone. I don't want the police to be monitoring me while I'm planning. Right?'

'A what?'

'A burner phone, cloth ears.'

'A burner phone!' she repeated. 'Whatever is that?'

'You don't need to know. Just ask them in the shop. They know what it is,' he said brusquely.

Against her better judgement, Beth, softened her reluctance and again did his bidding.

She told Ben and JC that she needed to go into town because she'd forgotten something.

'Do you want me to drop you off?' JC offered.

'No, it's OK. I quite like taking the bus,' she fibbed. 'It's no hassle. There's a regular ten-minute service these days.'

After arriving in town, she then had to decide which phone shop to go to. Unused to buying phones without Ben's help she was confused by the considerable number all promising special offers. Finally, she chose one shop that looked 'nice' and studied the bewildering display. Eventually picking a mobile up, she nervously approached the counter.

'Excuse me I'm after a burner…burner phone. Is this one, one of those?' she asked naively, showing the woman her choice.

'Well, yes. But actually, they don't use specific phones these days,' the assistant informed her.

'No?' Beth was wrong footed. Now wallowing out of her depth.

'No. They use a burner phone app, which you download from the internet,' the shop assistant informed her. 'It provides the same secrecy functions that the old burner phones used to.'

'Oh, OK. Thanks…umm…I've chosen this one, but I'm not sure which one to get,' Beth puzzled looking at the nearby display of over twenty phones.

'I'd recommend a Samsung Galaxy with EE. They are doing a good deal at the moment.'

'OK thanks. In that case, I'll go with your recommendation.'

Beth duly paid with her credit card and, with her purchase in hand returned home to be greeted by an inquisitive Ben.

'Hi Mum. Did you get it?'

'Get what?' she said defensively, wondering if he'd watched her buying the phone. Her heart rate rising with guilt.

'The shopping that you went into town for?' he reminded her.

'Oh…oh that. No. I…I…they didn't have it.'

'So that was a waste of time then,' Ben surmised.

'Yes, yes. It was. Excuse me I…I must get some air.' She said heading for the back door.

'Where are you going now Mum?' Ben asked. 'Are you feeling alright?'

'Yes. Yes perfectly…I just… hot flushes, that's all.'

'Do you really need to take your handbag though?'

'Yes…I… umm …I have a runny nose,' she lied.

Getting the mobile phone to Mike was proving to be more difficult than she thought with her eagle-eyed son watching her every move.

Beth stepped out into the garden, the dog followed and ran down the lawn barking.

'Why does the dog keep going down the bottom of the garden? Ben asked.

'I don't know. Perhaps there's a hedgehog or something down there,' Beth replied nervously. 'Can you take her in please. Her barking isn't helping my headache.'

Ben called the dog, who went back to him immediately.

Ensuring that Ben had gone back into the house, Beth made her way to the annex and tapped on the door.

'It's me,' she whispered. 'I've got your phone.'

Mike was in his underpants and made his way to the door, unlocked it, and opened it a chink.

'Oh, it's you. You got it then?'

'Yes.'

'What kept you?'

'I was as quick as I could. There were so many phones and I...'

'Yes, yes. I know, I know,' he said irritably, cutting her off. 'Right, hand it over then.'

He opened the door wider, while she dug into her handbag and retrieved the phone. He took it from her and closed the door without saying thanks.

Beth was not surprised at his ignorance.

'He hasn't changed over the years. Why do I keep letting him walk over me,' she thought as she returned to the house.

CHAPTER FIFTY

Ben was suspicious about his mother's recent strange behaviour of going to the bottom of the garden, so say 'to cool down from a hot flush.'

Or was there something more sinister? He had a feeling of dread that Beth had fallen off the wagon. Was she drinking again and using the annex to hide her habit.

As a young carer for his mother during his childhood years, Ben recognised the pattern of lies and excuses that she used to try to hide her clandestine substance abuse.

Reluctantly, he decided to investigate and to try to catch her out. Although hoping against hope that she wasn't descending into an alcoholic nightmare again. He felt the angst and had flashbacks of dealing with the disgusting consequences of her drunken episodes, whilst he was only a child.

It was the last thing that he needed right now as he was close to the emotional 'edge' himself. The issues surrounding Mike's escape, his trial, the accident, and inquest, were getting to him.

Now at least, if she has started drinking again, he wouldn't be alone this time. He would get help from JC. Their friend and landlord was now dry himself after living an alcoholic's life on the streets of London for a long time. Consequently, JC had his own personal knowledge and experience of the medical dangers of excessive drinking, having had a liver transplant.

Ben chose his moment to investigate the annex while his mother and JC were out of the way. He made his way down the garden and tentatively tried the door. It was locked.

'Bugger, it's locked. I'll need a key. Looks like it's a big key, not a yale,' he assessed, examining the lock. 'Looks like it's been oiled recently too,' he observed, running his finger in the damp stain on the woodwork and sniffing it. WD!' So, it looks like she is using it. Damn,' he thought. I'll have a look in the key drawer and see if I can find one there,' he thought.

He returned to the house and got a few large keys that he thought could fit. But when he tried them, none worked.

After half an hour trying the various keys, he gave up. 'Oh, I can't be arsed,' he admitted returning the keys. 'If she wants to destroy herself, let her go ahead.'

Inside the annex, disturbed by the noises coming from the door, Mike had jammed the door with a chair so that it wouldn't open anyway. He knew it wasn't Beth because she always knocked first, then whispered his name.

CHAPTER FIFTY-ONE

A few days later, alone in the house, Ben was feeling down. The prospect of his mother going back on the booze and the forthcoming investigations for the inquest was weighing heavily on his mind.

'Come on Ben,' he urged himself. 'What you need is a nice bar of chocolate to cheer yourself up. Now where does mother hide her chocolates?'

Ben looked unsuccessfully in her usual hiding places and turned his attention to one of the kitchen cupboards. As he was feeling around on the top shelf his fingers brushed upon a key.

'Hello, what's this key doing here?' he wondered. 'It should be in the key drawer. Perhaps Mum or JC are losing the plot and put it in the wrong place,' he reasoned.'

Then 'the penny dropped.'

'Or... is this the key to the annex that mother has been hiding?' he guessed. 'Only one way to find out.' Ben had accidently stumbled on the second key.

Making sure that his mother still hadn't returned from her ladies coffee morning, he picked up the key and went down to the annex. He tried the door it was locked as expected.

He inserted the key in the lock and was relieved to see that it turned. He opened the annex door and stepped inside.

It was empty.

Fortunately for Ben, Mike had gone into town to get a passport from one of his mates. Whilst there he got some medical bits to dress his injured arm himself, it was the only thing that Beth had found some courage to stand against Mike. She had refused to tend to his injury.

Mike had gone in 'disguise,' wearing a baseball cap and his overcoat, which concealed his grubby bandaged arm.

'Well, somebody's using this place,' Ben said, looking around at the unwashed cup, unmade bed, and general mess on the floor.

Then he spotted the bottles of wine which Beth had bought at Mike's insistence for his own consumption. He counted six empty bottles.

'Oh mother! Oh, damn it!' he said unhappily. 'Mother IS drinking again. I knew it,' he muttered. 'Sod it! She's fallen off the wagon. After all that time of being dry!'

Having seen what he really didn't want to see, he closed and locked the door, his heart heavy. 'Oh God I don't want to go through all that nursing crap again. Cleaning up her vomit. Pissing herself.'

He went back into the house, returned the key to its hiding place, and went to his bedroom.

He texted Janie. '*Hi, As if I haven't got enough going on in my life. I've just discovered that Mum is back on the booze.*'

He debated with himself whether to tell JC, but decided he'd confront his mother first.

The following day, Beth again announced that she was having another hot flush and was going outside to cool down.

On the way out, she surreptitiously went to the cupboard and removed the key to the annex and went into the back garden with her handbag.

Ben waited a few moments and then quietly followed his mother down the garden, determined to catch her in the act and challenge her.

As he expected, after a cursory glance around, she went to the annex door.

Ben hid behind a tall bush and watched her knock on the door and then unlock it and go in. As she crossed the threshold, he heard a voice from inside that made his blood run cold.

'About bleeding time too, slag,' Mike berated her.

'Oh, my days! That's Mike! What the hell is he doing in there? I can't believe it. So mother is sheltering him from the police. What the hell is she thinking of?'

Ben was devastated. 'After all that bastard has done to me. She lets him in to our house! What the hell is going on?'

Ben's head was spinning. He typed a message to send to Janie.

'*Janie my problems just get worse. Mum is hiding Mike from the police in the annex. What should I do? I can't dob my Mum in.*'

But he stopped before he sent it.

'I can't let anyone know about her doing that, otherwise she will go to prison. Perhaps I ought to persuade her to get rid of him,' he thought. 'Or should I go in there myself and confront him?

No, that would be suicidal. He would probably kill me. How otherwise could he stop me giving evidence about him and his lousy business partner? I suppose he could kidnap Mum instead. Oh shit! I didn't think of that.'

At that moment, the annex door opened, and Beth stepped out. She was obviously upset. Ben watched as she locked the door again and went past his hiding place and into the house.

He felt angry, but totally helpless that Mike was upsetting her. His fears about her drinking again were overshadowed by a worse situation. Hiding Mike and doing his bidding was a criminal offence.

CHAPTER FIFTY-TWO

Mike was bored being stuck in the annex with only the TV and a daily visit from Beth to break the boredom.

'I hope my mates sort out my transport soon so I can get over the channel hidden from the authorities,' he thought. 'Just seeing only her is doing my nut in.

Perhaps I'll contact that Suzette. Then again, I don't want to get involved with her and her problems again. 'The danger is she could drag me into issues surrounding her sister's death. I don't want that,' he thought.

But on the other hand, she's been extremely useful and proved her worth by getting me my freedom. The trouble is, I haven't got any documented evidence that incriminate that Scout Leader and his sidekick to give her. On the other hand, that solicitors clerk was quite forthcoming.

I suppose that I ought to show the woman some sympathy for her loss. but it's hard as I'm glad that her sister is dead. I hope the evil bitch is rotting in hell.

But the more that he thought about it the more favourable it could be contacting her. Afterall, he needed funds to make his escape to Spain once he was across the channel.

Beth was telling him she couldn't fund him anymore and nothing was forthcoming from his mates. Suzette might be a source of money, a fresh credit card to drain.

And in time, it would be nice to have the lovely Suzette as another notch on my bedpost,' he fantasised.

Mike used the burner app on his phone to ring Suzette, after a short while she answered.

'Hello. Who's calling,' she asked, suspiciously.

'It's me,' Mike informed her.

'Mike! Mike is that you?' she queried, excitedly.

'Yes.'

'Where have you been? I thought I'd lost you. Where are you now?' she asked, avalanching him with questions.

'What do you want me to answer first?' he said flatly, already wishing that he hadn't called her.

'Where are you?

'Somewhere safe.'

'Why didn't you come back to me?' I did wait for you,' she explained.

'Something came up.'

'Anyway, it was just as well that you didn't, because shortly after you'd left, the police surrounded me, and I was arrested.'

'I expect they clocked the number plate,' he suggested unhelpfully.

'And now I'm on bail thanks to you,' she informed him angrily.

'Well, you knew the risks. If you want to clear your sisters name, you got to take risks,' he pointed out coldly.

'Yes, I suppose. I was a bit naïve to think that I would get away Scot free.'

'Well, the reason for my call is ....'

'Yes?' Suzette asked, expecting him to say that he had the evidence.

'Is… that I need money to get the files of information that we need,' he lied.

'So, you've tracked down the evidence then?' she said, excited at the prospect of clearing her sister's name.

'Well, no…not yet. That's why I need the money,' he fibbed.

'How much are we talking about?' she queried guardedly.

Mike hadn't actually thought of a figure and blurted out the first number that came into his head…'five hundred…'

'Five hundred! Yes. OK, I can do that,' she interrupted.

'Thousand,' he added. 'Five hundred thousand pounds.'

'What! Half a million! You've got to be joking,' she said in horror.

'No, I'm not. There's a lot of people to bribe. Your sister was telling me that this harassment goes all the way back to when her ex, Rupert had just divorced her. Just after they split, he inherited millions in a will from his Godfather. Money which she reckons that she was entitled to, fifty percent of it, anyway.'

'But if they were divorced,' Suzette observed.

'Well, she reckoned that, fortunately, at that stage the divorce wasn't finalised.'

'Yeah, OK, I hear what you say. But how is that proving they were conspiring against her?

'Well, it's all based around this legacy. They were all in it to stop her getting any money.'

'So, you're saying we need money to release more money?' Suzette queried.

'Yeah, that's it, in a nutshell,' Mike confirmed.

'I don't know where to get that sort of money from,' she informed him. 'Five hundred thousand! That's monopoly money.'

'Didn't you say that your brother had a ranch in Australia?'

'Yes, but he isn't going to give me any money. We had a big falling out before I left. He won't want to have any dealings with me anyway. And, as I discovered, I was adopted by his family. So, he's really my stepbrother.'

'Mmm…that's a bit of a challenge then. Why don't you tell him that you have discovered an unmissable opportunity to invest in a new UK company which is growing at an incredible rate. If you say that, and tell him that he's bound to make a killing, if he invests early via me?' Mike suggested.'

'Are you sure that there is no other way of getting these documents? Can't we pursue it through the courts?'

'That's likely to take for ever and it's going to be even costlier. No, the only winners will be the lawyers,' Mike suggested, desperately thinking of another money raising idea.

'Then it isn't going to be possible. We aren't going to be able to prove her innocence,' Suzette observed resignedly.

'Well, there is a third option,' Mike proposed.

'Which is?'

'To steal the stuff. I'm sure I could find some burglars who would like to take it on for a few grand,' Mike proposed.

'For a few grand!'

'A few grand each of course.'

'Oh dear. Let me have a think,' Suzette said. 'I'll see what I can do to raise the funds. I can't do too much at the moment as I have to report to the police daily.'

'Right,'

'Is this the phone number that I can reach you on?' she asked.

'Yes. But don't take too long. My contacts are busy people,' Mike urged.

'OK,' she said miserably, wondering how to raise the money quickly.

'Gullible bitch,' he thought, ending the call. In reality there was no other party that he had to bribe. Mike was filling his own pockets. What's more, he had no documented evidence. It was all hearsay from listening to Sue groaning on and the solicitors clerk spilling the beans.

CHAPTER FIFTY-THREE

Ben was beside himself with the discovery that his mother was harbouring Mike, an escaped prisoner. He'd churned the whole thing over and over in his mind, until he was wound up like a tight spring. He couldn't let it go. 'I need to protect Mum from herself.' he thought.

Consequently, he decided the only way out was to tackle his father 'head on' and get him to leave. This would save his mother being dragged through the courts.

He waited until the house was quiet and his mother had gone to bed, then he crept out, trying not to disturb the dog.

Unfortunately, despite the normal walk around the block, the old dog was as attentive as ever and wagged her tail, pleased to see him, as he went past.

'Hello Rusty. You stay in your basket. That's a good girl,' he said quietly.

The dog wagged her tail again, and did as she was told, put her head down on her paws, and didn't move.

Ben retrieved the annex key from its usual hiding place and walked quietly down the lawn to the annex.

He could see through a chink in the blinds that his father was stretched out on the old two-seater settee watching television.

His heart in his mouth, he quietly inserted the key in the lock, but to his annoyance, found that it only went partially in.

'Damn,' he thought. 'Mike has left the other key in the lock the other side of the door.

Ben was now faced with a dilemma, whether to leave and go back to bed and try again another day or to get Mike to open the door.

He was feeling pretty scared, dry mouthed. This would be the first time that he'd seen his father since rescuing him from the fire at the farm.

However, he decided if he left it, he wouldn't have enough courage to attempt it again. He needed to act now in order to get his mother out of the mess, before it was too late.

Taking his courage in his hands he knocked on the door.

From inside he heard his father blaspheme.

'What the effing hell do you want at this time of night, you dozy cow,' he shouted, shuffling over to the door.

Ben stood back, wondering if he'd thought this through properly. Wondering what he was hoping to get out of the meeting. Hopefully, persuading Mike to leave would be a good outcome,' he decided. And not being killed in the process would be an even better result,' he thought.

The door opened a crack. Mike peered out.

Ben could see that he was standing there in a filthy, stained white vest and black underpants. Completing his ensemble, on his feet, black ankle socks, with his big toes poking through.

'Well, well, well. Who the effing hell have we got here?' Mike said, smiling, and immediately grabbed

Ben by the shoulder, and dragged him in to the building. 'It's boy wonder!' he beamed.

However, the dog had decided she wanted to be with Ben, so had escaped from the kitchen through the dog flap and dashed through the open annex door before Mike could close it.

Seeing Ben being roughly handled, she barked loudly and snarled at Mike, attempting to protect her master.

Used to noisy animals on the farm, Mike ignored the yapping dog, and quickly closed the door.

'Look what the cat dragged in,' Mike slurred, gazing at Ben's frightened face. 'I think that's a good description that fits your mother, don't you? A lazy cat' he laughed.

Ben bristled at the insult and wanted to hit his father for his unpleasantness.

'Ben you're just the person that I wanted to see,' Mike revealed.

'Well, you're the last one that I wanted to see,' Ben murmured.

'Now, now. Don't be like that. I haven't seen you for a while. You see I've still got my arm?' He said, showing Ben the filthy bandage. 'Despite your efforts to give me blood poisoning from that filthy horse trough.'

'I saved your arm by dropping the temperature, you ungrateful bastard,' Ben ranted.

'Here, watch your language! You don't talk to your father like that. Do you?' he shouted, grabbing the front of Ben's clothes with his good arm' and hoisting him up so that Ben was standing on tiptoe.

'Get off me,' Ben shouted defiantly, staring into his father's face.

Rusty joined in the heated conversation and nipped Mike's leg.

'Ouch you bloody thing,' Mike shouted, kicking at the dog.

Fortunately, the dog danced away, out of harm's way, still barking loudly and snarling at her master's assailant.

'Mike let go of Ben's clothes and stood in front of the door, blocking any opportunity for Ben to escape.

'Now you listen, and you listen good. When I go to trial...IF, I go to trial. You are going to say that it was that bitch Sue, which kidnapped you. And she forced me at knife point to get involved. Right?'

'Yeah, but that's not what happened is it?' Ben reminded him.

'Don't argue with me you horrible little shit. Obviously that useless creature of a mother didn't drag you up properly. You need to respect your elders. Understand? No of course not. She's incapable of doing anything sensible. She was probably pissed out of her drunken head, wasn't she?'

'Don't you dare insult my mother. You were the cause of all of her problems in the first place.' Ben ranted. 'I should have left you in that blazing barn. Instead, I carried you out and saved your life.'

'In your dreams. That's not the way I remember it,' Mike said.

'No, you've got a convenient memory, haven't you? I saved your arm from having to be amputated, too,' Ben reminded him. You ungrateful sod. You don't deserve to exist.'

Mike's backhander caught Ben across the cheek and knocked him off his feet.

The dog went for Mike, barking and baring her teeth.

Mike kicked at her to keep her away, the pair circled each other in a cacophony of aggression. The dog barking hostilely.

In spite of the blow, Ben stood up, rubbing his cheek. 'Is that all you've got old man?' he shouted, defiantly. Provoking his father.

'So, what pathetic scheme brings you here Mummies boy?' Mike demanded, ignoring Ben's jibe and the barking dog,

'Getting rid of you out of our lives, and out of Mum's hair.'

'Yeah! You and who's army?' Mike sneered.

'The police,' Ben bluffed. 'I've told them that you're here.'

'You what?' Mike queried angrily.

'I've told the police. They will be here any minute,' Ben repeated his bluff.

'If they are. You've just dropped your mother in the shit.' Mike said, studying the boy's face. 'No. As thick as you are. I don't think that you'd do that to your mother. Would you?' Mike goaded.

'Wouldn't I?' Ben postured.

Mike stared at Ben to gauge the truth of his boast.

Ben brazened it out and stared back without blinking. 'You'll soon find out if I did won't you,' he provoked.

'You little bastard, I should have drowned you at birth along with that litter of unwanted puppies that I got rid of.'

Red hot with anger, Mike grabbed Ben's clothes and threw him against the wall. Ben's head hit the wall and the impact took the wind out of him. He collapsed, knocked out, cold.

The dog continued to bark, angrily, and finally sank her teeth into Mike's leg.

CHAPTER FIFTY-FOUR

When Ben regained consciousness, Mike had gone. But Beth was in her dressing gown staring down at him from the open annex door.

'Oh, my god! Ben, are you alright?' What are you doing here?' Where's Mike?' she spluttered.

'I think he's gone Mum. Mike's gone. What were you thinking of hiding him in here?'

'I...I felt sorry for him and.... I know it was a stupid thing to do. I wanted to help him.'

'Help him! After what he did to me?' Ben said, amazed at his mother's naivety.

'He said it was that Sue woman that made him do it.'

'That's bullshit. He knew what he was doing.'

'But why did he leave? Has he gone for good?' Beth asked nervously.

'I told him that I'd called the police and he got angry. He knocked me out.'

"What have you done? Ben you silly boy,' she said, cuddling him. 'He could have killed you.'

'I know,' Ben said, rubbing the back of his head and feeling a lump.

'Did you? Had you called them?' Beth queried anxiously.

'No. Of course not. Otherwise, you'd be in trouble, wouldn't you?' Ben revealed, struggling to stand. 'More's the point, what are you doing here?'

'The dog's barking woke me up. I've never heard her bark like that before,' Beth explained. 'And I came down and found you.'

'Just as well that JC isn't here. Did he know about this?' Ben asked.

'No. I never told him. He would have been terribly upset at what I was doing.

You know that Mike will be back? This isn't the end. He will haunt us forever,' she sobbed.

'No. It will be alright Mum,' Ben reassured her but mainly himself. 'He'll be back behind bars soon and then when I give my evidence and tell them he wanted me to lie. He will be banged away for a long time. Honest,' he said positively.

'If only that were true,' Beth filled up again and hugged Ben.

'Why did you help him, Mum?' the boy asked again.

'So...so he would leave us alone,' she lied.

Her son wouldn't understand that Beth still loved Mike, even after all the horrible things he'd done to them both.

Beth's actions proved that '*Love is blind.*'

CHAPTER FIFTY-FIVE

'Where's Rusty? Ben said, suddenly realising that the dog wasn't there. 'She was here,' Ben revealed, anxiously looking around. 'She was protecting me when he grabbed me,' he explained.

'Good girl,' Beth said, looking in the other rooms and calling the dog. 'Rusty, Rusty. Here girl. Did she bite him?' Beth asked.

'Yes, I think so.'

'Good for her.'

'Oh my god! You don't think he's hurt her, do you?' Ben said, concerned.

'No. As horrible as he is, he wouldn't hurt her. Would he?' Beth pondered, now unsure. 'He works with animals. He respects them,' she said naively.

'He doesn't respect people though Mum, does he?' Ben said quietly, catching his mother's eye.

'No...no, probably not,' she blustered, knowing exactly what Ben was inferring.

'I heard him shouting at you. Calling you a slag,' Ben admitted.

'Well, you know, some people have a tough upbringing and have difficulty expressing themselves. He probably doesn't mean it,' Beth explained, defensively, not wishing to condemn Mike. Anyway, it's like water off a ducks back. I take it with 'a pinch of salt.'

'Yeah, right!' Ben said, in disgust. 'Anyway, forget about him. More importantly, let's look for the dog.'

'Yes let's. Have you got a torch?' Beth asked.

'I got my head torch here,' he said, getting it out of his pocket.

'Perhaps she's gone back to her basket. I'll check the house,' Beth said, trotting off.

They left the annex together and went off in separate ways. Calling for the dog.

Ben wandered around the back of the building and saw a broken fence panel.

'Mike obviously decided he needed a faster escape route,' Ben thought. 'I wonder if the dog chased him off. Good for you Rusty if you did.'

Then Ben made his grim discovery. His torch beam washed over a dark shape.

'Oh no,' he pleaded.

The dog was lying nearby, under a bush. She had defended Ben to the last and had chased Mike off but had paid the price for her loyalty.

'Oh Rusty,' he sobbed, kneeling down by her. 'Rusty please be alright?' he implored, hugging the limp animal. 'Please be alright.'

At that moment Beth returned.

'Ben, Ben,' she called. 'Where are you? She's not in the house.'

'I'm here. By the fence, he shouted. 'I've found her,' he said thickly.

'Oh, thank god for that,' she said, rounding the corner.

Then she saw the dog as her torch beam swept over Ben and Rusty. 'Oh no! Don't tell me...she's not...'

'I don't know. She's not moving. Let's get her to the vets. It looks like she's got an injury to her head. I wouldn't be at all surprised if he didn't kick her.'

'The bastard,' Beth exploded. 'After all I tried to do for him.'

Beth joined Ben kneeling by the dog and stroked her still body.

'Oh Rusty,' she sobbed.

'I think she must have been seeing him off. Still trying to protect me,' Ben suggested tearfully.

'Good girl,' Beth said, quietly stroking the dog. 'Good girl. Carry her to the car Ben. Let's get her to the vets.'

CHAPTER FIFTY-SIX

After knocking Ben out by slamming him against the wall and fighting off the barking dog. Mike got dressed quickly and stuffed his possessions into his rucksack, fearful that any moment the police would arrive.

Stepping over the unconscious Ben and dodging the barking dog he hightailed it from the annex.

Unsure whether Ben had been bluffing or not, he quickly ran to the fence and put his boot into a panel as the dog went for him again.

He silenced her with a kick to the head. She went down like a sack of spuds and didn't move. 'Thank Christ for that. Silence at last,' he thought.

He gingerly stepped into the alley, relieved that there was no one walking along it and followed it to the road.

As he left the passage, he kept a low profile. 'Easier to escape at night,' he thought, 'because the headlights of approaching vehicles can be seen long before the car arrives.'

Thanks to a lifetime of hunting and fishing, he felt at home in the dark. Poaching had honed his night-time senses, whilst having to keep an eye out for the Gamekeepers and Bank wardens.

Fortunately, no police cars appeared as he made his way through the darkened streets.

'I wonder if he did call the police after all,' he pondered. 'The little shit is actually more like me that I want to admit,' he thought.' On the other hand, perhaps the police have already got it staked out. I guess I'll never know.'

'Pity about having to leave the comfort of that annex. As shitty as it was, it 'ticked all the boxes,' he thought. 'Can't go back now though, just in case.

Pity to leave that stupid bitch Beth too,' he thought. 'Silly cow just wanted to wait on me hand foot and finger. She couldn't do enough for me. Ha! Another few days and I'd have had her on her back. Sod it.'

Mike stopped in the shadows and reviewed his next steps.

'So where am I going to get some shut eye tonight? I don't fancy sleeping on the streets. I'm bound to be fingered there.

No. Best to find somewhere else. Ah now. What about that Suzette?' he suddenly thought.

'Yes, that's it. Having helped me escape, she's right in it now. I'll call her and she can put me up. Perhaps if my lucks in, I might be able to sneak into her bedroom later.'

Mike dug his phone out and rang Suzette's number. It rang out for several minutes before a sleepy voice answered.

'Hello... Who is this?'

'It's me. Mike. I need your help. I've had to leave my previous hideout and I need somewhere to stay. I thought you might help?'

'Oh. I'm not sure about that.'

'I could sneak into your hotel and...'

'I'm not in the hotel anymore. I'm renting a place,' she informed him.

'Even better. Give me the address and I'll come round.'

'Umm...I'm not sure,' she said hesitantly.

'Come on. I need to get off the streets, he said urgently. 'The police are out looking for me.'

'Well...it's difficult,' she explained.' The term of my bail is that I'm not supposed to have any contact with you. And if you telephone me, I've been told that I should call the detectives.'

'Look, I'm offering to help you get the murderers of YOUR sister behind bars. I won't be able to do that if I'm behind bars myself, can I? I need to stay out of prison, don't I?' he rationalised.

'I'm not sure. I'm lucky not to be behind bars myself now. If I help you, it will break the terms of my bail,' she repeated.

'Don't worry. You'll be alright, trust me. I've been around the legal system many times,' he blustered. 'They can't do anything. The courts are so busy. They won't get around to your case for at least twelve months.'

'Well...I...' she struggled with the uncomfortable dilemma.

She would be sharing the rented house with an escaped prisoner, in spite of helping him to escape, in reality, he was someone that she barely knew.

'Suzette, please. I promise I won't be any trouble. You won't even know that I'm there. I need a base to work from, to sort out the sources of evidence. It's all for YOU, after all' he emphasised.

Finally, she 'caved in.' 'Oh, OK. On the condition that you produce the proof, to get justice for my sister.'

'Yes. Yes of course, I'll do that,' he lied. 'Scouts honour!'

CHAPTER FIFTY-SEVEN

Suzette reluctantly gave Mike her address and within ten minutes, he was walking along the street to her front door.

The house was a small two-bedroom new build property. It was an infill, jammed into what was formerly the vegetable gardens of two adjoining 1930s houses.

Since his call, she had been pacing up and down and peering out of her upstairs window, apprehensively awaiting his arrival.

On seeing his approach, she rushed down to open the door before he could knock, fearful that he would disturb her 'curtain twitching' neighbours.

Indicating for him to be quiet, she stood aside as he entered the lounge diner, and she quietly closed the door behind him.

'Hello Mike,' Suzette whispered.

'Hi. Thanks for…helping me out again,' Mike said, undressing her with his eyes. 'The house is a bit small though, isn't it?' he observed.

'Sssh, don't talk too loudly. Noise carries,' she instructed, putting her finger up to her lips. 'The estate agent called it cosy. But it's big enough for me,' Suzette said, already uncomfortable at his lecherous gaze and modestly rearranging the flimsy dressing gown up to her neck to cover her cleavage.

Unfortunately, as the gown was quite short, the effect was to expose her long shapely legs as she did so.

Mike's eyes letched at her exposed limbs. 'I'm going to enjoy living here,' he thought, already starting to feel horny.

'I'm sorry but there is no bed in your room,' Suzette apologised. 'But I have put a sleeping bag down on the floor for you though.'

'Oh...that'll have to do, won't it?' he said. 'Hopefully it won't be too long before I get into your bed anyway,' he thought.

'I only had time to grab a few bits and pieces and stuff it into my rucksack, so I won't be taking up too much room,' he explained, as he slipped the pack off his shoulder and dropped it on the floor.

'Let me show you around. 'It won't take long,' she informed him.

'OK.'

'Obviously, this is the lounge diner, I only have the two armchairs. There's the cooker, fridge, and sink,' she said, pointing at the compact kitchen arrangement. 'I tend to eat off the work top using the stools rather than having to buy a table and chairs.

The stairs here go up to the two bedrooms. Yours is quite small, and there's the combined shower and toilet up there as well.'

'They've certainly crammed this lot in, haven't they? At least the paintwork looks fresh,' he observed.

'Yes, I think that I'm the first tenant to rent it, 'Suzette said. 'Now you've arrived. I'd like to get back to bed if you don't mind?' she added.

'No, that's perfectly alright. I'll follow you up,' Mike announced.

'No, you go up first,' Suzette instructed, conscious that if he followed behind her, her short dressing gown would reveal more than she wanted. 'Your room is on the left. I will just lock up down here first.'

Mike reluctantly accepted that his lecherous intentions would have to wait and made his way upstairs. Suzette locked the front door and followed him up.

Mike opened his designated bedroom door and was not impressed. He thought he was stepping into a cupboard.

'God this is small,' he said, immediately stepping onto the sleeping bag that she had laid out for him.

'Yes, sorry. It's the best I can do. I have emptied it of all my bags and bits and pieces to give you a bit more room. I think it's supposed to be eight by four,' she explained from the landing.

'What, eight inches by four inches? I'll barely have room to turn over without banging my nose on the other wall,' he grumbled.

'Sorry,'

'And worse, it smells of paint,' he moaned.

'As I said it's a new build. I can't do anything about it. Sorry. You don't have to stay. At least you've got a roof over your head.'

'Yes, I know. What's your bedroom like?' he asked walking towards her.

'Um, well its…its…quite bijou, I'd say,' she explained.

She moved away as he invaded her personal space. Nevertheless, he deliberately brushed past her and went to her open bedroom door and looked inside.

'Oh, this is nice,' he said, looking at the sparsely populated room. 'This is twice the size of mine. In fact, it's big enough for two,' he remarked, looking at the folded back duvet on the bed.

'Yes, but occupied by one,' she was quick to add. 'So, you can forget that for a start. Any shenanigans and you're out.'

He took a deep breath. 'Your perfume smells wonderful. There's no new paint smell in here either,' he observed.

'No. And now, if you don't mind, I will get back into my bed and we'll discuss things in the morning.'

'Right Miss. I know my place,' he said, turning and reluctantly going back to his bedroom. 'Oh, have you got some antiseptic wipes. A bloody dog was nipping at my legs, and he caught me several times. Bleeding thing. I booted it though and that did it. It went away whimpering,' he lied.

'What were you doing to antagonise it?' she demanded.

'Nothing,' he fibbed.

'Let me have a look, I'm a trained nurse.'

'They feel bruised too,' Mike added and wasted no time in dropping his trousers, rather than rolling the legs up, and exposing his bites.

'Oh yes, there are several nasty bites and lots of bruising. Nothing serious though,' she said, inspecting his exposed legs. 'You're fortunate that it didn't bite any chunks out of you. I'll get the wipes so you can clean yourself up. You might need a plaster or two on the puncture marks,' she added.'

'Aren't you going to tend to me?' he asked hopefully.

'No. Sorry. I'll provide the medical stuff. You can provide the medical treatment,' she told him firmly.

'Do you think I will need a tetanus or Rabies jab,' he asked.

'That's up to you. If you do, it's a trip to the hospital. There are no 'off the shelf' jabs that you can use.'

'Thanks for your help,' he said sarcastically.

Suzette provided the plasters and wipes that she'd promised and went to bed.

'Good night, sleep well,' she chuckled to herself.

CHAPTER FIFTY-EIGHT

Beth had called the Vet's out of hours number and the pair rushed the dog to the surgery.

Sadly, the Veterinarian confirmed what they already knew. The dog was dead.

'Yes, there was a blow to her head, but I don't think that would have killed her. No, her heart gave way, I suspect. She was old after all. Did you say that she was barking at an intruder?'

'Yes, and I think she bit him as well,' Ben said proudly, thinking about Rusty's defence when Mike was assaulting him.

'The contusion is obviously where the intruder kicked her?' the Vet surmised.

'Yes, that's what I thought, the bastard,' Ben said quietly, stroking the dog.

Beth on the other hand was feeling guilty for the dog's death.' Had I not let Mike stay,' she berated herself.

'You should report the incident to the Police in that case,' the Vet advised.

'Oh, yes, we will. We will,' Beth lied.

Ben gave her a sideways glance to see if she was genuine, knowing that informing the police would get Beth into serious trouble.

'Did you want to take her home or would you like us to …'

'No. We'll take her home,' Ben said quickly. 'I'll bury her at home.'

'Thank you anyway for turning out,' Beth said tearfully.

The pair left the Vets and drove home in silence.

When they got home, Ben carried the dog into the back garden and gently lay her down.

With tears in his eyes, even though it was the middle of the night, he dug a large hole for the dogs grave.

'I'll get her favourite blanket,' Beth said, going into the house and retrieving it from the dog's basket.

Ben laid the blanket down and gently lifted the dog into the grave. He wrapped her up in another blanket and started covering the body with dirt.

Both of them were distraught as the last part of the dog disappeared under the soil.

'I'll make a cross for her in the morning,' Ben said sadly.

'OK. We ought to go to bed now,' Beth said putting her arm round her son's shoulders.

Ben moved away from her. 'This is your fault Mum, letting that maniac in to our home. What the hell were you thinking of, allowing him to stay here? Now look, Rusty is dead as a result. JC won't be happy either when he gets back and sees the damage to his fence.

'Yes, I know Ben. I'm so…so… sorry I didn't think. I'm so, so sorry,' she cried and ran into the house.

CHAPTER FIFTY-NINE

Mike spent an uncomfortable night tossing and turning on the hard wooden floor. His bites painfully reminding him of Rusty's revenge, as the sleeping bag rubbed against them. Consequently, he was up early.

He wandered downstairs, found the kettle, discovered the tea bags, and made himself a cup of tea. He wondered whether to take her one and get a glimpse at her lightly clad body. But unfortunately, she thwarted his plan by coming down fully dressed in her day clothes.

'Good morning Mike. Did you sleep well?' she asked cynically.

She already knew the answer, having heard him tossing and turning all night as she also slept lightly. In her case, her fitful sleeping was to guard against any unwanted intrusion from this stranger.

Consequently, to her shopping list she'd added a set of tools and a door bolt for the inside of her bedroom door.

'No, it was effing awful. You're going to have to buy me a bed and some bedding,' he commanded.

'I'm going to have to do what?' she sparked. 'You've got a nerve. I don't appreciate being lectured about what I have to do.'

'You'll do what I tell you to do,' he shouted. His sleepless night making him equally irritable.

'Right, let's get this sorted before it goes too far. If you want to stay here. You follow my rules,' she said firmly. 'My house, my rules.'

'And if you want to clear your sister's name. You play by my rules,' he countered forcefully. 'Remember you're already a criminal for helping me escape. So, you are in no position to dictate to me what is going to happen. Right?'

'Don't be so sure that I won't tell the police where they can find you,' she threatened.

'And if you do that, they will also find a dead body, bitch,' he seethed.

'Oh yes. You don't scare me, with your idle threats. After begging for a roof over your head, you'd better get a grip,' Suzette screeched. 'Or you're gone.'

'Right, let's both calm down,' Mike said, realising that Suzette wasn't going to be the pushover that Beth and the other gullible women were.

'Calm? I'm not the one who is ranting,' she said, defensively.

'OK, let me put it another way. I would appreciate if you bought me a bed and some bedding.'

'What's the word?'

'Word! What word?' he puzzled.

'The polite word when asking for something,' she lectured.

'I don't know what the effing hell you're talking about,' he said angrily.

'It begins with a P,' she hinted derisively.

'P word!' he puzzled. 'You're talking a foreign language to me lady.'

'I'll give you a clue it rhymes with peas.'

'What! You really are pissing me off now. Stop playing effing games and tell me what you want me to say.'

'Please….the word is PLEASE.'

'Oh, for God's sake. Please. Tell me, please.'

'Idiot. that's the word you say when you're asking someone to do something. You say PLEASE. Did your parents not tell you that? she lectured.

'My parents. Ha! They were a waste of space. Always at the pub never told me or my brothers and sisters nothing.'

Suzette hesitated to correct his grammar but thought better of it.

'OK. I will buy some suitable stuff. How much can you afford?' she asked, expecting him to plead poverty.

'Afford! I can't afford nothing. I've been in prison remember.'

Up until now he had been fortunate that, Beth had been subsidising him, with money and the purchase of his mobile.

'Buy me some shaving cream too,' he added.

Suzette just glared at him.

He took the hint. 'Please,' he said grudgingly.

CHAPTER SIXTY

When Suzette had finished her shopping, she returned home exhausted, only to find Mike lazing on a lounge chair with his leg over one of the arms, watching daytime TV.

She dumped her armful of shopping on the floor.

'Look at this place. Look at the mess you've made. What have you done to it? I knew it was a mistake to let a slob like you in,' she ranted.

Unfortunately, as she turned away after berating him, she walked straight into an open wall cupboard door that he hadn't closed, and she banged her face.

'Ouch! That hurt. Can't you even shut cupboard doors. You slob,' she shouted, holding her eye. Hoping that it wasn't bleeding.

'You should look where you're going,' he shouted, unsympathetically. 'Silly bitch.'

'I suppose that you've been sitting there all morning while I've been doing this shopping.' Suzette said tersely, getting a wet flannel and holding it over her eye.

'No, I've been busy doing stuff too.'

What she didn't know was that the 'stuff' he had been doing included going into her bedroom, with a perverted pleasure of ferreting through her underwear drawer and fondling her knickers and bras and sexually caressing her pillow.

'Make me a cup of tea, Mike...please. I think I'm going to have a black eye,' she said, dabbing her eye with the flannel. 'My face is throbbing.'

'If I must,' he said, reluctantly getting out of his chair.

'It's the least you can do. I'm knackered from carrying this bleeding bed in for you,' she bristled.

'Bed!' he queried looking at the pile of stuff she'd brought. 'Unless I'm going blind, there's no bed there.'

'It's an inflatable one,' she explained. 'There was no way that I was forking out for a proper bed. You aren't going to be here long, and I've only got a short lease on this place. It will be alright. According to the label, It's air cushioned luxury,' she said optimistically, hoping that it would live up to its billing.

'It had better be,' he said threateningly.

'After you've made me a cuppa, why don't you go and try it,' she suggested, holding the wet flannel over her eye, and collapsing into the other armchair.

'I ain't your bleedin servant,' he protested.

'Neither am I yours. Now unless you get me the tea, you will be going hungry too. There is no food in the fridge, and I will go and eat out. Up to you,' she threatened.

Mike reluctantly made her a cup of tea and grudgingly brought it to her.

'Thank you,' she said taking it from him. 'So, what have you actually done today, apart from sitting on your arse watching tv?'

'Well, you might like to know that I have found something that you might be interested in. But you must be extra nice to me if you know what I mean?'

'Listen slime ball. You ain't getting any 'favours' off me, so get that in your thick skull. So, what have you found?'

'Some very crucial evidence,' he revealed joyfully.

CHAPTER SIXTY-ONE

'Your sister was set up by a man called Geoffery Foster.'

'So it's true.'

'Yes. He tried to get her done for attempted murder.'

'Attempted murder!' she said in amazement. 'Whose murder?'

'His own.'

'What! Why would somebody recruit someone to kill themselves?' Suzette queried.

'Well apparently, he did. He was dying of cancer, and he persuaded her to help him out of his pain. I think they call it euthanasia,' Mike revealed.

'How? By murdering him!' Suzette said gobsmacked. 'That doesn't make sense.'

'Mercy killing, I think they call it. Yes.'

'And what happened? Did she, do it? Did he die?'

'No, he didn't die. It was a set up. But it was all recorded to make it look like she was attempting to murder him, when in fact she was helping him to commit suicide, as he'd requested.'

'How do you know all that?' Suzette asked, suspiciously.

'I have my sources,' Mike said, thinking of the great coincidence of sharing a cell with an alcoholic solicitors clerk and swapping telephone numbers, whilst they were both on remand.

'Sue was due to get a quarter of a million for helping him. If she succeeded,' Mike revealed.

'£250,000 !' You've got to be joking?'

'No, apparently that was the deal.'

'So, what happened?' Suzette demanded.

'She was just following his instructions when this Andy, his nurse, burst in and stopped her just in time. She was set up.'

'Is it the same Andy that was involved in her crash?'

'Yes. The Scout Leader bloke is also a hospice nurse. That's what I'm saying. It was a conspiracy against your sister right from the start.'

'This bloke Andy again. I'm starting to see the pattern here,' Suzette observed.

'Then after setting her up, they alerted the police, and she was arrested and charged. They denied all knowledge that this Foster bloke had asked her to help him commit suicide.'

'Poor Sue. No wonder she was on the warpath,' Suzette observed.

'But there's more. In addition to all that, she was due to get some big money too from a legacy.'

'A legacy from whom?

'From the very man who she was accused of trying to kill. This Geoffery Foster. So that was a double whammy against her. Her former husband Rupert, was a Godson of Geoffery Foster and inherited five million.'

'How do you know all this?'

'Part of the evidence that I got for you. My contact sent me a copy of the letter on my phone.

It was a letter that Geoffery Foster wrote to your sister's former husband, Rupert. Dated October 1st, 2011.

Dear Rupert. This letter will come as a great surprise to you. We have not seen or communicated with each other over many years. However, I would like to redress this omission and meet up with you. Currently my health isn't too good and I'm now resident in the Dorothy and Tom Hospice at Hamptonleck near Cheltenham, having recently left my former home in Monaco. Hence, I would like to see you as soon as possible. I can assure you that it will be to your financial benefit to meet me. Sincerely, Uncle Geoffery Foster.

'Financial benefit!' Suzette latched on to the term.

'Yes. Apparently, the financial benefit turned out to be five million pounds. But it was in his will. So, no money was available at the time. It obviously came later after he died.'

'Five million! Well, that would solve a lot of problems, wouldn't it?'

'Of course, Sue was entitled to half of that as she was married to Rupert but unfortunately was divorced shortly before the money was awarded.'

'Yes, she would have been eligible for some of it.' Suzette agreed.

'Well Sue battled over many years with the executor of Geoffery Foster's will. His name?... guess.'

'No can't guess. I give in. Don't know,' Suzette capitulated.

'Andy Spider.'

'Not that man again? The one from the inquest.'

'Yes. And this is the same Andy guy, who was the executor of the Geoffery Foster will. And also, it appears that he has become Sue's executioner too.'

'I don't follow,' Suzette queried. 'What do you mean. Executioner?'

'Well of course he was the one driving the other car, wasn't he?'

'The other car?' Suzette puzzled. 'I don't follow.'

'Yes, when you sister's car crashed. He was the driver of the other car that was following and allegedly pushed her car over the edge,' Mike said, distorting the truth. 'He hated her because she stood up to him.'

'So, he did have a motive to kill her?' Suzette concluded. 'That proves it then, doesn't it?'

'Yes, it certainly looks like he did,' Mike encouraged.

'I knew it. Sue was bullied,' Suzette concluded.

'However, something else that you should be aware of, which might cloud the issue. The reason behind Sue's divorce was that she was accused of domestic violence against her husband, Rupert. He had lots of injuries.'

'Yes well, Sue told me that he was a bit unsteady on his feet. She said that he was accident prone and kept falling over and hurting himself. Yes, she said that she was blamed for inflicting various injuries and accused of domestic violence by this Andy chap.'

'So, as well as being involved at the hospice, where this Geoffery bloke was setting your sister up with the assisted suicide bid, this Andy was involved with her husband Rupert's claim of abuse.'

'Now it's starting to make sense,' Suzette said.

So, you see they ganged up on her. Obvious, isn't it? They murdered your sister.'

Suzette was hooked. As each part of the story was revealed, she was feeling angrier and angrier. She was now fully focussed on getting Andy and Ben charged with murder. No matter what the cost was going to be.

Now she had the facts, but not any concrete evidence. Would they stand up in court?

Could she find this money to give Mike to get the evidence? She owed it to her sister to get her justice. Didn't she?

CHAPTER SIXTY-TWO

Mike's freedom was short lived. Suzette's elderly next door neighbours had become alarmed by the shouting between Suzette and Mike in the normally quiet cul-de-sac.

They reported it to the police as possible domestic violence against the charming Australian girl by an abusive man, whom they'd seen arriving in the middle of the night. Possibly an illegal immigrant.

The policeman knocked loudly on Suzette's door and stood back waiting for someone to open it.

'Who's that?' Mike asked Suzette quietly.

'I don't know. I'm not expecting anyone,' Suzette said, moving to the window and peered through the lace curtains. 'Oh god it's a policeman.'

'Don't answer the door,' he ordered.

'I've got to. He saw me at the window.'

'Stupid bitch. I'll go and hide,' he said and shot upstairs.

Making sure he had settled down; Suzette went to the door and opened it.

'Hello,' Suzette said to the young PC.

'Hello Miss, sorry to bother you. But we've had a report about some shouting going on.'

'Oh, that's a nasty looking blackeye,' his female colleague said, joining them on the doorstep.

'Yes, I damaged myself. I walked into an open cupboard door. Silly accident, wasn't it?' Suzette gushed, putting her hand up to her eye.

'Would you mind if we came in?' the policewoman said, stepping in without waiting for an answer.

Suzette stood back as the pair entered.

'So, do you live here alone?' The policeman asked, walking around the ground floor looking for signs of multiple occupation.

'Yeah…yes I do,' Suzette stuttered.

'Only your neighbours heard a man's voice arguing with you,' the policeman said, spotting two used mugs on the table.

'Oh! They're elderly. They must be confused. I expect it was on the telly. I do tend to have my television turned up quite loud.'

'And you say that you live here alone?' the Policewoman said, looking up the stairs.'

'Yes. That's correct,' Suzette confirmed.

'So do you mind if I have a look upstairs?' the policeman asked.

'Well. I'd prefer if you didn't. I…I was about to go to the doctors. Um, I have an appointment,' Suzette lied. 'You know how difficult it is to get an appointment these days. I don't want to miss it.'

'It shouldn't take a minute,' the PC said, striding up the stairs.

Suzette's heart sank. She was going to be found out.

'If you want to get your coat on so that you're ready, that would be OK,' the policewoman suggested.

'My coat?' Suzette wondered, looking apprehensively up the stairs.

'Yes. For your Doctors appointment, remember?' the policewoman prompted, knowing full well that it was a lie.

'No. it's ok. I err... I need to use the bathroom first.' Suzette muttered, her heart going 'nineteen to the dozen' as she listened to the policeman upstairs going from room to room.

Then the sound she didn't want to hear.

'Hello Sir. What are you doing hiding under the bed? Out you come now.'

Suzette could hear Mike sliding out from under her bed and then he was running, leaping down the stairs two at a time heading for the door. Closely followed by the PC shouting for him to stop.

But the policewoman had already moved in front of the door and was in the process of withdrawing her taser.

Mike stopped and looked around desperately trying to find another exit point.

'Right Sir. Let's just calm down, shall we? Take a seat please. What was that all about?' the PC asked.

Mike sat down as ordered. 'I...I thought you were some gang members after me,' Mike lied.

'Yeah right,' the PC muttered sarcastically.

'We've had a report of possible domestic violence going on in here. What do you say to that?' the Policewoman asked.

'Nothing like that. As I say I did this myself walking into a door,' Suzette repeated.' Honestly. Just a silly accident.

'Yes, that's right she did. I left the cupboard door open. Bang, she walked into it. I had no sympathy for her. Stupid bitch.' Mike elaborated. 'Clumsy, aren't you dear?' he said, looking at her to confirm his story.

'You know it's surprising the number of women who suddenly become careless and walk into doors...they usually end up in a sheltered women's refuge,' the policewoman said, vociferously.

'Yes, well, I hear what you say,' replied Mike. 'But it's true. Honest.'

'Let's have some names then shall we,' the PC requested.

'Why? We haven't done nothing wrong,' Mike said.

'Just routine. There's nothing to worry about,' the policewoman said, remaining in front of the door. 'Miss?'

'Umm,' Suzette cleared her throat. 'Suzette...Suzette Brown.'

'Thank you. You from Australia?'

'Yes.'

'You've got a good rugby team, haven't you?' the policeman commented, putting her details into his 'tablet.'

'Never been to Australia myself. I know somebody that walked over the Sydney Harbour bridge though. You done it yourself miss?' the Policeman said conversationally.

'No. It's more of a tourist thing,' Suzette replied quietly, expecting any moment to be rumbled.

'I'd love to do that,' the policewoman added.

After a few minutes, the PC looked at the screen of his tablet. He walked over to his colleague and showed it to her. 'I see that you're out on bail at the moment Suzette, for assisting an offender to escape,' he said, looking at the two of them.

'Yes, sorry,' she confessed awkwardly, colouring up.

'Who would that offender be?' the policeman probed.

Suzette gave Mike a sideways look, which the policewoman picked up.

Realising there was no point in bluffing as the Policeman had all the details on his tablet anyway, she said. 'Umm…it was a man by the name of Mike…Mike Benson,' Suzette admitted.

'Oh yes, I remember now. He's still on the run, isn't he?' the policeman moaned turning to his colleague.

Mike stood up, ready to make a break for it and push the policewoman out of the doorway. But sat down again as she put her hand on her taser.

'And you Sir? Your name.'

'Umm…Andy…Andy Spider,' he lied.

Suzette tried not to react to his lie but failed. The policewoman again spotted the slight change in Suzette's body language.

The PC put the name into his tablet as Mike shifted uncomfortably on his chair. 'So, what do you do for a living Mr Spider,' the PC said, studying his tablet.

'I err…I er work at the Hospice. I am a counsellor,' he lied. 'You know people dying and that.'

'Must be a very challenging job,' the policeman said, typing in Mike Benson's name.

'Yes, it is. End of life stuff, you know,' Mike flannelled. 'Very intense job.'

'I see that you have a bandage on your arm. What have you done to it?' the policewoman asked.

'Oh I…I scolded myself. Careless really, with a kettle,' Mike bluffed.

The policeman showed his colleague the tablet which now displayed Mike's face and a report of his bandaged arm.

The policewoman drew her taser out fully and Mike realised that the game was up.

'OK. You know who I am. No point in pretending anymore.' Mike confessed. standing up. 'This is your stupid fault,' he barked at Suzette. 'If you hadn't been such a bolshy bitch, this wouldn't have happened. Now you've dropped both of us in it.'

'That's enough, Mr Benson. I'm arresting you for being an absconder and for domestic violence. You caused this yourself. You shouldn't have belted her one.'

'I didn't. She did genuinely walk into a door herself,' Mike said passionately.

Suzette nodded in agreement and burst into tears as the policewoman approached her with her handcuffs out.

'I'm sorry darling. I can see that he has bullied you into this. But I am arresting you for harbouring an offender.

Mike turned around with his hands round his back waiting for the handcuffs to go on. Which the policeman duly obliged him with.

CHAPTER SIXTY-THREE

Back inside, and under lock and key, Mike got a message to Beth via his solicitor, that he wanted to see her before his trial.

Although initially reluctant, eventually Beth again succumbed to his persuasive charms.

'In any case if I see him, I can get my anger off my chest about the way he abused my hospitality,' she convinced herself about the morality of her decision.

So she didn't have any awkward conversations she ensured that Ben and JC were elsewhere, and she visited Mike in prison.

Beth went through the normal security checks and made her way to the Visitors room. Mike was waiting for her.

She quickly spotted him and took a seat opposite. He smiled at her. She glowered back.

'I'm not sure that I should be here,' she said quickly.

'Why's that?'

'Because after everything I'd done for you, you killed our dog,' she said vehemently.

'No, I didn't. It was alive when I left,' he lied. 'I've still got the bite marks on my leg to prove it.'

'And why did you have to beat up Ben? He's your son for heaven's sake.'

'He was being lippy. I can't stand lippy kids. You ought to get him under control before he really talks himself into some serious trouble.'

'So, whatever you want, the answer is NO,' Beth surprised herself by saying it firmly. And she stood up ready to leave.

'Look Beth, I'm really grateful for you putting me up while I was on the run,' he said quickly, surprised by her intention to leave.

'Gratitude at last,' she thought. But her bubble was about to burst.

'But you know that it's a criminal offence to harbour an offender? And you sheltered me.' he reminded her, cruelly.

'Yes, but I ... I was...doing you a favour,' Beth said, 'winded,' and sat down again, shocked.

'And I was grateful for your kindness,' he said, unconvincingly. 'And of course, I won't tell the police about you hiding me.'

'No. Thank you,' Beth said, warily.

'But...but I'd like to ask you for a family good deed,' he suggested.

'What do you mean, a family good deed?' she puzzled.

'We, you, and I, are family, aren't we? You're Ben's mother and I'm his father.'

'Well, Yes. I suppose so,' she said suspiciously. 'But I wouldn't actually call us a family.'

'Well, whether you like it or not we are, and as family, we stick together, don't we?' he suggested.

'Go on,' she said, guardedly, waiting for the sting in the tail.

'So, we don't drop family into bother with the law, do we?' he suggested.

'It depends,' Beth said cautiously.

'What I'm getting to is that I haven't told the old bill that you hid me. And committed a criminal offence.'

'Thank you, I appreciate that,' Beth said, surprised at his uncharacteristic thoughtfulness.

'So, to even things up then. Tell Ben not to testify against me,' he instructed, malevolently.

'What!' Beth said in disbelief. 'I knew it wasn't going to be that simple.'

'Or you will find yourself in the dock too. Understand?' Mike threatened.

Beth stared at him dumbfounded. 'You want me to do what...' Beth stood in shock.

'All he's got to do is persuade the jury that I was coerced into it by that bitch Sue.'

'I can't ask him to do that,' Beth rejected.

'And If you don't comply when my sentence is over. I know where you both live. Don't forget.' Mike said, vehemently.

Beth burst into tears and made her way blindly out of the visiting room.

Mike watched her leave. A broad grin across his face.

CHAPTER SIXTY-FOUR

Beth was in a quandary; she didn't know what to do. If she didn't tell Ben not to testify against Mike, he would probably carry out his threat and report her.

If she didn't comply, she'd have the threat of revenge hanging over her head every day that he was in prison, fearful of the day when he was released.

On the other hand, she didn't want to add pressure to Ben's already traumatic life by telling him about Mike's threat.

And besides, her relationship with Ben was still pretty rocky after she foolishly sheltered Mike in the first place. Ben blamed her for exposing him to Mike's brutality and worse still, Rusty's death.

Beth was clearly depressed with the additional pressure from Mike taking its toll. But fortunately, Ben recognised that there was something troubling her and sought to help.

'Mum, if this is all about my accusation the other night. I'm sorry. I know you were under pressure from that…bastard, Ben apologised.

'No, it's not that,' she said quietly.

'What is it then?'

'It's nothing. Nothing that I can't sort out myself,' she said, stubbornly.

'Come on Mum, I know you better than that. You can't fool me. You've been to see him, haven't you?'

'See him! See who?' she feigned innocence.

'Mike. You've been to see Mike, haven't you? I can read you like a book. Oh Mum, when will you ever learn?'

'I feel sorry for him,' she confessed.

'Sorry for him! After what he did to the dog and me!'

'Yes, well. He hasn't got anybody and…'

'So, what lies was he making up this time to get back in your knickers?'

'Ben! There's no need to be crude.'

'Well. What fantasy has he created for you?' Ben demanded.

'He…he. Oh, I can't…say it.'

'Can't say what?' Ben probed.

'He…he wants you not to…to not give any evidence against him.'

'Yes, I know he's already told me…even threatened me!'

'He has?' So, will you, change it? Beth said hopefully.

'No. There's fat chance I can do anything about it.

Oh Ben, why? Beth's hopes were dashed.

'I have made a statement to the police and the Prosecutor knows all about the vile man and what he did to me.'

'Yes, but he reckons that the jury could be persuaded that he was forced to do it…if you modified your…'

'Mum. Do you realise what you are asking me to do?'

'You don't have to fib…just a…just a half-truth…a white lie! Hold back some of the detail. Emphasise about Sue's role and don't mention Mike's.'

'Has he threatened you? Because if he has, we need to tell the police.'

'The police! No, not the police. That's the problem. He is threatening to tell the police that I hid him when he was on the run. And they will put me in prison for harbouring him.' Beth burst into tears. 'Ben, I don't want to go to prison,' she sobbed.

Ben put his arms around her, 'The ungrateful bastard, after all you did for him,' Ben ranted. 'Don't cry Mum. I'll see that you won't go to prison. It'll be alright.'

'It will never be alright. He said if you don't help him, no matter how long that he goes down for, he will find us when he finishes his sentence. And he'll sort us out.'

'Mum it's all bull. You know him better than me. You know what he's like. He's full of bullshit.'

'I don't want to get you into any trouble. I know that you have been a good boy for many years looking after me, and I shouldn't be asking you this but...'

CHAPTER SIXTY-FIVE

Following her breach of bail conditions by contacting Mike, Suzette had been remanded in custody. She was also charged with harbouring an escaped prisoner. Consequently, she was behind bars and was unable to attend Mike's trial.

On the day of his trial, Mike was brought up from the cells and stood in the dock with a prison guard either side of him.

With the jury in place and members of the public in the gallery, the court was ordered to stand as the judge entered.

Mike hated the pomp and ceremony at the start of trials, of which throughout his criminal career he had seen many.

'For god's sake, just get on with it,' he thought.

The clerk of the court read out the charges.

'Michael Benson. You are accused of kidnap, extortion, and actual bodily harm. With an additional charge of escaping from custody. How do you plead?

'Not guilty. It was that bloody woman, Williams-Screen that…' Mike ranted.'

'Silence,' the Judge ordered sternly. 'You will have your opportunity to speak later.

Ladies and Gentlemen of the jury, throughout the trial you will hear the name of Sue Williams-Screen whilst hearing evidence. This person is not sharing the dock with Michael Benson today because she had evaded police attempts to arrest her and tragically was killed in a road traffic accident.' The Judge explained.

However, had she still been alive she would have been jointly accused and been on trial. So, whilst listening to this case, you will need to divorce yourself from any sympathy for the deceased woman.'

'Please make your opening remarks,' the Judge instructed the prosecution lawyer.

The prosecutor stood up and made his way to the jury box.

'Thank you, Your Honour. Today, members of the jury, we are dealing with a profoundly serious series of crimes involving Kidnap, extortion and causing actual bodily harm.

It is important for you to recognise the dangerous nature of the character that you see on trial here.

I am sure that you will be horrified to learn, that not only did this man violently kidnap his own son, but he also injected him with some noxious substance to render him unconscious. Having done so he then made a series of calls demanding a five-million-pound ransom.

However, I must explain that due to the strained relationship to the defendant, his son has asked to have a curtained screen placed in front of the witness box, so there is no eye contact between the two.

Should it please the court, the witness will give his evidence behind the screen.'

'Yes. Approved,' the judge confirmed.

The court usher duly pulled the curtain across the witness box blocking the view of the occupant of the dock.

'I would like to call my first witness. Ben Bird.'

Despite Andy's reassurance that it wasn't him that was on trial, Ben felt very apprehensive as he went into the court. However, he was further assured by the curtained screen that had been put in place. The last thing he wanted to see and be intimidated by, was his father's withering gaze, as he gave his evidence.

'All you have to do is tell the truth,' Andy had reassured him.

Unfortunately, after Mike's threat to implicate Beth in harbouring a known felon and getting her sent to prison, Ben didn't know what version of the truth he was going to tell.

Consequently, as he entered the austere surroundings of the court room, he was visibly shaking.

He felt conspicuous, as he walked to the witness box. As if everybody's eyes were burning into him.

'Take the bible in your right hand and read from the oath card,' the usher directed.

'I do solemnly, sincerely and truly declare and affirm that the evidence I shall give shall be the truth the whole truth and nothing but the truth.' Ben said quietly, now slightly lightheaded.

'Ben, the court is very conscious of the enormous pressure that you are under in giving evidence against your own father. But I remind you that the oath that you have just taken is a solemn and binding obligation on you to tell the whole truth. Is that understood?' the prosecutor reminded him.

'Yes Sir.'

'Please explain to the court how you were kidnapped.'

'Umm…Well my f…father,' the word stuck in his throat…' he, Mike…came and told me that my mother was ill. He said that she had been taken to hospital, but he would drive me there. I thought it was strange because my parents were not together, and he was not part of our lives anymore.'

'Our lives?' the lawyer queried.

'Mum and me.'

'Thank you for the clarification. But you still went with him. You trusted him! Why?'

'Yes, because my mother had previously suffered… err…ill…ill health.' Ben had been advised not to mention her earlier alcoholic 'addiction challenges.' 'So, I had no reason to doubt him.'

'What happened next?'

'I got into his car.'

'Was he alone?'

'Yes, Well, I thought he was. I was just anxious to get to my Mother, so I didn't look.'

'And then what happened?'

'As we drove off, suddenly a black hood was placed over my head.'

'A black hood?'

'Yes.'

'So, if your father was driving, surely he couldn't place the hood over your head?' The lawyer amplified.

'No. He didn't.'

'So, who placed the hood over your head?'

'It was that horrible woman…Sue Williams-Screen.'

'But I thought you said the defendant was in the car alone?'

'Yes, so I thought. She is, was, not very tall and must have been hiding in the back passenger seat area. But it was definitely her.'

'What happened then?'

'She dragged the hood tightly back against my headrest preventing me from moving my head. It was so tight that it was cutting into my throat. I had difficulty in breathing.'

'If she was behind you, how do you know it was her?'

'As...as she pulled harder on the hood, she whispered into my ear. And I'd know that voice anywhere.'

'Please continue.'

'Don't struggle,' she said. 'It will be much harder if you do.'

'You resisted?'

'Yes of course. I put my hands up to pull the hood off. That was when I felt a sharp prick in my thigh.'

'And the cause?'

'A syringe was plunged into my leg.'

'Who do you think did that?'

'I...I err...don't know.' Ben said, 'softening' his allegations.

The barrister looked at his notes taken aback by Ben's vagueness, expecting him to accuse his father.

'Are you sure that you don't know?'

'Yes, I'm sorry,' Ben squeezed the edge of the witness box, uncomfortable at modifying his original accusation, that it was his father.

'That's my boy,' Mike thought.

'You are not sure who did it?' the brief said, pursuing the point.

'No, Sir. I...'

In the public gallery Beth stood up and shouted. 'Tell him the truth Ben. It doesn't matter if I have to go to prison for hiding him. Just tell the truth. He did it to you. Your own father.'

Mike clenched his fists in frustration, his plan had failed. 'Bitch! She will pay for that,' he thought.

'Silence in court. I will not have my courtroom turned into a circus,' the Judge ordered. 'Anymore interruptions and you will be taken down for contempt.

'He threatened us. We had to lie for him,' Beth continued.

'Madam, I won't tell you again. Bailiff, I want you to remove this person.'

'Yes, Your Honour.'

'Whilst doing so, can you please establish the facts behind this outburst. If this is true, the prisoner has been up to no good, intimidating the witnesses.'

'Yes, Your Honour.'

'I suggest a short adjournment,' the Judge added.

'All rise,' the clerk ordered, as the judge left the courtroom.

The case was duly stopped while Beth was interviewed by the Bailiff and the facts of Mike's threats were established.

CHAPTER SIXTY-SIX

The case was reconvened with Ben in the witness box and a frustrated Mike back in the dock.

'Mr Bird, I have to remind you that you are still under oath to tell the truth.' The Judge reminded Ben. Clearly, your earlier evidence was compromised due to intimidation by the accused and therefore biased in his favour. This serious breach will be dealt with by this court later. Please continue your evidence.'

'Prior to the break and to remind the jury, The question was, who Mr Bird thought had plunged the syringe in his leg,' the prosecutor explained.

Now as the threat over his mother had been removed, Ben went back to his original statement.

'Well as I was sat next to my father in the front passenger seat, It could only have been him. Mike Benson.'

Mike grimaced; his warnings of exposing Beth had failed. Her outburst was completely out of character from the old Beth that he used to control.

There was a gasp from the public gallery.

'And what was the effect of this injection?'

'I became unconscious.'

'So, you were injected with, what we believe was, sodium pentothal?'

'If you say so.'

'And to where were you taken?'

'A farm building. A barn. It was an unused cow shed. My…fath…Mike Benson lived there in a tied cottage. He worked on the farm.'

'During the time that you were there, were you unconscious all the time?

'No.'

'How were you detained?'

'I was tied to metal bars.'

'Tied? Restrained. By your father?'

'Yes.'

'To what were you tied?'

'A grid. Normally used to tether cattle.'

'So, while you were tied there, I believe Michael Benson then made a call to your home demanding what?'

'Yes. I was later told that it was £5 million for my release.'

'That's an extraordinary demand for, you'll pardon my terminology, an ordinary boy. You're not from a high-class aristocratic background. Why such an outrageous amount of money?'

'I can only think that it was because the millionaire Geoffery Foster had given several people £5 million each in his will.'

'Several people! Who are we talking about precisely?'

'Mr Foster's Godsons.'

'Mr Foster! Who was Mr Foster?'

'He was a nice man. A multimillionaire that used to live in Monaco. He had cancer and died in a hospice in the Cotswolds. He left his money to his Godsons.'

'So, the defendant made a call to one of the Godsons in order to get money off him for your release?'

'Yes.'

'Anyone in particular?'

'Yes. The man that my Mum and I live with. James Charles.'

'But James Charles is not your father. So, it seems strange that he would pay a ransom?'

'Yes, that's right but he is a good friend.'

'Not your father?'

'No. I didn't know who my father was until recently.'

'Why didn't you know who he was?'

'My mother brought me up, single handed.'

In the gallery Andy glanced quickly at Beth and thought, It was more like Ben had brought his mother up, than the other way round. Ben had been her 'young carer' for many years as she wallowed in an alcoholic haze.

'So, your mother didn't tell you?'

'No. My mum was a single parent. Because he...'

'Please clarify. Who is this he?' the Judge demanded.

'Mike Benson, the defendant Sir. He left her shortly after making her pregnant. She was terribly upset when he deserted her...'

'Yes, we see it in the court room too often. Men escape their responsibilities, while women are left with the consequences,' the Judge commented.

...and she drowned her sorrows in alcohol,' Ben revealed.

In the public gallery Beth gasped as her squalid private life was revealed to the court.

'And you were actively looking for your father?' the defence barrister asked.

'Yes Sir.'

'Why did you want to find him?

'I was looking for him to help me look after Mum and…to feel…to feel…wanted.'

'Wanted? So, what sort of relationship did you have with your Mother if you didn't feel wanted?'

'Objection. What is the purpose of this line of questioning?' the prosecutor demanded.

'I am just trying to establish the relationships that he had with his parents.'

'Overruled.'

'Please continue Mr Bird,' Mike's barrister invited.

'Mum told me that it was a mistake to try to find him. But like a fool, I ignored her,' Ben admitted.

'What did you do?' the prosecutor asked, taking over the questioning.

'I asked Mum directly if it was him. To put me off the scent, Mother denied that I was his child. His love child.

When I told him what Mum had said, he belittled her. He said, that's a laugh. There was no love between your mother and me. It was pure sex. She was a slut.'

Beth filled up at the revelation. Kay, chaperoning her, squeezed her hand. 'Don't listen to Mike's rubbish. You know what the slimy bastard is like,' she added.

'So, what did you do? Mr Bird'

'I got angry with him for saying horrible things about Mum. He told me that if he had known about her pregnancy, he would have arranged an abortion. So, I didn't deserve to be alive anyway.' Ben explained.

'Didn't deserve to be alive! Ladies and Gentlemen of the jury. Is that a discussion that you'd expect from a caring father to his son? So that gives you an idea of the callous uncaring person that Mike Benson is.'

The jury shuffled uncomfortably and looked at each other.

'So, we have established that Michael Benson was in on the extortion. Who else was part on the ransom demand?' The lawyer asked.

'Sue Williams-Screen.' Ben revealed. 'But she tried to keep out of my sight. But I told her that I recognised her voice. So, there was no point in hiding.'

'And then what happened?'

'She told me that she was going to kill me after they'd got the money.'

CHAPTER SIXTY-SEVEN

'Kill you?' The prosecutor repeated.

Again, another gasp from the public gallery.

'Yes,' Ben confirmed.'

'And what did your father say about that?'

'He surprised me. He defended me. He told her that, *she never said anything about topping me. He said that I thought once we had the money, they'd release me and then just disappear.*'

'So, he was horrified to hear of her intentions?' the defence lawyer interjected. 'In truth, he was actually safeguarding his son's life. 'Indeed, your father was not condoning her intention of killing you at all was he?'

Ben became annoyed that Mike was now being portrayed in a good light.

'No. But he kidnapped me, didn't he? If he hadn't, I wouldn't have been there and in danger,' Ben shouted angrily.

'Please Mr Bird, there is no need to shout in my court,' the Judge warned him. 'Restrain yourself.'

Ben looked sheepishly at the floor. 'Yes Sir.'

'How were they intending to prove that they had actually kidnapped you?' the prosecutor continued.

'They wanted me to do a voice recording,' Ben explained.

'A voice recording for what purpose?'

'Asking my Mum to pay the ransom. But initially I refused to do it.'

Beth sobbed quietly into a handkerchief.

'What happened then?' The lawyer asked.

'She started torturing me.'

'Who is she?' the judge asked.

'Sue Wiliams Screen.'

'Thank you. Continue.'

'Torturing you! How was she torturing you?'

'By grabbing a small handful of my hair at the nape of my neck and viciously twisting it.'

'What was your father doing at this stage?' the lawyer probed.

Ben's heart rate increased as he was mentally transported back to the incident. Painfully he described the awful events of the torture session.

'He was on her side saying, *Come on Ben. Son. Just do as she says. She will continue to hurt you if you don't cooperate.*'

'I told him, *Don't you dare call me your son. You're no father of mine.*'

'And then she said' *Have you ever had a splinter behind your fingernail, 'I can assure you, that it's very painful.'*

Another gasp from the public gallery.

'But your father didn't hurt you?' the defence lawyer interjected. Underlining his client's innocence in the episode.

'No. It was her,' Ben continued.

'But your father was advising you to cooperate to save you from more punishment?' the barrister continued.

'Well, yes. I suppose so. And I held out for as long as I could. But in the end, I made the recording,' Ben confessed, feeling like a coward by admitting his weakness.

'But shortly after making the recording, I gather you escaped?' the prosecution lawyer reminded him.

'Yes, when they'd left the barn, I was able to cut the bindings, as I had a knife in my pocket, and I was able to release myself. Then I escaped from the barn.'

'So, you now had your freedom. What did you do? 'the lawyer asked.

'I ran to a phone box and spoke to JC. But they caught me in there before I finished telling him about what was going on. They dragged me away from the phone box. That woman was terribly angry.' Ben recalled.

'Williams- Screen?'

'Yes. And after they caught me that woman stuck a needle in my leg. The last thing that I remember was… was that my father was holding me while …while she did it,' Ben reflected emotionally.

'I am shocked at the barbarity of their actions on a child.' The prosecutor said. 'I find it incomprehensible that a father would be party to committing this sort of violence against his own son. This is not without precedent, members of the jury. This is the second time he has aided and abetted in allowing his son to be abused. An obvious and clear case of causing actual bodily harm.'

People in the public gallery shifted uncomfortably at the description of the assault.

Satisfied that he had 'teased out' evidence that underlined proof of the ABH charge, the prosecutor sat down.

The defence lawyer took over the questioning.

'Your honour, I have been sitting here allowing a gentle line of questioning and well frankly I find young Mr Bird's evidence difficult to believe. It is a fantasy made up by an overactive teenage mind, based on computer games.'

Objection, the defence is belittling a truly fearful episode in a young person's life.' The prosecutor stated.

'The defence is merely stating an alternative scenario. Objection overruled.' 'Thank you, Your Honour,' the defence lawyer crowed, smiling at winning a point of protest. Knowing that it would put doubt in the minds of the jury.

CHAPTER SIXTY-EIGHT

'Do you recall regaining consciousness?' the defence barrister continued.

'Yes.'

'Were you restrained again?

'Restrained? What do you mean?' Ben asked naively.

'Tied up?'

'No. I wasn't.'

'What did you see?'

'I came round in the farm building again. But I was surprised to see two ladies, Helen, and Nadine in there with me. People that I knew.

'For clarity and to help the jury, please explain how you knew these people.'

'Helen is Andy, my Scout Leader's, wife and Nadine was a former girlfriend of Geoffery Foster, the deceased millionaire that I had met several times.'

'Were they tied up too?'

'No. They said they'd come to rescue me.'

'How did they know that you were there?'

'I'm not sure. But somehow Nadine knew.'

'OK, we'll explore that later. Where was your father, at this time?'

'He was in the barn too. But he was tied up.'

'Tied up?' the defence barrister looked at the Jury and repeated the words 'TIED UP. Who would have tied him up? Not the two ladies?'

'No. it was the Williams-Screen woman. I believe that she had beaten him up too.' Ben revealed.

'Why would someone who is supposed to have been part of the kidnap plot have been beaten up by a co-conspirator?' the defence lawyer asked looking at the jury.

'He cocked her ransom scheme up,' Ben told him.

'By which you mean, he disrupted her plans?' the lawyer amplified.

'Yes, I suppose you could say that. And also, for not searching me properly and discovering the knife in my pocket. That's how I managed to escape the first time.'

'So, perhaps your father was trying to help you? Perhaps, by allowing you to escape, he paid for his fatherly thoughtfulness by being beaten up?' the barrister surmised.

'Suppose' Ben said, now wondering if he had misjudged his father.

'Clearly, he paid the price for his sympathy whilst trying to right the wrongs of his partner in crime. Given this scenario, I put it to you that it is obvious, he was helping you. The protagonists had obviously fallen out,' the defence lawyer suggested. 'The Williams-Screen woman, and Michael Benson had become antagonists; enemies suddenly.'

'Sorry,' Ben puzzled. 'I don't know what you mean by protagonists and antagonists.'

'Put simply co-conspirators becoming opponents,' the brief explained.

Ben was fearful that this clever talking lawyer was going to get his father off and the jury would rubbish his evidence.

'Ladies and Gentlemen of the jury, I suggest that his father, Michael Benson, was not a willing volunteer in all this. He was forced to kidnap his own son against his paternal instincts,' the defence lawyer suggested. 'The case against him is based on hearsay. Furthermore, you will hear that Michael Benson was again severely punished for standing up for his son.'

'Please continue Ben. 'What happened next?'

'I was told that the woman, Williams-Screen came back into the barn and kicked Mike in the stomach.'

'Why didn't he fight back?'

'She had tied him up earlier,' Ben explained.

'Members of the jury, does that sound as if Michael Benson was a willing volunteer in this story of mayhem? Williams-Screen had already attacked him and now unable to defend himself, she had viciously kicked him in the stomach.'

'She told him that she was going to get rid of the evidence by burning the barn and its occupants. That would have been me as well as my fa...Mike.' Ben revealed.

'So, Michael Benson was going to be burnt to death alongside his son. He wasn't a villain, he was a victim,' the defence lawyer pointed out, sitting down.

Beth was beside herself imagining what would have happened to Ben had that awful woman's horrific plans come to fruition.

Kay, Tim's mother, comforted her.

'Continue Ben please,' the prosecutor coaxed.

'My friends heard the woman sprinkling petrol around the outside of the barn and setting it on fire,' Ben added.

'So why didn't you and the others leave the building?'

'Apparently, while I was still unconscious, that Williams-Screen woman had locked the only exit, the sliding door.

'You were to be burnt alive because your father had brought you into a dangerous situation, which he knew exposed you to the actions of an arsonist. It was unfortunate for him that she turned against him. It does not make his own crimes any less serious. No further questions.'

The defence barrister addressed the jury. 'So, Sue Williams-Screen was getting rid of her partner in crime? Obviously not an important part of her team. A foot soldier only. Cannon fodder. The case against my client is looking pretty weak,' the defence barrister pointed out.

CHAPTER SIXTY-NINE

'Please continue with your evidence, Mr Bird,' the lawyer invited.

'When I came round after being dragged out of the telephone box, the fire was already raging. It was spreading quickly around the barn,' Ben continued. 'Thick black acrid smoke was everywhere.'

By this time, I was now fully conscious. The ladies said we ought to try to escape but they told me that Mike was in the building too. But he was tied up. They said that they'd tried to free him, but they'd only been able to undo the rope on one of his arms. They were expecting him to undo the other arm himself and to come and join them. But he didn't appear!

So, despite the ladies telling me not to, I set off to find him. The roar of the fire and thick acrid smoke was awful.'

Beth sobbed loudly at the terrible thought of Ben being trapped and burnt alive.

The judge looked up at the public gallery and said, 'I appreciate the details are quite harrowing for you, but unless you can be quiet, I will have to ask you to leave.'

Kay hugged Beth and stroked her hair. 'Sssh. He's safe. Forget what might have happened, Be proud of what he did. He is your hero.'

'I was shouting to Mike to find out where he was,' Ben continued. For all I knew, he might have already escaped. But then over the roar of the fire, I heard him.'

Mike's screams filled Ben's head again as he mentally revisited that awful ordeal.

'At last, I found him. As I got to him,' Ben recalled. 'He was hysterical. He grabbed hold of my clothes. He was desperate and kept shouting, Ben, Ben you got to help me. My arm is tied. I can't undo the rope, he screamed.'

'But because of the thick, choking smoke, I couldn't even see my hand in front of my face either. Ben paused.

'No rush, take your time,' the Judge directed.

'I felt along the length of Mike's arm, feeling for the rope strands. But I was surprised that I couldn't feel the coils. Then I realised that the polypropylene rope, used to tie him up, had melted in the heat.'

The court was riveted at Ben's recollection of his rescue.

'I couldn't think straight with his screaming and the noise from the fire, so I told him to be quiet and to help me save him. I asked him for my knife which he'd taken from me'

Ben was struggling with his emotions in recalling the terror he felt at the time.

'He was obviously in great pain because he was saying that his arm and hand was on fire. He begged me to help him,'

Several members of the Jury were visibly upset as the story unfolded.

'I told him that was what I was trying to do and asked again about my knife. As the smoke got thicker and thicker, I had difficulty breathing. My eyes were streaming.

'He eventually told me that it was in his jacket pocket. But all the time he was screaming 'help me. I don't want to die.'

'There is an irony to this situation, Ladies and Gentlemen of the jury, for until a short time before the fire, apparently, he had no qualms about killing his own son,' the prosecutor stood up and observed.

Ben was totally focussed on telling his story and continued with his halting delivery.

'I put my hand into Mike's smouldering jacket pocket and felt something hard...the knife. I felt relieved, I had the knife.

I quickly got it out and opened the blade. I ran my fingers down his arm until I found the rope where it was wrapped around the metal bar that he was tied to. I made sure that I was clear of his hand and arm then I started hacking at the melted mass.'

'You must have been close to collapse because of the noxious gases from the inferno,' the prosecutor suggested.

'Yes. I was. It was the smoke. I was feeling stranger and stranger as the fumes filled my lungs.

It was killing both of us. Mike's screams and thrashing around became less frantic as the fumes took their toll on him too.

After what seemed for ever, suddenly the rope parted, and Mike was free. In his blind panic, he pushed me over and ran towards a gap where the door used to be.'

'Pushed you out of the way,' the lawyer laboured the point looking at the jury. 'After what you'd done?'

'Yes, but he only got a few steps before he fell over and lay halfway out of the building on glowing embers.

I scrambled to my feet and ran to him. I don't know

how I did it, but I managed to pick him up and carry him outside.'

'So, in spite of being in a smoke logged room, the boy found some maniacal strength, picked up the dead weight of his father from the embers and somehow got the pair outside. What exceptional bravery this young man exhibited,' the Judge observed.

'I remembered my burns training that Andy gave me. So, I dragged Mike to a nearby water trough and plunged his severely burnt arm into it and held it there until the ambulance people eventually came.'

'Ben. No further questions,' the lawyer said.

Ben came out of his mental rerun of the events upon hearing his name.

'Ben Bird you may step down.'

Sweating profusely, with his head down, Ben walked out the courtroom. Glad that the ordeal, which he'd been dreading for months, was now over.

Although he felt drained, he wanted to hear Andy's version of events. More importantly he wanted to hear if the jury found Mike guilty or not.

Aware of the judge's sensitivity to extraneous noises, he crept quietly into the public gallery to join his mother and Kay.

He flashed a reassuring smile as he sat on the wooden bench next to them. Beth reached for his hand and squeezed it.

CHAPTER SEVENTY

Andy was called to the witness box next.

'Mr Spider please take the bible in your right hand and take the oath, the clerk directed.

Andy duly swore his oath and was immediately plunged into the sensitivities of the case.

'I assume you have no request for the privacy curtain to be in place?' the Judge asked.

'No thank you your honour,' Andy said.

'Clerk please store the curtain.'

The court usher duly did as directed, giving Andy a clear view of Mike in the dock. They briefly exchanged disdainful glances.

'Mr Spider tell the jury how you know Ben Bird.' the prosecution lawyer asked.

'I am a Scout leader. Ben is a long-term member of my Scout Group. I have known him and his home life for a long time.'

'Tell me a little about his parenting.'

'Objection Your Honour the parenting issue has nothing to do with this case,' the defence lawyer said.

Your Honour, I intend to prove that there is no parental bond between Ben and his absent father.'

'Objection overruled. Continue your line of questioning.'

'Mr Spider tell me briefly about Ben's parental support.'

Andy thought for a moment not wishing to raise the spectre of Beth's drinking record or Ben's care role.

'To my knowledge, Ben has been brought up solely by his mother. His father was absent. Ben wanted a father figure, which apparently in his eyes, I am embarrassed to say, that I represented.'

'So, you had a close relationship with the boy?'

'Yes, Within the safeguarding rules of the Scout Association, I became like a surrogate father to him.'

'So, you were protective of him?'

'I'd like to think so. Yes.'

'You were obviously aware of Ben's kidnaping?'

'Yes. I was devastated to hear that he had been kidnapped. I knew that the police suspected Sue Williams-Screen as the abductor. But I was led to believe, they didn't know where she was,' Andy explained.

'But you stumbled on to her location whilst rescuing your wife from a farm fire, is that correct?'

'Yes.'

'Please explain the events leading up to it, if you wouldn't mind,' the barrister said.

'I was attending a training course and it finished early. When I got home, I was surprised to see our babysitter at home rather than my wife. The babysitter told me that Helen, my wife, had gone off in her car with a foreign sounding woman. Obviously, it could have been anyone, but I knew Nadine was in town and I guessed it was her and I had concerns.'

'Who is Nadine?' the Judge asked.

'Nadine Mondegan is a former partner of the late multimillionaire Geoffery Foster.

The multimillionaire, whose legacy to his Godsons is at the centre of many of the issues surrounding this case your honour,' the barrister explained. 'I believe we have a statement from Ms Mondegan to submit to the court later.'

'Right, please continue.'

'Your honour. Now Mr Spider, what was your concern?'

'The two ladies have...have clashed on previous occasions and I was concerned for my wife's safety.'

'What do you mean clashed. Are you suggesting physical violence?' the lawyer probed.

'To my knowledge there has never been any instance of physical violence. Antagonism certainly. Definitely no love lost between them.

Helen hadn't left a note to tell me what was happening. And I was unaware of any circumstances that would bring them together requiring a car journey.'

'So, what did you do?' the lawyer asked.

'I decided to investigate where she was.

'If she hadn't left a note of her intentions, how did you do that?' the lawyer probed.

'I traced her location from a tracking app that I'd put on her phone.'

'That's very invasive isn't it,' the Judge remarked.

'No, it's very handy in managing our lifestyles your honour. It means that we know where each other is at any time.'

'I assume she gave you permission to track her every move?' Otherwise we are exposing coercive control.

'Yes your honour.'

'Please continue.'

'I was able to see her exact location,' Andy continued. 'So, I drove out to the location indicated and after a short car journey, I found her car. It was parked by a building which was on fire.'

'Was your wife in the car?' the lawyer asked.

'No, but I could hear her shouting for help from inside it. As I ran over to the building, I called the emergency services.'

'Why didn't she ring you for help on your mobile?'

'In her panic to find Ben, both she and Nadine had left their mobiles in the car.'

'What did you do?'

'I quickly concluded that they were trapped in the building and needed rescuing.'

'How did you rescue them?'

'I was desperate because I couldn't find a door, so I broke through a boarded-up window and fortunately found them close by. I reached in and dragged my wife and Nadine out through the window. Both were suffering from the effects of inhaling smoke.'

'And what about Mr Benson and his son Ben?'

'I didn't know that they were in there. Until Helen recovered slightly. She told me that Ben was in the building but had gone to rescue his father.

I waited by the window from where I'd rescued the women, shouting for Ben. But the smoke and flames was so thick. I had to back away and thought nobody could have survived that inferno.'

'Then what did you do? Did you search for the boy and his father?'

'No, I thought they'd perished in the fire. I was devastated. I assumed that Ben had died in a heroic bid to save his father.'

'But in fact, they had survived, and they were both OK?' the lawyer clarified.

'Yes. I later discovered that they were at the other end of the old barn and were actually being treated by an ambulance crew. I was overjoyed when I eventually heard.'

'Members of the jury the dramatic rescue culminated in Michael Benson being whisked away by helicopter to a specialist burns hospital,' the lawyer explained. 'The quick thinking by his heroic son definitely saved his life. And likewise due to his rapid first aid actions he also saved Mike Benson's arm from being amputated. Such was the severity of the injuries.'

In the dock, Mike subconsciously rubbed his bandaged arm at the mention of his rescue.

The defence lawyer continued, 'Michael Benson was clearly as much a victim as was his son. He is still receiving treatment for his injuries and bears the terrible life changing scars caused by this woman. I believe that his injuries should be taken into account during the judgement,' the barrister proposed. '

'I will be the judge of what is, and not, included in my judgement,' the judge said firmly, gazing over his glasses.

'I believe the young man deserves a medal for his bravery,' Andy added. 'He certainly doesn't deserve a father like you,' Andy said vehemently, looking at Mike.'

In the public gallery, Ben attempted a smile.

'Please stick to answering questions Mr Spider,' the judge admonished. 'It is not your role to make allegations against the defendant.'

'No further questions,' the lawyers said.

'You may stand down.'

Andy left the court and joined Ben, Beth, and Kay in the public gallery.

CHAPTER SEVENTY-ONE

I'd like to call Helen Spider to the stand, the prosecution lawyer announced.

Helen nervously entered the court room.

She was duly sworn in and confirmed her name.

'Mrs Spider, what is your relationship to Ben Bird? The prosecutor asked.

'Ben is like a stepson to me and Andy,' Helen smiled, looking up to Ben in the public gallery.

'On the day in question you went to a farm building. Correct?'

'Yes.'

'Why did you go to that particular farm building?' the lawyer probed.

'Out of the blue, I had a visit from Nadine, and she told me that Ben had been kidnapped and was being held there.'

'May I stop you there. This Nadine?' the Judge asked. 'What is her relationship to yourself?'

'She and I...we...err...didn't exactly see eye to eye,' Helen said, uncomfortably.

'Can you explain the reason for this tension?' the prosecutor asked.

'Yes. I...err...I thought she was having...having an affair with my...my husband, Andy.'

There was much muttering in the public gallery as the revelation of this juicy bit of gossip was exposed.

Quiet in the gallery,' the Judge ordered.

'But I was wrong...no she wasn't. It was a... misunderstanding.'

'Sorry for the interrogation, but we need to ensure that the jury have a clear understanding of the complexities of the case. Please continue.'

'Nadine visited me and told me that the evil woman...'

'Can you be more specific? Who is this so-called evil woman?' the Judge quizzed.

'Sorry Sir. In our circle of friends anyone who has had dealing with Sue Williams-Screen calls her the evil woman,' Helen explained.

'Quite so. But this is a court of law. Please use her correct name.'

'Yes Sir. Sorry.'

'Thank you, please continue.'

'The woman's name is Sue Williams-Screen,' Helen explained. 'The same woman whom we all believed was dead. It was assumed that she had previously drowned in the River Severn. However, she was very much alive and amongst other crimes she had also kidnapped Ben.

Nadine told me where they were holding Ben,' Helen repeated.

'I thought that you said it was Williams-Screen.'

'Yes, it was,' Helen confirmed.

'Then. Who are they?' The Judge demanded.

'Sorry, it was Williams-Screen and Ben's father, Mike Benson.'

'Members of the jury. This is crucial to this trial. Let me repeat what has just been said, It is alleged that Ben's father kidnapped his own son.' The prosecution lawyer said, looking at each member of the jury as he repeated it slowly. 'Michael Benson had kidnapped his own son.'

'That's what she told me. Yes,' Helen continued. 'And they were going to ask for a ransom for his release.'

'A ransom, for his own son. The boy obviously meant nothing to his father,' the lawyer emphasised, staring at each member of the jury, driving home the severity of Mike's cruelty. 'The boy's status was demeaned. He had become just a bargaining chip to extort money.'

'Nadine told me that once the ransom had been paid, she...Williams-Screen, was going to kill Ben. Nadine didn't want to get involved with it, so she came to see me.'

'And what did you do?'

'I suggested going to rescue Ben.'

'Why didn't you call the police?'

'Unfortunately, Nadine had been coerced into helping Williams-Screen financially. That's how she knew where Ben was being held. She said if the police were involved, she would leave without taking me to Ben's location. And if she left, well I wouldn't know where to look. So, I really didn't know what to do. I was stuck between a rock and a hard place.'

'What about calling your husband?' the lawyer asked.

'I tried, but he was on a training course. Phones were banned and he couldn't be disturbed.' Helen explained. 'Well, I knew I had to do something, so I agreed to go with Nadine, and she took me to the farm, and we attempted to rescue Ben.'

'That was terribly brave or terribly fool hardy of you,' the lawyer observed.

'When we arrived at the farm building, we heard angry voices. Somebody was shouting. Then we heard a door sliding shut. Then it went quiet. So, we wandered round the building and discovered the sliding door. We slipped inside the building, hoping to find Ben.'

'Was your quest successful?'

'Yes, but not straight away. It was very dark inside. After a short search in the gloom, we discovered, a person with his head on his chest and his arms tied and bound. He was crucified against a metal cow pen. You know, arms straight out, like being on the cross,' Helen revealed.

Up in the public gallery Beth squeezed Ben's hand.

'We hoped that it was going to be Ben, but as the person lifted his head, we could see it wasn't him. It was Ben's father, Mike Benson. We were shocked to see that he had been beaten up. He had a bloody and bruised face, and his eye was injured.' Helen relayed.

Mike gestured at his face. Only to be admonished by the Judge.

'If you continue this disrespectful conduct to the court, I will have you sent down. Do you understand?'

'Yes Judge.'

'Please continue, Mrs Spider.' The Judge directed.

'Thank you, Sir…As shocked as I was for the condition of his poor face, I was relieved to see that it wasn't Ben,' Helen explained. 'Although he was injured, he was however semi-conscious.'

'This again confirms his level of involvement in the scheme was slight,' the defence barrister repeated.

'At first, I thought, Williams-Screen had kidnapped Mike as well as Ben, but Nadine explained that he was part of the gang who was after the ransom money.'

'So, you are confirming that he kidnapped his own son?' The prosecution lawyer said, turning to face the jury to reinforce the point.

'Yes, I believe so.'

'Please continue.'

'I asked Mike where Ben was, and he muttered something which I couldn't understand.'

'Why was that?'

'It was because his lips were swollen from the beating. So, I asked him to repeat it and after several failed attempts, he turned his head indicating something towards the back of the barn.

So, Nadine and I went to where he was indicating and found Ben. He was drugged, unconscious.'

'So, the boy had been heavily drugged thanks to his father's compliance,' the prosecutor summarised. 'What occurred then?'

'That evil…sorry…Williams-Screen woman came back into the building and shouted at Mike. It was a shock seeing her, as I said, I thought she was dead. Fortunately, in the gloom, she couldn't see Nadine and me.

She told Mike that she was going to burn the evidence, including him and Ben. Fortunately, she didn't come to the back of the barn where we were hiding near Ben.'

'Let me get this right. So, Williams-Screen told the defendant that she was going to burn him alive, correct?' The defence lawyer probed.

'Well, yes.'

'Members of the jury is this what you expect from a gang leader to do to one of her soldiers? This surely is an indication that the defendant was coerced and under the threat of violence to do her bidding,' the defence lawyer explained. 'He had clearly rebelled against her vile scheme and was paying the penalty. Please continue Mrs Spider.'

'Thank you. Williams-Screen then left the barn and closed the door. We could hear her splashing something on the woodwork outside...and then we smelt it. It was petrol... And then she...she...she set fire to the barn... With us in there.'

'That must have been frightening.'

'Yes, it was. We were very scared. Within a few minutes the old wooden building was well ablaze and... and it...quickly became...became an inferno.' Helen recalled haltingly. 'We thought we were going to...be... burnt...alive...to die.'

'Take your time Mrs Spider,' the Judge said kindly.

'Thank you. Helen said, gripping the edge of the witness box. She caught her breath for a moment, as the jury looked on sympathetically.

'We...it was obvious that we had to get out of the building, and we tried to carry Ben. But he was still unconscious and just too heavy. So, we needed Mike to help us. We went back to him, and he was panicking as the building filled with smoke. He agreed to help us, so I started to untie him.'

'Cleary the defendant was reviewing his involvement in the kidnap of his son and was intending to help to save his son's life,' the defence lawyer observed.

Helen continued, 'I undid the rope around one of Mike's arms and...and told him to undo the other arm himself.'

'So again, he was cooperative and willing to help, when Williams-Screen wasn't around,' the defence barrister reiterated.

'The front of the barn, where we went into the building was well alight, so Nadine and I started looking for a backdoor out of the barn while Mike untied his other arm. But all we could find was a few boarded-up windows.

Fortunately, Ben started coming round and was semi-conscious.'

'So, the defendant joined you in helping to carry his son out?'

'No. Helen sobbed. We were waiting for him, but he didn't join us. We thought he had gone and left us. Because the smoke was so thick, we couldn't see him.'

'So, he hadn't deserted you then?' the lawyer prompted.

'No, I gather for some reason that he couldn't untie his other arm. By now Ben was more with it and I explained that we were waiting for his Dad to join us, but he hadn't arrived.

Ben shouted for his father to come to us. But all we heard was some panicky screaming.

Ben was clearly agitated...his father continued screaming. It was an awful sound. To hear...to hear a grown man screaming hysterically.'

'Yes, we can only imagine how terrifying it was for you.' The Judge observed.

'I don't know whether it was the drugs or what, that made Ben do it, but despite the thick smoke and intense heat, he left us and went looking for his father. I begged for him not to go, but...he did...we couldn't persuade him not to.'

Helen looked up into the public gallery and saw Ben's pale face as he recalled his close call with death.

'So, the boy, who had been brutalised by his own father, braved the fire and went looking for him?' the prosecutor said. 'A very courageous thing to do, especially after being kidnapped and abused by that very same man. Few people would have the courage to do that.'

There was a sharp intake of breath from several members of the jury and silent tears from Beth in the public gallery.

Ben was again transported back to that moment; the acrid smoke, feeling the intense heat, as if his face were on fire. His thoughts were interrupted as Helen continued.

'The smoke was so thick and acrid. I...I could hardly breathe, my...my eyes were streaming. In desperation Nadine and I were screaming, shouting for help,' Helen filled up and wept.

'Just take your time. That must have been terrifying for the both of you.' the Judge said sympathetically. 'Do you want a break? I appreciate reliving this harrowing experience is such a drain, but it is so important for the jury to understand the enormity of what happened.'

'No, I'm OK thank you, your honour.' Helen said, clearing her throat.

'Ok when you're ready, please continue,' the Judge directed.

'We had been shouting for help when suddenly... suddenly one of the boarded windows caved in and a hand came in and grabbed me. It was...it was my husband, Andy. He pulled me out and then I grabbed Nadine's hand, and he took us away from the building.'

'And what happened to Ben?' the prosecutor asked.

'We thought he was dead, she sobbed. 'We didn't see Ben or his father again. We assumed that they had been killed in the fire.'

'But as we have heard testimony from Ben earlier, he is very much alive, thankfully,' the defence lawyer was quick to point out.

'No further questions.'

'Right, you may stand down.'

Helen joined the others in the public gallery.

CHAPTER SEVENTY-TWO

'May I ask the court's permission to allow the written evidence given by Nadine Mondegan, a Monegasque, a native of Monaco, to be used Your Honour?' the prosecutor asked.

'Clerk of the court can you clarify please?' the Judge directed.

The clerk leafed through several files and informed the court of his findings.

'Yes your Honour, as she was a significant part of this incident her documented evidence meets the necessary criteria.' 'I am in possession of that written statement;' the clerk explained.

'However, she is not here in person.'

'And why is that? Was she not called?' the Judge questioned.

'Yes, Your Honour, she was called. But, unfortunately, after experiencing significant trauma associated with this case, she is suffering from mental frailty,' the clerk explained. 'She has sought to be excused on medical grounds.

'I can imagine that being trapped in a burning barn is enough to affect anyone psychologically,' the judge observed. 'Which is why Mrs Spider's testimony was such a brave step in recounting her dreadful experience and facing her own demons.'

Helen heard the judge's praise from the public gallery where she had returned. On her arrival, she'd received a brief hug from Andy.' Well done,' he'd whispered.

'However, as a major actor in this serious crime, was extradition not considered to bring Ms Mondegan to this trial?' the Judge asked.

'Yes, it was, Your Honour. But the CPS decided that it was not appropriate because of her fragile mental state and sought an alternative solution, a written statement.' the prosecution lawyer explained.

'Your honour, although Ms Nadine Mondegan appears to have been financing some of the gang's activities. In mitigation, she was a victim of extortion herself when Michael Benson stole her credit card and forced her to give them the pin,' the prosecution lawyer explained. 'Indeed, there was an attempt on her life where, unfortunately, a hotel security guard was shot and killed,' he continued. Clearly it was very traumatic for Ms Mondegan who was present at the time of the fatality and had been the intended target.

"I presume that this incident is not part of this case?' the judge asked.

'No your Honour, the crime is believed to have been committed by Williams-Screen in a vendetta against Ms Mondegan and was being investigated by the police.

'Thank you for the clarity. Please continue,' the judge ordered.

'Thank you, your Honour. So, this gives a brief insight to the reasons for her mental sensitivity,'

'Quite so.'

'So they have been spending her money to finance their criminal activities,' the prosecutor advised the court.

'A point of clarity. You have used the terms them and they. Surely if it was Williams-Screen it should be her?' the Judge observed.

'Sorry Your Honour. Them and they refer to two people, Williams-Screen, and the defendant Michael Benson. Both were extorting money from Ms Mondegan.'

'Your Honour, I seek the court's permission to read the statement from Nadine Mondegan,' the clerk asked.

'Permission granted, but before you do, let me first advise the jury of the legality of this process. Whilst a signed statement from a complainant is enough for a charge, it is not necessarily enough to secure a conviction. The complainant must be able to convince the jury or magistrates that the defendant is guilty beyond reasonable doubt. So please bear that in mind when you consider your verdict. You may continue.'

'Thank you, Your Honour.'

CHAPTER SEVENTY-THREE

The clerk cleared his throat and started reading.

'*My name is Nadine Mondegan. This is my signed statement in relation to the trial of Michael Benson.*

I declare the following to be true as witnessed by myself. My purpose in providing this statement is to assist in obtaining justice.

I am not appearing in person due to health issues caused by the trauma surrounding this case.

Since my arrival in the UK, in pursuit of my legitimate share of my former boyfriend, Geoffery Foster's legacy, I have been slandered, libelled, mugged, sexually assaulted, verbally abused, physically attacked, blackmailed, extorted, nearly burnt alive as well as being shot at.'

'I think going through that amount of trauma is enough to make anyone ill,' the Judge interrupted. 'Not exactly the welcome that promotes the UK to visitors, is it? Please continue.'

The clerk did as directed.

'*The background to my involvement in this case, is based on my legitimate claim on my former boyfriend's estate.*

I was his partner for 6 years before he sadly died. During that period, I helped him create his wealth.

However, we split up just before he died. Hence, I was not included in his will.

Instead, the money was distributed by Geoffery's hospice nurse, Andy Spider, as the executor of the will, to Geoffery's three Godsons. Of whom he had never met since they were babies during their christenings.

In pursuance for my rightful share, I travelled to the UK to meet the executor and was unfortunate to bump into Michael Benson.

Whilst shopping, I was mugged of my handbag and Michael Benson, who witnessed the theft, chased after the thief, and retrieved the bag for me.

As a 'thank you' for his bravery, I treated him to dinner at my hotel.

Unfortunately, he misread my gratitude for more salacious reasons and made a sexual advance. Which I immediately rejected.

However, at his insistence, I had foolishly given him my card containing my mobile telephone number on it.

I was unaware, at the time, that Mike Benson was involved with Williams-Screen, but, to my cost, I soon found out when she rang me.

I later found out that Michael Benson was sheltering Sue Williams-Screen in his filthy cottage.

Unfortunately, as I'd had a previous antagonistic 'run-in' with her the pair ganged up on me and blackmailed me into becoming involved in their evil crimes.

Previously, she threatened to blackmail me over some photographs she had taken of Andy Spider and me in Monaco. I had asked him, innocently, to my hotel apartment for late-night drinks.

Andy's toes curled to hear the accusation of the fictional secret affair being aired in public. It had taken him some explaining to placate Helen and convince her that nothing had happened. Andy reached out and gripped Helen's hand.

Helen too felt uncomfortable at the public exposé and coloured up in embarrassment.

The clerk continued to read the statement.

'*I met with Williams-Screen, and she revealed that she was pursuing money from her former husband Rupert, who was a Godson of my former partner Geoffery Foster. This was money which I believed was rightfully mine.*'

'So, the pair were both after financial gain?' the Judge summarised.

'Quite so, Your Honour.'

'Continue. I hope that we'll soon get to some relevance for this case,' the Judge observed.

'Yes, I think this is the relevant information,' the clerk suggested.

Following Michael Benson's suggestion, Williams-Screen plotted to kidnap Ben. He informed her that one of the Godsons had received five million pounds legacy from the multimillionaire. And that Godson was Ben and Beth Bird's landlord, known as JC.

They blackmailed me to give them some start-up funds by threatening to publish photoshopped pictures of Andy and me and make them pornographic.

Unfortunately, I succumbed to their blackmail, and I gave them money to fund their scheme. I then discovered that Michael Benson had stolen my passport and credit card, and then forced me to give him my pin. As a result, my account is now thousands in the red.

Because of Michael Benson and Sue William Screen. I will never be able to pay it back. My credit rating is now Zero. And I am bankrupt.

'So, we have established a link to the extortion and blackmail charge against Michael Benson,' the prosecutor interjected.

'Please continue,' the Judge directed the clerk.

'Michael Benson manufactured an incident and arranged with a schoolboy to fight with Ben in a nearby park. Ben was abducted by his father from there.'

'Just to be clear, members of the jury. So, Michael Benson actively planned and abducted his own son by arranging this so-called fight, 'the prosecutor announced.

The clerk continued reading.

'Sue Williams-Screen and I subsequently fell out in a big way when she discovered that I had told the police of her plot and that I had helped rescue Ben.

She attempted to murder me by setting up a shotgun in my hotel room. It was configured so that as I entered my room the gun would go off. I was a bit suspicious about an earlier visitor and arranged for the Hotel security guard to come with me to my room. Unfortunately, as he opened the door, the gun went off and he was tragically killed. It should have been me.

As a result of this experience, I am psychologically damaged and I'm currently receiving psychiatric assistance.

The only positive aspect of all this, is that I was able to help save Ben's life by taking Helen to the barn. And together we rescued him.

Mike Benson is a devious, strong character, a lying rogue. He is a partner, not a slave to Sue Williams-Screen.'

Signed Nadine, Mondegan. Witnessed by Henri Buzane (Lawyer)

'Nicely put Nadine. That's another nail in Mike's coffin,' Andy thought.

'Thank you,' the Judge commended the clerk. 'I think we have a clear indication of the defendants involvement in this element of criminality.' The Judge observed.

CHAPTER SEVENTY-FOUR

'I would like to call Mr Michael Benson to the witness box,' the clerk announced.

Mike took his place.

'May I remind you that defendants in any criminal trial have to decide whether to give evidence themselves,' the Judge informed Mike. 'As a defendant you are entitled to remain silent at trial and leave it to the prosecution to prove its case. How do you wish to proceed?'

'No, no it's OK Judge, I'll be pleased to give my side of the story,' Mike replied.

'In which case, please read the oath from the card.'

'I...I...er... haven't got my reading glasses, sorry,' Mike stalled.

'I have spare pairs here,' the clerk said, offering Mike a pair.

'Oh! Thanks. It's just that I...err... don't do a lot of reading and a...I'm a bit rusty on some of the words,' Mike explained, awkwardly.

'Don't worry, I will help you if you get stuck,' the clerk offered.

'Oh, OK.' Mike put on the glasses and held the card at arm's length.

'Yeah, I can see the writing,' he said joyfully.

'Just get on with it,' the Judge directed.

'I do...what's that word?' Mike asked the clerk, pointing at the card.

'solemnly.'

'I do solominee. And this next word?'

'Sincerely.'

'I do solominee and since-er-lee and truly...don't tell me. I'll get this next word myself..., d-e-c-l-a-r-e; declare and,' Mike smiled in self-congratulation. 'Affirm... what's an affirm? Is that a firm like Ford?'

'I am running out of patience,' the Judge said angrily. 'Just get on with it. Otherwise, I shall be sending you down for contempt, and then you'll have to wait on remand for a retrial.'

'Sorry sir, it's only that reading wasn't ...you know... at school.'

'Clerk, read the outstanding words so he can repeat them after you,' the Judge ordered, irritated by the farcical delay.

'My Lord.'

The clerk turned to face Mike. 'Now say after me.'

'Right,' Mike smiled mischievously.

'that the evidence'

'that the evidence.'

'I shall give'

'I shall give.'

'shall be the truth.'

'shall be the truth.'

'the whole truth'

'the whole truth'

'and nothing but the truth.'

'and nothing but the truth.'

'How did I do? Mike said, giving the reading glasses back to the clerk.

The clerk took the glasses and turned away without comment.

'It'll have to do. Right, now that painful exercise is over, please proceed,' the Judge directed.

'Your Honour. Mr Benson, you are accused of some serious crimes, physical and sexual assault, kidnap, extortion and causing actual bodily harm,' the prosecutor said.

'Yes, and it's not true,' Mike insisted.

'I won't tell you again,' the Judge said sternly. 'You were not asked to comment.'

Mike looked sheepishly at the floor.

'We have heard during this trial that you have been seen to be actively complicit in several of these activities,' the prosecutor explained.

'Have I? Complicit! No sorry you can't stick that one on me. I've never been complicit in my life.'

'Do you understand what complicit means?'

'Well actually...no. But I doubt that I have been. Otherwise, I would have remembered if I had. Wouldn't I?'

'Complicit means that you have been involved with others in an activity that is unlawful.'

'Oh, I suppose you could say that I have been then. Yeah.' Mike accepted.

The judge, clearly irritated, was about to intervene, but decided to hold off.

'Can you give me any reasons why you have, for instance, been involved in the kidnap of your own son Ben Bird?'

Mike shifted uneasily. 'Well, it wasn't as though we were, we were like, close.'

'Closeness in a relationship is not a parameter whereby you discharge your paternal responsibilities,' the Judge lectured. 'You have continual responsibilities that are inalienable. How would the world function if all parents failed in their parental duties?'

'Pretty shit, I should think,' Mike observed.

'Mr Benson. Please watch your language. Remember where you are. You are in a court of law, not down your local pub,' the Judge admonished.

'Sorry sir,' Mike grovelled. 'I was forced to do it Sir. That Sue Williams-Screen threatened me that if I didn't do what she told me, she would kill me. Which as you can see by my injured arm that she very nearly succeeded in doing.'

'So, are you saying that you have been a pawn in her criminal games?' the lawyer probed.

'I'm not sure what you mean. But I have been pushed around by her, yeah.'

'I put it to you that you have enjoyed the power of being her sidekick. That you have luxuriated in the authority that you have held over your victims?'

'Never thought of it that way, but I suppose it does make you feel macho when you're bossing people around. Yeah.'

'So, you admit being part of the Gang, but clearly, not the brains behind it,' the prosecutor said. 'No further questions.'

The defence lawyer stood up and said, 'So members of the jury, we have heard Mrs Spider suggesting that Michael Benson was a victim too?'

Several of the Jurors looked at each other puzzled.

'You'll recall that she overheard Williams-Screen's conversation with Michael Benson when she had returned to the barn.'

'Wake up, she'd shouted. Remember, he was tied up in a crucifix stance and couldn't defend himself. She then kicked the defendant in the stomach.' The lawyer related and checked his notes.

The defence lawyer latched on to the phrase and repeated the words slowly. 'K i c k e d i n t h e s t o m a c h. T i e d U p! Members of the jury, does that sound like a team at work?

I contend that Michael Benson was also a victim of coercion himself and under the influence of an enormously powerful woman.'

'Yes, that's right, I was,' Mike added, smiling, much to the concern of his lawyer who feared Mike would discredit the point that he was trying to make.

'She bullied me and was very violent as you heard. She beat me up something rotten. She was a nutter,' Mike concluded.

The prosecution lawyer stood and picked up the point.

'I agree with my learned colleague that it doesn't sound like they were always acting together. But he WAS her partner in crime, whether he was coerced or not and no matter how incompetent he was.

He set up and kidnapped his own son. Put him in danger at least twice by physically restraining him while he was injected with some noxious substance. An unprofessionally administered injection alone can be deadly by injecting air into the bloodstream, let alone the potency of the substance being injected.

Ms Mondegan has accused the defendant of a sexual assault and theft. This wasn't something that he was coerced to do. I suggest that he is playing the victim too much and you, the jury will see through his masquerade.

His escape from custody wasn't anything to do with Williams-Screen either. So, rather than being the victim, as he claims. I put it to you that he had equal billing with Williams-Screen who, unfortunately, will never be brought to justice. But I believe that the full weight of the law should fall on Michael Benson's shoulders.

I rest my case.'

CHAPTER SEVENTY-FIVE

The judge made the closing remarks.

Members of the jury. You have heard the arguments for the prosecution and defence.

The crimes that were committed in this case are at the top list of criminality. Please remember that this is not a trial of the chief instigator, Sue William Screen, but of one of her henchmen, Michael Benson.

Although the death of an innocent man, the security guard is not directly attributable to the defendant, he was part of the criminal environment that perpetuated the crime.

You might think that the confident manner in which the defendant delivered his evidence is a clear indication of a strong strength of character. And as such his personality would prevent him from doing anything that he didn't want to do. In other words, in the vernacular, he was his own man.

On the other hand, the manner of his 'cheery' articulation might be a sign of nervousness and vulnerability. In which case you might consider that he is susceptible to being coerced and find him innocent.

You have to decide, in mitigation, whether he was forced or coerced into undertaking this misconduct.

Michael Benson's appalling treatment of his son is not a proof of guilt per se, but it is an example of child abuse of the worst kind.

There is a lot of complexity for you to ponder. The prime motive for all the misdeeds that occurred in this case was money, pure greed.

Please retire and consider your verdict. You have to tell me that by considering all the evidence presented to you, whether the defendant Michael Benson is Guilty or Not Guilty of all the charges against him.

Please take the jury 'to the jury room. And ensure that no one speaks to them,' the Judge directed the Clerk.

The jury argued the pros and cons of the case for a modest two hours and notified the jury bailiff that they had reached a verdict.

The bailiff duly notified the judge, and the court was reconvened.

The advocates returned to court and the defendant was returned to the dock. Members of the public returned to the public gallery. Finally, the jury were brought back in, and the judge entered the courtroom.

The court clerk asked the jury foreman to stand and asked.

'As the spokesperson for the jury have you reached a verdict upon which you are all agreed? Please answer 'Yes' or 'No.'

'Yes'

'In respect of each individual count against Michael Benson. What is your verdict on the count of kidnap?'

'Guilty.'

On the count of extortion?'

'Guilty'

'On the count of actual bodily harm?'

'Guilty.'

'On the count of physical and sexual assault?'

'Guilty.'

'Members of the jury, thank you for your important public duty,' the Judge acknowledged. 'I have to remind you that although your involvement in the case is now over, you are not entitled to discuss what took place within the jury room; for to do so amounts to a criminal offence.

'Prisoner in the dock. As part of the 'faster justice' initiative, I am in a position to sentence you today.

You have been found guilty of all four charges. I have taken in to account the seriousness of the charges of kidnap and actual bodily harm in what amounts to be child abuse of your own son.

You have bullied your way into involving an innocent woman to hand over her credit card and pin and helped to cause her terrible trauma for which she is heavily in debt. Your extortion is a dastardly crime and will be punished accordingly.

Your intimidation using physical and sexual violence of this same woman has left her with permanent psychological issues for which you have shown no remorse or even acknowledged your crime.

The tariff allows me to give you a life sentence for the crime of kidnap alone. But I have taken into consideration signs of your reluctance to follow some of the directions given to you by Sue Williams-Screen. You are fortunate that others have noted and reported it.

I have also taken into account your escape from custody whilst on remand. I therefore sentence you to eight years with a restraining order on your release not to approach your son or his mother at the risk of a further eight years imprisonment.'

Mike looked aghast and mouthed 'eight years,' followed by an expletive.

'I trust that during that time in prison that you will reflect on your life of crime and come out a better person,' the Judge added. Take him down.'

In the public gallery Ben hugged his mother. But the tear in Beth's eye was not for Ben, but for her former lover being taken down to the cells. She still wished that things would have worked out between them.

Andy and Helen embraced each other, their ordeal over. Now it was only the inquest to get through and hopefully life would at last return to normal.

CHAPTER SEVENTY-SIX

The group of friends exited the court and went into an excited group hug on the pavement outside.

Ben, Janie, Andy, Helen, Beth, JC, Joanne, Kay and Carrie, all locked arms in a big scrum, much to the annoyance of passers-by who had to step into the road to get past them.

Tim and Rupert were absent from the proceedings. Carrie had banned Tim from attending the trial because of his volatile nature and short temper. She had told him that he was likely to shout at Mike and subsequently end up in jail for contempt.

Rupert was babysitting little Jeffery and Joanne phoned him with the good news.

'Well, at least we got one of the perpetrators behind bars,' Andy said, beaming.

'Yes, thank goodness that's all over. I was dreading going into court and giving evidence,' Ben confessed.

'You were very brave,' Janie said, squeezing his hand and nuzzling up to him.

'I'm glad that they put that curtain up though, so I couldn't see his face while I was giving my evidence. He can give scary looks,' Ben admitted.

'Yes, it looked like he was really 'throwing daggers' at you, especially when you said he stabbed you with that syringe,' Janie said.

'When you think of it, eight years isn't much for what he did to you though,' JC observed. 'Kidnapping, his own son. I mean, the man's got no morals.'

'And after I heard that he'd escaped from prison, I was pooing myself.' Ben admitted. 'Then when I found him in our annex, I nearly had heart failure.'

'That must have been horrible for you,' Janie sympathised.

Their comments were like daggers to Beth's heart. Ever since that dreadful night when Ben was assaulted and the dog died, she had been beating herself up and was overwhelmed with guilt. To hear them talking about Ben's awful experience added to her guilty conscience.

'Yes, it was. As you know he knocked me out throwing me across the room,' Ben reminded them. 'And then, effectively he killed the dog too.'

'Poor Rusty. He should have been charged with killing her too,' Janie added.

'I'm so sorry Ben. It was my fault.' Beth said crestfallen. 'He was desperate and I...I just felt so sorry for him.'

'He's a maverick,' Carrie said, vehemently. 'He didn't deserve your sympathy, Beth. But I understand why you felt as you did, despite the fact that he had almost killed your son.'

Beth felt the accusation deeply and sobbed.

'I'm sorry Beth that was a bit thoughtless of me. Sorry,' Carrie said quickly, giving her a hug. 'But I could never forgive him. You know the dreadful things that I suffered as a result of that pair's cruelty. It's a pity she wasn't on trial too. I would have loved to see that evil smirk wiped off her face.'

'No, It's OK. I probably deserved it,' Beth admitted, wiping her eyes.

'Well at least, after his escape they caught him quite quickly. And that woman we met at the inquest, that Sue look-alike, is getting done.'

'Just goes to show what a cunning character that Mike is, doesn't it? Not only did he persuade her to help him to escape but then let him stay in her house.' At least they didn't charge you as well Beth for harbouring a felon.'

'No, I was half expecting it, I must admit,' Beth said nervously. Secretly jealous that he had allowed another woman, Suzette, in his life.

'The police were called after I shouted out in court, and they told me that in view of the circumstances they wouldn't press charges. But they warned me in no uncertain terms what would happen if I did it again,' Beth admitted.

'Just as well that he's gone away for a long time then,' Kay added.

'And he has that restraining order against him too,' Ben said, relieved that the law was going to protect them after Mike had served his term.

'Catch me having any dealings with him,' Helen shuddered.

'Now the next big challenge is when they reconvene the inquest,' JC reminded them all.

'Don't remind me,' Ben muttered.

'Yes, it's a bit like having the sword of Damocles hanging over you.' Andy observed.

'The sword of what?' Ben asked. 'What does that mean?'

'Damocles. It's a fourth century myth. It's when something terrible is about to happen.'

'What do you mean? That we're going to be found guilty of pushing her over?' Ben puzzled.

'No. It just means we dread the uncertainty of it all.' Andy clarified.

'Don't worry Ben,' Janie said, quietly. 'I know you did your best to save her.'

'Yeah, but the coroner doesn't. Nor that sister of hers.'

'Talking about her sister. Her trial for aiding and abetting an offender is coming up soon, so I'd heard. Are you going?' Andy asked.

'No chance. The least contact that I have with that family, the better. I don't want to keep being reminded of that evil bitch, Sue.' Carrie said firmly.

'She looks just like her sister though and I keep having flashbacks of when Williams-Screen tried to kill me after she kidnapped me and tried to drown me.' Carrie revealed. 'In spite of me rescuing her from my sunken car. The bitch was so full of hate that even as I rescued her, she still tried to kill me,' Carrie recalled.

'Anyway, we've got a good lawyer representing us at the inquest.' Andy said confidently. 'He'll make sure the truth comes out and we're acquitted of any blame.'

'I hope so,' Ben said quietly. 'I've heard that some lawyers boast of getting innocent people banged up. They have a league table of winning cases whether their clients are guilty or not.'

'Just ignore it,' Andy encouraged.

'That's just idle gossip. It'll be fine,' Janie said kissing Ben on the cheek. In any case, I'm going to make you a special cake to celebrate.

'A cake? What sort of cake?'

'A chocolate Ganache.'

'A chocolate what?' Ben queried.

'A Ganache. It's a glaze, icing, sauce, made from chocolate and cream.'

'Oh yes please,' Ben drooled. 'Chocolate and cream! Yummy.'

'Anyway, enough of the doom and gloom. We have to celebrate our success,' Carrie said. 'Who's for a healthy big Mac?'

'Yeah, sounds like a good idea. It means I don't have to cook,' Helen said, smiling at Andy.

'Oh, I was hoping for the panache that you've been telling me about,' Andy told her.

'The what?' Carrie asked.

'Oh, he's just being silly. I've been watching a cookery programme on the TV and quite liked the term Panache. It's a French cooking term for a mixture of a variety of different vegetables. That's all,' Helen explained.

'I'm not sure that they do that healthy option, where we're going,' Carrie said.

'Never mind, I will look forward to tucking into a panache another time then,' Andy smiled.

In buoyant mood, the group headed to the nearest McDonald's restaurant while Mike headed to jail in a prison van.

CHAPTER SEVENTY-SEVEN

Chris Cooper had got wind of Suzette's arrest and had visited her in prison.

'What are we going to do with you? he asked rhetorically. 'I said, if you needed help to call me.'

'I know, I didn't know what to do. I was so confused when Michael Benson called me in the middle of the night,' she said.

'Well now you're in the system, I can't do anything to help you. Best of luck. Keep your chin up and I hope things work out for you.'

'Thank you anyway for your concern,' she said quietly, wondering why the policeman was even interested in her problems.

Likewise, his colleague, Marcus Williams shared the same thought. 'What is Chris up to with that woman?'

While Mike's trial was being held, Suzette was on remand in prison, consequently she was unaware of the details of the serious allegations about her sister's criminality.

However, because of a Ministry of Justice initiative, to clear the backlog of cases, fortunately Suzette did not have to wait long as her trial was fast tracked and downgraded to be heard in a Magistrates Court.

Nevertheless, the enormity of being a prisoner had had a dramatic effect on her and a petrified Suzette stood white faced in the dock, fearful that she was going to be deported.

A small consolation to her fears came when she saw a familiar face and spotted Chris Cooper in the public gallery and gave him a weak smile. He smiled back and nodded an encouragement.

'Suzette Brown you are charged with facilitating the escape of a prisoner and furthermore of harbouring that escaped prisoner. How do you plead?'

'Guilty.'

'As a newly arrived Australian citizen, how did you get involved with Michael Benson?' The defence solicitor asked.

'I arrived in England from Australia to meet my sister only to be advised that she had died the day before in a traffic accident.'

'That must have been devastating news,' the defence lawyer said compassionately.

'Yes, it was. We had been split up when we were only babies and I had just tracked her down. We were meeting for the first time. I was overwhelmed when I heard the awful news,' Suzette explained tearfully.

'How did you come to get involved with the prisoner that you aided and abetted?'

'After the inquest into my sister's death, unexpectedly Michael Benson contacted me via my solicitor.'

'For what reason?'

'He wanted to meet me. I was reluctant at first, because I didn't know anything about him. And then he told me he had evidence that would exonerate my sister from all the accusations against her. I finally decided to go and visit him whilst he was on remand in prison,' Suzette revealed.

'And what was the outcome of this meeting?' the solicitor asked.

'He told me that my sister had been murdered,' Suzette explained.

'Murdered! He told you that your sister had been murdered?' the lawyer repeated.

'Yes.'

'Is this all relevant to the charges she is facing?' the chief magistrate interrupted. A charge of murder is beyond the authority of this court.'

'Yes, I appreciate that. But we won't be considering the murder charge. However, I believe it is important for the mitigating circumstances of the defendant's conduct to be revealed,' the solicitor explained.

'Carry on, but be as brief as possible,' the Magistrate instructed.

'Yes Sir, I will, thank you ....So, Miss Brown, Michael Benson was informing you that your sister had not died as a result of a road traffic accident? But instead that she had been murdered?'

'That's correct,' Suzette confirmed.

'That must have been dreadful news?'

'Yes, it was. It was devastating. I didn't know what to think. Michael Benson said that he could get some evidence to prove it too,' Suzette revealed.

'Did he say from where he was going to get this evidence?' the solicitor asked.

'No. He said that people were 'bad mouthing' my sister Sue to make her look guilty, so that would justify her murder.'

'So, what did you plan to do with this 'evidence'?'

'I reckoned if I had evidence of collusion then, although I couldn't bring her back at least I could clear her name. She has been accused of some terrible things,' Suzette said passionately.

'What did he want from you in return for providing you with this evidence?'

'I had to help him escape from his remand prison.'

'And did you help him escape?'

'Yes. But I was very reluctant. It took some time before I agreed to do it. I didn't want to break the law, but I thought I owed it to my sister to find her murderers and to clear her name. I am deeply sorry for my actions,' she said, looking at the magistrates.

'How did you assist with his escape?'

'He had it all planned. I had to pick him up from the hospital carpark after he'd received his daily treatment for the burns to his arm.'

'Then what happened?'

'Over a series of meetings, we agreed on a day, and I met him in the carpark as planned and…well it wasn't like I was breaking him out of jail. I mean it was just like… like picking someone up after a hospital appointment.'

'Nevertheless, you knew that what you were doing was illegal?' the chief magistrate reminded her.

'Yes sir. And I'm terribly sorry.

'And where did you take him?' her solicitor continued.

'I dropped him off in town, and I waited for him to come back. But he didn't return. So, I didn't know what to do.'

'But you continued to wait patiently for his return?'

'Yes, And then as I waited, suddenly my car was hemmed in by three police cars. And I was arrested.

'What were you charged with?'

'Assisting an offender. And then I was let out on Police bail and summoned to attend a magistrates court.'

'Did Michael Benson contact you during this period?'

'Yes. But I didn't hear from him for probably two weeks. I thought he had conned me and wasn't going to do what he promised.'

'You must have been angry with him?'

'I suppose I was. But I was angrier with myself for letting him con me. Then one night unexpectedly, he rang me and said he wanted shelter. He said that the police were on to him. He was desperate."

'So, you'd got him out of prison, and he'd not been in contact? Why ever did you want further dealings with him?' the Magistrate asked. 'What made you change your mind?'

'He said that he had the evidence that would clear Sue's name.'

'So, he was now luring you into his trap, again?'

'Well, I suppose you could look at it like that. But he said that unless I helped him, he wouldn't be able to fulfil his promise of helping put Sue's murderers in prison.'

'What did you do?'

'I didn't know what to do. I was in a tizz. But I gave in and allowed him to stay in my rented house.'

'For how long?'

'For several days.'

'Even though you knew that it was illegal to harbour an offender?'

'Yes. But I was desperate to do anything for my sister's sake.'

'Did you get to see this 'so called' evidence?'

'No.'

'And why was that?'

'He hadn't got it. Unfortunately, someone reported that I was the victim of domestic violence. And the police arrived to check the complaint out.'

'And were you being violently abused?'

'No. Although, we had lots of noisy rows. He never hit me. I had given myself a black eye by accidentally banging my face on an open cupboard door. Unfortunately, the police officers didn't believe me and thought I was lying to protect the man.'

'And you weren't?'

'No. Not in this case. I was telling the truth, but during the discussion they recognised Mike as being 'on the run' and we were both arrested.'

'But you knew that helping a prisoner to escape and harbouring a felon is a criminal offence?'

'Yes, and I'm very sorry.'

Sir that is all the evidence in mitigating Ms Brown's behaviour that we wish to present.'

'Thank you, for outlining the context in which these misguided actions were taken,' the chief magistrate said. 'Suzette Brown.'

'Yes.'

'You realise that you have committed a serious crime?'

'Yes.'

'However, taking into consideration all the various issues going on in your life at the time. I believe that your judgement was impaired by grief due to the tragic loss of your sister.

Michael Benson sought you out at a point in your life where you were very vulnerable, and he manipulated you.

I note that you are formerly of good character and have not got a criminal record in Australia. Indeed, as a nurse you normally exhibit a high stand of morality. Have you anything to say before I pronounce sentencing?'

'No, just that I'm very sorry,' Suzette whispered, her mouth dry.

'As you have pleaded guilty, I am able to give you a lower tariff. I therefore sentence you to two years...'

Suzette gasped in horror.

'...suspended for two years.'

Suzette gripped the edge of the dock and sobbed.

'Thank you,' she croaked. 'Thank you.'

Outside the magistrates court, she thanked her lawyer for her assistance.

'Thank you for helping me through with that. Not a good start in a new country, is it?' Suzette said, reflectively.

'No. But in the circumstances perfectly understandable. You just 'lucked out' by bumping into that villain. Good luck in clearing your sisters name. If I can be of any help, here's my card.'

'Hopefully the coroner will get to the bottom of it, and we can clear her name as well as identifying her murderers.'

Chris Cooper sidled up to her. 'Well done, it looks like you got off lightly again.'

'Thank you for supporting me. It was nice to have a friendly face in the court.'

'My pleasure. Can I offer you a lift home?'

'Oh, I'm...I'm not sure,' she faffed.

'Don't worry, It's only a lift home that's on offer,' he smiled. 'I'm going your way and I would think what you've been through recently you could do without the hassle of catching buses. True?'

'Yes, true. Thank you.'

'My car's around the back in a magistrates parking space, he informed her.

'Is that allowed?' she pondered.

'Didn't bother to ask,' he laughed.

CHAPTER SEVENTY-EIGHT

Chris Cooper dropped Suzette off and, much to her relief, didn't proposition her.

'Goodbye Suzette. Try to keep yourself out of mischief,' the policeman advised. 'I don't want to do anymore prison visiting.'

'I promise. I'll keep a low profile from now on. Except...'

'Except?' He queried.

'...The reconvened Inquest.

'Oh yes. I anticipate that I shall be in the Coroner's court too, So, I'll see you there. Cheers.'

'Yes, goodbye and thanks for the lift.'

Suzette walked up the path as the neighbours curtains twitched at her return.

'They've let her out,' the old woman said, watching Suzette. 'We don't want those drug dealers living around here.'

'No dear,' her husband said with his head in the crossword.

'I shall write to our MP and complain.'

'Yes' dear,' the old man replied, disinterested.

Meanwhile Suzette unlocked the door and stepped in. She closed it behind her and leant heavily against it.

A sense of relief rushed over her that she had evaded being locked up and deported.

'What is going wrong with my life? she moaned. 'What have I done to deserve this shit?' I came to meet a sister that I never knew I had, that failed miserably. I came to start a new life, that's now in doubt. And I end up in prison with a criminal record. So now what do I do?'

She gazed tearfully at the ceiling, as if looking for an answer.

Then suddenly galvanising herself into action, she moved into the kitchen and put on the kettle.

'Come on Suze,' she encouraged herself. 'Get your act together. Self-pity won't help you. Pull yourself together.'

She fished her mobile charger out of a kitchen drawer and plugged it into her dead phone.

As she made herself a cup of tea, the phone bleeped several times as messages came into the now charging phone.

'Who's been sending me messages?' she wondered.

With her mug of tea in hand, she collapsed into an armchair and casually looked at her phone. She could see that she had received several messages.

She listened to the messages, one of them was a voicemail from her mother in Australia.

'Suzette, pick up the phone. (pause)... I don't know what you're up to but someone in England is trying to track you down. You'd better call them back.' She then gave a phone number that the caller had left.

Her mother sounded terse. 'If only she knew what is going on here, she'd have a field day undermining me,' Suzette thought. 'I wonder what this is all about. Perhaps they're going to deport me after all?'

Eventually she worked up enough courage to ring the number. Curious, but fearful about the reason that someone was trying to track her down, Suzette rang the number.

After a few rings, the call was answered. 'Hello, Family Reunite, Sarah speaking. How may I help?'

Expecting to be greeted by a terse officious response, Suzette was taken aback by the friendly greeting.

'Hi...umm...I've...I've been given this number to call. Who did you say you were?

'Family Reunite. We are a specialist global family tracing organisation.'

'Oh...I see.' Suzette puzzled. I believe you want to speak to me. Someone rang my folks in Australia, apparently they were looking for me?'

'Yes, that's quite likely. Could I ask your name, please?'

'Yes, it's Brown, Suzette Brown.'

'Just a second.'

In the background Suzette could hear the receptionist typing away on a keyboard.

'Ah yes, here we are. I will transfer you to one of our researchers. Hold the line please.'

'Ok, thanks.'

The line went dead as she was transferred to another phone. And then within a few moments it started ringing again. Immediately the call was answered.

'Good morning, Suzette, thanks for calling back. My name is Jacqueline, Jacqueline Ruberg.'

'How did you know it was me?' Suzette queried.

'Our telephone system is linked to our computer system and transfers data from the point of entry into our company to the nominated assistance point.'

'Oh, that's clever.'

'Yes, it is isn't it.? Now I understand that you are looking to find your birth parents, 'the researcher revealed.

'Yes, but how do you know that?' Suzette puzzled.

'Because you have registered part information on the national Adoption Contact Register.'

'Yes, that's correct,' Suzette confirmed. 'I couldn't fill in all the details because I didn't know my birth father's or birth mother's names. So how did you track me down?"

'We conducted a DNA check against yours and obtained a match with your father's DNA.

'My father's! But my DNA search company told me that they couldn't find a match when they did a global check,' Suzette puzzled. 'They only found my...my sister.'

'Yes, that's quite likely.'

'Oh why?'

'Because his DNA was not available to all search companies,' the researcher informed her.

'That's strange. Is there a reason for that sort of secrecy?'

'Yes. But rather than discuss it over the phone. Would it be possible for you to come to our office in London to talk in more depth?'

'Well, yes. I suppose so. But are you sure that it is really my father?'

'Yes. His DNA matched the parental signature with your own.'

'Wow. That's intriguing,' Suzette exclaimed excitedly. 'What about my mother?'

'No, sorry. No joy there.'

'At least we have my father's. Right now, I could do with some good news,' Suzette confessed.

'How is your diary fixed for the next week?' the researcher asked.

'Oh, it's pretty empty at the moment,' Suzette volunteered. 'The sooner the better please.'

'Ok lets' say next Tuesday 11 am,' the researcher suggested. 'I have your contact details from the Adoption Register, so I'll email you with the details on how to find us.'

'Thank you. This is brilliant news. I'm so excited. I can't wait,' Suzette gushed.

'I'm pleased that we are able to help. I look forward to meeting you.'

'Likewise, thank you. Oh, by the way. What's my... my father's name?'

'Sorry I can't tell you that information, until we do some security checks with you,' the other informed her.

'Oh! I guess that's OK.' Suzette said. 'Thank you, Jacqueline. Look forward to seeing you,' she said, hanging up. Her mood was now buoyant. 'Well, I'll be. Finding my real Dad! Perhaps my luck is going to change after all.'

CHAPTER SEVENTY-NINE

Ben couldn't settle, the whole court experience had made him very tense. The trauma of giving evidence and listening to the others, then waiting for the jury's verdict had taken a toll on his nerves.

The successful incarceration of his father for eight years should have been an end to his tension. However, seeing occasional glimpses of Suzette around town, reminded him that there was still the ordeal of the suspended inquest to undergo.

This constant reminder of the unfinished business surrounding Sue was 'getting to' Ben. He needed a break to help him unwind, so he headed out with Janie on their bikes into his comfort zone, in the hills and valleys of the Cotswolds.

The pair rode their mountain bikes over the undulating tracks that crisscross the beautiful Cotswold hills, diving into the steep sided valleys, taking air, bunny hopping their way over small obstacles en route. Losing themselves in the joy of mountain biking and challenging each other to undertake technical parts of the routes.

Following a gruelling half mile uphill 'slog,' the pair finally stopped for a rest.

Unclipping their shoes from the pedals and removing their helmets, they 'dropped' their bikes and sat on the smooth trunk of a 'harvested' ash tree.

'My god, you really worked me today Ben. I've never seen you so fired up. Not even when you were in a race.' Janie panted, wiping the sweat from her face. 'I had difficulty keeping up with you,'

'I needed that. To be honest, I was shitting myself giving that evidence in court. I know I've been to court before, but this was different. It was me against…him,' Ben confessed. 'Mum warned me against looking to find out who my Dad was, but like a fool I ignored her. I knew best. Huh! What a pig-headed fool I was. I wish I'd never laid eyes on him,' Ben said, filling up.

Janie put an arm around his shoulders. 'It was something that you needed to do though Ben. I could see that the uncertainty was 'eating you' up. You weren't to know how it would turn out. He could have been the best Dad ever.'

'But he wasn't, was he? He turned out to be a horrible human being. He didn't care about me. He didn't love me. He was, is, a selfish…a selfish bastard.' Ben choked at his realisation of his father's character.

'But it's over now,' Janie coaxed. 'So, forget it. It's water under the bridge.'

'No, it's not. If he behaves himself, he'll be out in four years and what happens then?'

'He's got a restraining order not to approach you or your mother,' Janie reminded him.

'Yeah, if he sticks to it… You know what really pisses me off though?'

'What?'

'He didn't even thank me for saving his life and doing first aid on his arm,' Ben said, now lost in his own trough of self-pity.

'At least you know that you haven't been missing out on anything. Not knowing who he was, didn't uncover any hidden benefits did it?' Janie queried. 'He's too self-centred to have done anything for you, anyway.'

'Well yes, I suppose that I found my father. But I wasn't expecting that demon.'

'Sshh, let it go Ben. It's over,' she cooed, kissing his cheek.

'No, it's not. The trial is, but there's the dreaded inquest to come. And I could be facing murder charges.'

'Now stop it. No, you're not. You're exaggerating. You're not facing a murder charge. It was her accident that killed her,' Janie reminded him. 'She killed herself.'

'Even Andy doesn't believe me,' Ben moaned, dolefully.

'Yes, he does. He knows you. He knows that you would have been trying everything to help her. Don't be so pessimistic.'

'It was all over so quick,' Ben reflected. I keep running it over and over in my head.

I keep wondering whether I did help her or did I just imagine it. You know, I'm not sure that I did help her. I'm beginning to doubt it myself.'

'I'm sure you did,' Janie reassured him.

'It happened so fast. One minute she was shouting obscenities at me and the next minute...the car disappeared into the blackness of the quarry and then blew up! I have nightmares about it. Her screaming voice... it was horrible. I saw her die.' Ben said dramatically.

'Oh, my poor Ben,' Janie said hugging him.

'I've never seen a person die before. I was numb. I didn't know how I should feel. Does that make sense? Does that make me callous?' Ben pondered.

'No not at all. I can only imagine how awful it was. I know that you would have done your best to save her,' Janie reassured him. 'I know that. I shouldn't say it, but I'm glad that she isn't around to harm you anymore.'

'Me too.'

'Enough of talking about horrible things. Let me cheer you up,' Janie said, planting her lips on his, and hugging him.

CHAPTER EIGHTY

'Suzette was beside herself with excitement. Butterflies filled her stomach as she alighted from the GWR train at the busy Paddington Station.

Although she had seen it from several thousand feet, as the plane circled waiting to land, she had never been to the capital before.

Her arrival in the UK had consisted of landing at Heathrow and then a trip in a Police car to Gloucester.

A lively buzz filled her ears, as the platform announcements mixed with the hubbub of chatting passengers. The hullabaloo was punctuated by intermittent guards whistles as another train was cleared for departure and clanked its way out of the station complex.

She was excited, eager to discover more about her roots, her family and especially her birth father. The period of time since she had made the initial call to the family reunite researcher and the appointment day had seemed to drag.

Carried along by the crowd of people leaving the platform, she joined the human tide cascading from the train station and down the concrete steps to the underground trains.

'Right. Now I need to get to Blackfriars station.' she said to herself, excited by the prospect of her first trip on the 'tube.' How do I get there?'

She stopped by a large underground route map and tracing the multicoloured spaghetti lines with her finger, she studied her route.

'Oh yes that's it. First, I want the Bakerloo line and then the District Line. So that's the brown and then the green lines then. Oh, this is exciting,' she thought.

'Take the Bakerloo tube from Paddington to Embankment station. And then, take the District tube from Embankment station to Blackfriars station. Right, here we go.'

She followed the direction signs through the labyrinth of tunnels and arrived on a platform just as a train was arriving.

As the doors slid open, an avalanche of commuters flowed off the train. Patiently she waited for the tide to stop and then she was unceremoniously pushed into the carriage by the crush of other passengers behind her.

'I hope this is the right train going in the right direction,' she thought. There were no empty seats, so she had to stand. She grabbed a handle to steady herself for the journey. Within a few minutes the tube train pulled out and quickly gathered speed.

Hanging on for grim death she smiled to herself. Not exactly how she had imagined her first trip on a tube train. But happy to be the filling in the sandwich of other commuters as the train raced underneath the streets of London.

Beaming widely with excitement at this new adventure, she looked at the other passengers, whose dead eyes refused to meet her own smiling eyes.

Listening to the train announcements and referring to the high-level tube map in the carriage, she was pleased to see that she was going in the right direction.

She eventually got off at Embankment station and followed the signs to pick up the District tube line to Blackfriars station. Within a few moments of arriving on the platform, the tube whooshed its way into the station and the exodus of passengers leaving the train was replaced by the hordes waiting to climb on board.

Suzette was quicker this time and managed to get a seat.

As the tube 'hummed' its way along the tunnels, Suzette was checking and rechecking the names of the stations against the map and was pleased to see that she was going the right way.

Counting down the stations, eventually, the tube arrived at Blackfriars, and Suzette joined a small group of other passengers disgorging from the carriage.

She followed the exit signs and found her way out onto the street. Puzzled at first, she consulted the app on her phone and followed it's directions to Queen Victoria street near Blackfriars bridge.

She had previously 'googled' the area and learnt that it was named after the Black Friars or Dominican monks. They were so called because they wore long black mantles over their white robes.

Another bit of trivia caught her eye on the screen was that the Blackfriars bridge, spanning the majestic river Thames, was opened in 1869. 'I might be able to use that in a quiz sometime,' she thought.

She was pleased to see that Google had got the office location right, it was near a statue of Queen Victoria regally staring along the Thames embankment.

CHAPTER EIGHTY-ONE

After ascending the steps from the underground station and arriving at street level, Suzette quickly found the multistorey building that she was looking for.

On the pillars outside the building entrance, there were several polished brass plaques. An indication that multiple firms used the building.

Suzette was pleased to see the name of 'Family Reunite' amongst them.

Taking a deep breath, to calm the butterflies, she went through the revolving door and strode up to the reception desk.

A smart, blazer coated grey haired man looked up as she approached the desk. 'Retired Policeman, probably,' she thought.

'Yes Miss, can I help?'

'I hope so, I've come to see Jacqueline Ruberg from Family Reunite. She is expecting me.' Suzette informed him.

'Certainly. If you'd like to sign in here,' he said, pushing an opened visitor's register and a pen to her. 'I will call Jacqueline for you,' he added, looking in a small directory.

Suzette had just completed printing her name in the register as Jacqueline answered the receptionist's telephone call.

He looked at the visitors register for confirmation of her name, and announced, 'Suzette Brown is in reception for you.'

'She will be down in a minute; he advised and gave Suzette a security badge attached to a lanyard.

'Please wear this at all times when you are in the building and return it to me when you leave,' he advised.

Suzette put the security badge around her neck, feeling like a VIP.

As she did so, the lift doors opened, and Jacqueline stepped out walking directly towards Suzette. The smartly dressed young woman was smiling and extended her hand as she approached.

'Hello Suzette. Thank you for coming. I see that Bill has got you all tagged up with your security pass. I just need to sign you in and then I'm responsible for you while you're here.'

Jacqueline put down the small briefcase that she was carrying and quickly scribbled her signature against Suzette's entry in the book.

'How was your journey?' the researcher asked.

'Oh, it was OK. Thankfully, no delays and I managed the underground successfully too,' Suzette volunteered.

'Good. Please come this way to our meeting room. Would you like a drink?'

'Oh yes please. I could murder a coffee.'

'If you need the bathroom, it's through that door there,' Jacqueline said, indicating a varnished door with a shiny chrome handle.

'No, I'm fine thanks,' Suzette said, following her.

'What coffee would you like?'

'Cappuccino, please.'

'How do you take it?'

'With one sugar please.'

'This is alright,' Suzette thought, feeling at ease. 'I wonder why all the secrecy?'

Jacqueline duly got their drinks from the free vending machine and gave Suzette hers.

The pair went into a small, well-furnished meeting room.

'Please take a seat,' the researcher invited, closing the door. 'I expect that you are wondering what this secrecy is all about aren't you?'

'Well, yes I am,' Suzette confirmed. 'Hopefully, at last my search for my family is finally over.'

'I think you will be happy with what I have to tell you,' Jacqueline said, opening her small briefcase and removing a folder.

'This is exciting,' Suzette said, barely able to contain herself.

'OK, Let me first tell you why your DNA firm were unable to find your father's match,' the tracer explained.

'Please.'

'Your father was a member of the aristocracy,' Jacqueline revealed.

'An aristocrat! Wow! An aristocrat,' Suzette squealed. She felt lightheaded at this revelation. 'Hang on just one moment. That doesn't sound like good news. You said, was! What do mean, was? Do you mean he is no longer an aristocrat, or ....' Suzette puzzled.

'All in good time. Bear with me. Let me explain a bit more. Your father came from a monied family. Unfortunately, he was forced into an 'arranged' marriage.'

'An arranged marriage! I thought that was outdated?' Suzette observed.

'No, I'm afraid it's not. Not in some…. Shall we say certain aristocratic families.'

'Certain aristocratic families! Intriguing. Who exactly?' Suzette pondered. Hoping that it wasn't going to be more unwelcome news.

'I can't tell you. It's…very…delicate, I'm afraid.'

'OK. Secret. I understand,' Suzette accepted, but really wanted to know.

'Apparently, his wife wasn't enthralled by having to marry him, either. And shall we say, there was never any chance of having a family.'

'You mean she was frigid?'

'Yes. For whatever the reason, she refused to have any intimate relations with him. That caused great consternation in the family. The possibility that an ancient blood line might come to an end because of her non-consummation, was a major issue in the family.'

'I bet.'

'But, coming from a big family himself, your father loved the idea of being a dad. And as often happens in situations where there is non-consummation. He became sexually frustrated and strayed.'

'Strayed?' Suzette repeated.

'Yes, he…he put himself around. Discreetly of course. But unfortunately for the family, he lost his heart to a young woman, a teenager.'

'A teenager! Oh dear. How old was he?'

At the time he was 24. Jacqueline revealed.

'What a scandal.' Suzette exclaimed, feeling uncomfortable with the revelation that her father was a 'cradle snatcher.'

'He had a long running, illicit, relationship with this young woman. Unfortunately, they became reckless in their passion, and she became pregnant.'

'Ooops, that was careless,' Suzette agreed.

'Yes. Sadly, before your father knew of the pregnancy the girl's family sent her away to have the baby.

Your father was heartbroken at losing her. And what's more, he didn't know that he was going to be a Dad until it was too late. So, he couldn't do the 'honourable' thing, divorce his wife, and marry her.'

'Pity. Things could have been so different,' Suzette thought.

'That woman was obviously your mother,' the researcher clarified.

'Oh my god! My mother was someone's mistress,' Suzette suddenly realised.

'The baby actually turned out to be not one but two. Twins, identical twins. Sadly, as soon as you were born, the family took you away from her and you were put up for adoption at an orphanage and all trace of the pair of you disappeared.'

'Oh my god. An orphanage!' Suzette exclaimed, filling up.

'In the early days, orphanages maintained a high level of secrecy about the parents of unwanted babies.

'How awful.'

Although, it's different these days.' Jacqueline explained.'

'Yes, I gather there is legislation to allow children to track down parents,' Suzette observed.

'Yes, that's right. However, when he finally met his young lover again and discovered the reason for her absence, he was devastated to learn about her pregnancy and their babies.'

'Didn't she pine for them?'

'Only briefly, because they were removed within hours of their birth, she didn't have time to establish a maternal bond with them,' the researcher added.

'What happened to their relationship?' Suzette asked.

'Her parents forbad her to see him again and they went to live in America.

'Oh, how sad.'

'Yes, it was. Obviously, he was heartbroken. But forced into the family business, he was unable to find time to track her down.'

'How sad. Poor Dad.'

'Quite recently, as a result of DNA developments, he employed heritage researchers to try and track down the pair of you, his lost family. They used all means available to them, including the new method of DNA matching.

Eventually he discovered that his babies were twins. Two girls, and their DNA were identical.

One had been brought up in England and one had been taken to Australia.'

'My real father was looking for us,' Suzette was overjoyed. 'That was my sister Sue here in the UK and me, in Australia,' Suzette added.

'Yes, that's correct,' Jacqueline confirmed, looking at her file.

'What was my father's name?'

'It was the honourable Lucien Clarkson.'

'So, I am a Clarkson?'

'Yes,'

'I like that name better than Brown, Suzette concluded. 'And my Mother's name?

'We were only able to uncover her Christian name. It was Sophie.'

'Lucien and Sophie. Very sophisticated,' Suzette thought.

'Unfortunately, before he could get to contact you, I'm sorry to tell you that he died when the helicopter he was piloting crashed, killing all on board.' Jacqueline explained compassionately.

Suzette's world fell apart again. Her hopes of being united with her parents were dashed.

'Not again, when am I ever going to get some good luck,' she sobbed.

'I'm sorry to be the bearer of sad news. Do you want a minute before I continue?' she asked sympathetically.

'No, no, it's OK. I'll be alright in a minute. Please continue.'

'He was never able to trace your mother, though, in spite of conducting DNA searches.'

'Unless she was doing a search of her own. Of course, it wouldn't be available. Oh, that's so sad.' Suzette reflected. 'So near, yet so far.'

'But we couldn't find any trace of her either,' Jacqueline explained.

'So, to all intents and purposes I'm an orphan,' Suzette concluded, resignedly.

'Yes. Most likely. Sorry,' the researcher said.

'So why bring me all the way to London to tell me the unwelcome news? You could have done it over the phone, surely,' Suzette said dejectedly.

'I'm sorry if we raised your hopes about finding your family,' Jacqueline apologised.

'It's ok,' Suzette said despondently. 'It is what it is. I am used to having shocking news. My mother was a teenage mistress, and my father was a cradle snatcher and is dead.'

CHAPTER EIGHTY-TWO

'However, amidst all the sadness, I do have some positive news, which is why I called you here.'

'I certainly could do with some,' Suzette said, dabbing her eyes.

'Your father was obsessed with the hope that you two girls might reappear one day, and he wanted to make up for his absent parenting, so he left money for you both in his will.'

'You mean...we...?' Suzette stuttered. 'We have a legacy?'

'Yes. After the sadness of not being able to see him, your day is about to get a lot brighter.'

'Really?'

'He left you both five hundred thousand pounds.'

Suzette couldn't believe her ears. 'Half a million pounds!' she said in shock. 'Half a million pounds!'

'Correct. But before we are able to authorise payment, we would like to do a DNA test to confirm that you are truly his daughter. Which we can do today.'

'No problem,' Suzette beamed.

'Do you have any contact with your sister, so that we can tell her the good news too?'

'My sister is...she...is...unfortunately dead. I came over from Aus. to see her but sadly, she was killed in a car crash the day before I got here.'

'Oh dear, I'm dreadfully sorry. Er...sorry for your loss. Well... in that case...sorry to sound callous. If you can provide a death certificate, we will be able to transfer her share to you.'

'Really?'

'Yes,' Jacqueline confirmed. 'It's in his will.'

'If only Sue had known about the legacy,' Suzette thought. 'She wouldn't have been so desperate to get her hands on half of her ex-husbands money.

Before she left the building Jacqueline arranged for a specialist nurse to take a blood sample from Suzette to confirm the DNA match with that of her father.

After the pleasantries, Suzette travelled back home on cloud nine. 'Now I know who I am. A Clarkson. And within a few days, I'm a millionaire too,' she smiled to herself. 'A millionaire. Wow.! Now I can get the best experts to find out the truth behind Sue's death.

CHAPTER EIGHTY-THREE

After the regular Scout meeting at Foster Lodge, Andy and Ben were restocking the new cupboards with crockery and cutlery.

'The decorators have done a good job to remove all the signs of the shotgun damage after that evil woman tried to kill us,' Andy said, admiring the décor following the complete kitchen refurbishment.

'She must have been gutted that she didn't get us though,' Ben smiled.

'Yes, she must have,' Andy concurred. 'But it wasn't from lack of trying though.'

'No, you're right there,' Ben agreed.

'I shall be glad when we've done this so that we can draw a veil over it though. Andy observed.

'What do you think that we need to do to prepare for the inquest?' Ben asked. 'I'm scared. I mean. What do I say?'

'Just tell them the truth. You'll be fine,' Andy advised. 'No need to get uptight about it. The coroner is a good bloke and...well, we'll see.'

'I hear that they have reconvened the inquest because there has been more in-depth investigations,' Ben added, nervously. 'Is that good or bad?'

'If it proves that we didn't do anything to cause her death then...'

'You mean ME. NOT WE,' Ben corrected. 'YOU weren't there when the car went over were you? I'M the one on trial,' Ben said dramatically.

'No Ben. Nobody is on trial. It's an inquest. Not a court of law.'

'Yes, but it could go that way, couldn't it? Which is why the coroner adjourned it in the first place. Wasn't it? To assess if there was an unlawful killing.'

'Perhaps, you're right.' Andy paused and looked at Ben. 'But there's something else on your mind though isn't there?' he probed.

'No...no...not really,' Ben replied hesitantly.

'Ben, I've known you long enough now and I know when you're lying. What is it? '

'No, really there's nothing.'

'Come on what is it?' Andy persisted. 'We don't hide secrets from each other.'

'Well...it's just...it's just that...you...you didn't believe me when I said that I didn't push her into the quarry. Did you?' Ben accused.

'Of course I did. I don't know what to say. I'm terribly sorry If I gave you that impression. Of course I believed you,' Andy insisted, perplexed that his young friend should make the accusation. 'What gave you that impression?'

'Well, after the crash, when you came back with the tow rope...you asked me...had I pushed...pushed her over.' Ben's mouth was dry as he tried to make his point to his mentor.

'And you said no, and I believed you,' Andy reminded him.

'Yeah, but why did you ask me that in the first place?'

'I…I don't know. I suppose because she had done so many horrible things to you, including turning your father against you that…it would be understandable if you did.'

'See that's what I mean. You think I could do that because of my background,' Ben suggested. irritably.

'No Ben, you are over thinking this. It was nothing of the sort. Remember I am more responsible for her death than you are.'

'Now the truth comes out. Responsible for her death! See you are accusing ME.'

'Yes, No. What I mean is. If I hadn't pursued her through those country lanes, she might not have lost control of her car and…died in that horrific way.'

'But you are saying that I was responsible too. I keep on telling you. Why don't you believe me? I didn't push her over. The car went over by itself. She moved in the car and stretched her hand out and…' Ben suddenly had a flashback of the moment…He shook his head to banish the mental image. 'No, I don't want to remember,' he thought.

Ben angrily pushed past Andy and got on his bike. 'I didn't Andy. I didn't push that woman to her death,' he shouted emotionally as he rode off.

Despite Andy's denial to Ben, he too was feeling the pressure. If they were being accused of murder and the coroners verdict went against them, they could end up in prison, accused of unlawful killing. The outcome was uncertain. A smart lawyer could swing things against them, he thought.

CHAPTER EIGHTY-FOUR

Andy checked his watch again.

'Come on Ben, you're going to be late,' he muttered under his breath.

Beth and JC came from the carpark alone and walked over to Andy who was stood by the main entry to the coroners court.

'Where's Ben?' Andy asked, concerned. 'We're going to have to go in shortly.'

'I couldn't persuade him to come out. He's sat in the car,' Beth informed him.

'We don't know if the coroner will still want us to answer any questions, but as we were the only witnesses to her death, I guess we might,' Andy explained.

'Yes, that's' what I told him,' JC pointed out.

'OK I'll go and see if I can persuade him,' Andy said, leaving the pair and ran round to the carpark. He spotted JC's car and went over to it. Ben was sat in the back looking frightened and gazing at his feet.

Andy tried the passenger door, it was locked. He tapped on the window and Ben looked up.

'Ben come on; we've got to be in the court in five minutes.'

'I'm not coming in,' Ben said and looked away.

'The coroner needs us to be there. He can get the Police to drag you in if necessary.'

'I don't care. Either way they are going to put me in prison, so it doesn't matter,' Ben said pessimistically.

'Come on, it's not going to be like that. This fresh evidence might be to our benefit.'

'No, I'm not coming in,' Ben said resolutely.

'OK well there's no point both of us being in contempt, so I'm going in. Cheerio.'

'Goodbye,' Ben whispered, self-consciously.

Andy turned on his heel and jogged back to where Beth and JC were still waiting.

'He's not coming as you say. Well hopefully the coroner won't call for him otherwise he's in stook.' Andy revealed.

The three went into the court room and sat down. But, within a minute the Coroner's clerk asked everyone to stand.

The court stood as the coroner entered and took his seat.

'Please sit,' the coroner instructed.

'I am reopening the inquest to the death of Sue Williams-Screen following further investigations by the police and new forensic evidence provided by an expert witness.

We have an unusual situation where I am informed that an expert witness, Mrs Deborah Young, has been employed by an unknown person and wishes to provide evidence to the court.

The reason for this unprecedented situation in fast tracking the resumption of the inquest is that Mrs Young is emigrating to Turkey. And as an independent expert she has no colleagues to present the forensic information to the court. I am therefore mindful to allow all opportunities to find the underlying cause of this death as soon as possible.'

'Mrs Young, please take the oath.'

While the forensic expert made her way to the witness box, a door on the opposite side of the court from Andy opened and Ben came in, holding Janie's hand.

The Coroner turned at the sound. 'I don't usually allow latecomers into my court. But if you take a seat quickly, you may remain,' the Coroner instructed.

'Thank you,' the pair replied and quickly sat in the nearest bench seat. Unfortunately, they were seated next to Suzette. Ben tensed up at seeing her and was about to get up, but Janie stopped him after seeing the Coroners disapproving look.

'No Ben. We have to sit here now,' she whispered.

Andy gave Ben a 'thumbs up,' which Ben didn't acknowledge.

Deborah duly took her place in the witness box and took the oath.

'Mrs Young you are an expert witness in what field?' the coroner asked.

'Vehicle collisions involving fire,' she replied.

'Please tell the court of your findings.'

'I need to explain that I was not involved in the case immediately following the accident. Identification of the body by DNA profiling had already been completed. I had to rely on some of my forensic evidence saved by scenes of crime officers from the local Police force, who may I say, did an excellent job of capturing the minutia of the accident scene.'

'Thank you for your professional assessment, I will pass your comments on to the Chief Constable.'

'Fortunately, the wreck of the car had been stored in a warehouse and guarded from cross contamination.

On examination of the burnt out MX5 hardtop. I was able to identify significant crease marks on the underside of the car's chassis indicating that it was balanced mid-point over an edge of some kind. The indentations on the cliff edge confirm this is the likely area where it had pivoted.

In a laboratory environment the metal used for the chassis structure was put in a test model. This simulated the various loads that would occur with the car balancing on the edge of the cliff. The coefficient of bending of the metal took three point two minutes to bend at the same angle as seen in the wrecked car.

This means that after the car crashed over the edge, it would remain balanced for approximately three minutes before the bending of the chassis would alter the centre of gravity to the rear and cause it to slip over the edge.'

'So, I was able to mathematically analyse the incident. Based on a calculation of timing between the crash and one minute arrival time at the crash scene by Mr Spider and Mr Bird.

In my mathematical modelling of the incident, I allowed for the circumstances and environment of when the accident happened.'

'Please explain,' the coroner asked.

'It was at night and deep in the countryside. There were no streetlights or light pollution to illuminate the site. The only light available at the scene was from moonlight, fortunately it was a clear night, and there was a small head torch and some illumination from Mr Spider's cars headlights.'

'And your conclusion?' the coroner probed.

'Clearly this would have made the timing of any rescue attempt to be very challenging, to say the least.'

'Have you any details that you can share with us?'

'Yes. In preparation for the inquest, I conducted an onsite simulation of someone exiting from a car similar to Mr Spiders and running to where the MX5 had been suspended. It was timed at thirty seconds.

So, let's do the maths. Three point two minutes before the car plunges into the quarry. Take off one minute for Mr Spider to arrive on scene; thirty seconds to get from the car to the balanced car site. That means that there were only ninety seconds to extract the woman from the damaged car before it went into its death knell,' the expert explained.

'So, you are saying that there were only ninety seconds for the rescuers to help the trapped driver before the car went over?'

'Yes, that's my conclusion.'

'Well, I think that timescale would challenge even the fire and rescue service, who are used to acting quickly in this situation,' the coroner observed. 'Let alone some shocked civilians.'

Ben picked up on the positivity of the coroners summation. His tension eased slightly.

'The witnesses report that the driver was conscious and in the driving seat,' Deborah explained. 'But the driver's door was severely damaged and jammed shut. So, rescue was only possible by the passenger door, the glass of which was shattered,' the expert explained.

'Rip marks in the wall of the front offside tyre contained traces of metal found in the barbed wire fence. A destroyed barbed wire fence was found at the edge of the field where the car is judged to have gone over. It is conceivable that the car could also have been temporarily restrained by the barbed wire.'

Andy recalled teasing Sue about releasing the barbed wire when he approached the stranded car. 'This woman's good,' he thought.

The expert continued. 'Tyre marks on the wall of the quarry and scrape marks caused by the exhaust pipe and silencer indicated that the car went down boot first. This is unusual in that the majority of the weight of the car is in the engine block, under the bonnet at the front. One would expect it to have flipped over and gone down nose first. This was not the case. It went down boot first.

The reason for this and the subsequent severe fire, was caused by a large quantity of petrol stored in the boot of the car in five large petrol cans.

'So, it sounds like she was planning to do more arson then,' Ben thought. He shuddered at the recollection of rescuing his father through the smoke logged barn and coughed involuntarily.

'The modelling shows that although there was a theoretical ninety seconds for the rescue, any movement inside the car would unbalance it and send it in to the quarry prior to that time. But, likewise, it could also have been delayed by the barbed wire entanglement,' the expert enlarged.

'So, you're saying that your ninety seconds has a plus or minus tolerance?' the coroner suggested.

'Yes, I can't be sure of the exact time in milliseconds, but I am confident that it was a truly abbreviated time to conduct a rescue,' Deborah clarified.

'I have a feeling of the urgency of the situation, which is helpful,' the coroner added.

'The police conducted a check on Mr Spider's car at the time of the accident. And there was no damage that would indicate external forces were used against the bodywork of the stricken car.'

Andy felt relief that her statement officially supported his claim that he hadn't hit her car. The forensic expert's findings disproved the suggestion of him nudging Sue's car over the cliff.

'Obviously, during a car crash massive damage can be caused to the car and occupants,' the expert continued. 'The impact of plastic and fibre's crashing together cause it to melt and fuse together, resulting in fibre and fusion marks. These marks are left on the car and on clothing.

The fusion marks are formed at 'point of collision,' and it is a highly significant indicator of positions of individuals in the car.

I was able to find fibre fusion marks in the passenger seat. Indicating that the driver was in the passenger seat when the car crashed at the bottom of the quarry.'

This confirmed Ben's story that he was helping her from the passenger side. Although she had a broken leg, she had at his insistence, unbuckled her seat belt, and slid over to the passenger side where he was. Unfortunately, in so doing she unbalanced the car, and it went over.

'The victim's body was not completely burnt. I was able to do forensic analysis on parts of it. Mr Bird's DNA was found on the decease's hand that survived the inferno. This was detached from the body and found several weeks later by a quarry worker.'

Suzette cringed at the image that the expert's explanation created.

'The contact patch of his DNA was found in a pattern consistent with the format of hand holding.'

'But surely DNA is invisible to the naked eye,' the coroner interjected.

'Yes, but it depends on what it is contained in. It could be blood, semen, phlegm, sweat. For this case I built up a mosaic from wipes around the flesh of the hand and was able to identify a shape similar to a hand grip.'

'So, I did reach her hand after all,' Ben was pleased to hear. And it did prove that he had not only reached her hand, as he thought, but that he had grabbed and held it.

'I further examined the images of the body shape indentation in the grass on the edge of the quarry. It confirms that a person of five foot five was lying down by the side of where the car was suspended. Earth scrapings from the toes of Mr Bird's trainers, taken at the time, are the same as that taken from the foot of the grass indentation.'

'And the implications of that?' the coroner asked.

'This indicates that Mr Bird was laying down on the edge of the quarry.'

'Which is what I told them,' Ben whispered, happy that she had again confirmed his evidence.

'That is the sum of my findings,' the forensic expert said, as she closed her file.

'Thank you for your comprehensive report, the coroner said, 'Are there any questions before I release Ms Young?' The coroner looked around. No? In that case I will allow her to stand down.'

Deborah took a seat in the court to listen to the Coroner's summing up.

'The forensic evidence appears to clear Ben Bird and Andy Spider from being the authors of Sue Williams-Screens demise,' the coroner concluded. 'Clearly the evidence of helping the deceased by grasping her hand provided by the DNA is a significant factor in collaborating Ben Birds' evidence.

'I will inform the Police of this vital evidence and confirm that I am satisfied that Mrs Sue Williams-Screen died as a result of a traffic accident. There are no suspicious circumstances that would indicate any malevolent actions. Case is closed.'

'Please stand,' the clerk said as the coroner left the court.

CHAPTER EIGHTY-FIVE

Ben wept as the stored-up tension left his body. Janie put an arm round his shoulders and hugged him.

Suzette stood and waited for Janie and Ben to disconnect.

'Excuse me,' Suzette said. 'Ben, I owe you an apology. The evidence is clear. You did try to save my sister. Thank you, thank you very much.'

Ben looked at the floor, embarrassed at Suzette's gratitude, it was something that would have never come from Sue's mouth.

Seeing Suzette talking to Ben, Andy hurried over to ensure that there was no conflict between them. He needn't have worried because Suzette was gushing about Deborah Young's evidence.

'That expert witness was brilliant and very thorough, wasn't she? I would never even thought about the things that she assessed.

I thought the wrecked car was so severely burnt that they would be unable to prove anything from it,' Suzette admitted.

'Do we know anything about the expert witness?' Andy interjected. 'Do you know if the coroner paid for her services,' he wondered.

'No, he didn't. Actually, it was me. I did,' Suzette confessed. 'I wanted to get to the bottom of Sue's death and obtain the truth of this horrible accident.'

'It just confirmed what we told the police,' Andy added.

'Sorry, but irrespective that you were actually there at the time of her death, I think that we. You and I, got that truth unambiguously explained today.'

'It must have cost a fortune to commission that detailed investigation,' Andy observed. 'I know these experts don't come cheap.'

'Yes, but fortunately, I had some good luck recently,' Suzette said, smiling. 'Thank you again Ben for trying to save my sister.'

Suzette stepped forward and unexpectedly hugged Ben. Taken aback by her familiarity, he nevertheless returned the hug.

'Peace at last,' Andy thought, joining the huggle.

After a brief moment, Suzette broke away from the others.

'Goodbye,' she said as she walked away from the group.

'Well, what about that then,' Andy said, amazed at the turn of events.

Had they known how Suzette had been able to fund it, they would have seen the irony of the exercise. The expert witnesses costs were paid from what would have been part of Sue's legacy from her aristocratic father's will.

The other irony was that the science which allowed Suzette to find Sue in the first place was also the reason for Ben and Andy to be cleared of suspicion of causing her death. Sue had, in effect, paid to clear Ben and Andy of any suspicion.

Suzette hurried over to the forensic expert, who had been patiently waiting. 'Thank you so much. I feel happier now that the dreadful thought of her being murdered has gone. I am still sad of course, but relieved. You have given me some peace of mind from a depressing situation.'

'My pleasure it was a nice 'meaty' challenge to get my teeth into and provide evidence that has exonerated two people,' Deborah explained.

'Hope your move to Turkey goes well,' Suzette added.

'Thank you.'

As the pair left each other Suzette thought, 'While she goes to Turkey, I shall be returning to Australia. There's nothing to keep me here anymore. Perhaps I'll even buy some land and breed cattle.'

At that moment Chris Cooper came over to her.

'Hope that you are happy with the result?'

'Yes, but I'd prefer if it had brought my sister back.'

'Not if you'd known the evil bitch,' the policeman thought. 'Would you like to celebrate with a drink or two?' he asked.

'Well...I...I umm...yes. What the heck. Celebrate success,' Suzette smiled.

CHAPTER EIGHTY-SIX

'Come on Ben, get in the car. Janie ordered. 'JC has volunteered to drive.'

'Drive! Drive where?' Ben demanded.

'All will be revealed. Now come on. In you get.' JC ordered.

'No. I'm not interested in going anywhere. I need to sort my bike out,' Ben insisted.

'Ben, come on. I have a surprise for you,' Janie encouraged.

'Thanks, but I'm not interested in surprises.'

'Come on. You need to cheer up.'

'Cheer up! Cheer up! What's there to be happy about?' he ranted.

'You have come through two trials and won both of them.'

'Yeah, but how long before I'm accused of something else that I didn't do?'

'Come on Ben. Celebrate success,' JC urged. 'You could do with a bit of fresh air and change of scenery.'

Reluctantly, Ben got in the car, and they left the four-bedroom house. The journey into the countryside took half an hour with a sour faced Ben sitting next to Janie.

'Right, we're here,' Janie announced as JC drew the car to a halt.

'What's this place?' Ben asked, looking around at the collection of farm buildings.

'You'll find out in a minute,' Janie informed him, trying to contain her own excitement.

'It's a farm,' he added, studying their location.

'Ten out of ten for observations,' JC said, 'I'll stay in the car and wait for you.'

'What are you getting me involved with now?' Ben demanded suspiciously to Janie.

'You'll see in a minute,' Janie said, grabbing his hand.

The pair walked through the farmyard and Janie jabbed at a bell push on the door jamb.

After a few moments, the door opened to reveal a jolly red cheeked country woman.

'Hello. You must be the person that rang earlier?' she said to Janie.

'Yes. We've come to see the puppies,' Janie informed her.

'Puppies?' Ben said in alarm.

'Yes puppies. You need something to take your mind off things and we have bought you a puppy.' Janie revealed.

'What the hell did you do that for?' Ben protested.

'Because we love you,' Janie added, squeezing his hand.

'I'm not interested,' Ben said resolutely. 'I'm done with dogs. They only break your heart when they... when they go.'

'Oh! In that case you won't be having it then?' the farmer said, looking at Janie.

'Ignore him,' Janie said, 'he's a bit of a grump at the moment. He'll change his mind when he sees them.'

'Ok. If, you're sure? Cause I'm not going to sell you a dog that isn't going to be loved and looked after properly,' she said firmly.

'Yes, I'm sure. He used to have a dog. But sadly, it died.'

'Was murdered,' Ben interjected.

'Once he sees it, he will go all gooey and love the animal, I know what he's like,' Janie reassured the woman.

'Well let me take you to the bitch with her litter,' the woman said. 'He might change his mind and want to take all of them.'

'That would be great,' Janie agreed. 'Perhaps not though. his Mum would go mad.'

The pair followed the farmer through the yard into a former stable.

In the corner of the old building the cream-coloured Labrador mother was stretched out on a sheepskin rug. Her litter of six, four-week-old puppies were crowding each other as they suckled greedily at her teats.

'There you are,' said the farmer. 'How can you resist that sight. Aren't they lovely?'

Janie knelt down by the bitch and stroked her.

'Look Ben. See how loveable they are?' Janie cooed.

Ben stood still, reluctant to show any emotion.

'I'm not interested,' he forced himself to say. 'Let's go.'

'How can you resist them, look,' Janie said, softly stroking one of the puppies. 'They're adorable.'

Ben reluctantly gave way and knelt down next to Janie. Hesitantly, he put his hand out towards the litter to stroke one of the puppies, and as he did so one disengaged itself from its mother's teat. The puppy wobbled over to Ben's outstretched hand and licked it.

'Looks like that dog has selected you,' the farmer observed, smiling.

'Well, I suppose he is really cute,' Ben admitted half-heartedly. 'Can I pick him up?'

'Yes of course. His mother has a calm nature. So, as long as you don't do anything to make him squeal, she will be content just to watch you handling her baby,' the farmer informed him.

'You're perfect little one,' Ben said, cuddling the warm pup to his chest.

It was as if the dog understood what Ben had said and in response licked his face. A tear appeared on Ben's cheek as at last he let go of his bottled-up emotions.

Janie put her hand on his back as he broke down and sobbed.

'It's OK Ben. Just let it all out,' she said, gently stroking his back. 'Ben's had a bit of a rough time recently,' Janie explained to the surprised dog breeder. 'He'll be OK in a minute. I think when the pup is old enough, we will be taking him away.'

END

Also, by the Same Author

Godsons – Counting Sunsets

Godsons – Counting Sunsets is a heartening story, charting the stubbornness of the human spirit to let the precious gift of life slip away without a fight to the bitter end.

Multimillionaire Geoffery Foster has been diagnosed with terminal cancer and has irrationally swapped his luxurious Monaco penthouse for a single room in a Cotswolds hospice in Gloucestershire England.

Determined to maximise his remaining days and impressed by the selfless humanity shown by his hospice nurse, Andy Spider, Geoffery decides to redress his neglected Godfather responsibilities.

Together Andy and Geoffery embark on a journey to track down and improve the lot of Geoffery's three Godsons.

But will resolving the problems of childhood Meningitis amputee Tim, the alcoholic 'drop out' James and the abused husband Rupert, be too much for Geoffery's frail health.

Added to his challenges, a drunken and intimate wedding reception encounter with a former girlfriend comes back to haunt Geoffery as he also gambles with his life in the hands of a woman spurned.

Counting Sunsets becomes the abacus on which Geoffery records his remaining days.

Proving, '*It's never too late to be who you could have been,*' *George Elliot.*

The Godsons Legacy

Andy Spider continues to be the glue that cements the three Godsons together as they expectantly await the release of their legacy from Geoffery Foster's will.

But surely even this pillar of society will be distracted from his task when tempted by the radiant beauty of Nadine.

Mesmerised by the exotic Monaco nightlife, his stoic resolve is weakened by lack of sleep and too much alcohol.

The eclectic mix of pallbearers wearing basques, death, destruction and serious crime occur as a consequence of Geoffery's legacy.

Such was his hold on his Godsons that he still controls their lives from beyond the grave.

The story is set in Gloucestershire England, near the beautiful Cotswold Hills

The Godsons Inheritance

The three Godsons have to work harmoniously to place the final piece in the inheritance puzzle for the release of their legacy.

But the wayward Tim makes it a challenging exercise. His self-centred, bloody-minded arrogance means the whole intricate web of relationships is jeopardised. Will his heart bring him back in line or will he still be ruled by his head?

Meanwhile Rupert is continually in fear of his vicious megalomaniacal wife and James is clinging on to life desperate for a liver transplant.

Young army veteran Carrie is haunted by the trauma of active service.

Ben a young carer for his alcoholic Mother inadvertently opens up old wounds by looking for his father. Can fellow young carer Janie help or hinder Ben's traumatic life?

Andy is having a tough time in his personal life, haunted by a late-night indiscretion, and frustrated by having to coordinate the activities of the three Godsons.

The story comes to a dramatic and exciting conclusion but is it the end. In this the third book in the Godsons series?

Godsons – That Woman

It all started so well with the lovely Christening in the ancient church on the hill, but then things started going on a downward spiral.

Someone was spying on the christening party as they left the church.

Then it got worse. A disputed will has triggered kidnap, arson, and murder.

Who's behind the blood lust? Surely the chief suspect is dead.

Ben carrying a knife is strictly a no-no, so how does it become a life saver?

Can Nadine survive her nightmare visit to the UK challenging Geoffery Foster's will?

An overstretched police force is being led a merry dance as suspicions fall on 'THAT WOMAN'

Unexploded Love

A love triangle is already an explosive situation without the added complication of an unexploded bomb.

But the Luftwaffe's 1944 legacy of a large bomb exposes a burgeoning romance and throws together the three people in the love match.

Trapped in a collapsed hole with a ticking WW2 bomb for company, the love cheat's hope of escape is in the hands of the man he is cuckolding.

Will the frantic race against time succeed? Or will the husband take revenge?

The stark outcome can only be a blast from the past or UNEXPLODED LOVE?

Gurney Leafmould - The Pied Piper of Calamity

With great DIY aspirations, there is nothing Gurney Leafmould won't tackle – but intent and results are poles apart.

For 'Do it Yourself' means upheaval when Gurney is holding the tools
   This is a lively and humorous tale of DIY disasters created by Gurney, a hapless DIYer.

His calamitous CV includes house demolition, a car blaze and a farm inferno coupled together with failed car maintenance and hospital chaos. All neatly wrapped in EU red tape. Not to mention a very delicate DIY surgical transplant.
   Many wives and partners will recognise some of Gurney's 'attributes' in their own DIY champions.

Willing but incapable, he is a first-class prat to his Mother-in-Law but to his long-suffering wife, Gurney Leafmould is 'The Pied Piper of Calamity.'

Contains 'Adult Humour'

Gurney Leafmould - The Ministry of Disruption

Gurney Leafmould was a hapless DIYer but is now legally restrained by an ASBO preventing him from undertaking any more DIY projects.

Unable to pursue his real passion, he turns to Journalism and proves he is good at it.

However, his decision to become an investigative Journalist has disastrous consequences when he stumbles on to a state secret, an organisation called the Ministry Of Disruption (MOD).

By subsequently joining this 'clandestine organisation,' Gurney hopes to 'blow the whistle' on their activities and get a major news scoop.

He discovers that the MOD, which was created during WW2 as a guerrilla force to disrupt invading forces; is still active today and conducting disruptive training exercises.

So, if you've been held up in a traffic jam; been stuck at an airport, delayed on a rail journey, the cause of which you could never find out…then it's likely you have been an unwitting 'casualty' of a MOD exercise.

This is the second humorous Gurney Leafmould novel.

AFGHAN BOY – The Impossible Dream

Mohammed (14) has been orphaned in a suicide bombing and rescued from underneath the debris of his destroyed family home by a British Soldier and his search dog,

However, the Soldier, the only person that seems to care for him, leaves shortly after the rescue, at the end of his posting.

But undeterred the boy travels halfway around the world to find the soldier in the hope he would adopt him.

The journey is fraught with danger, and the boy confronts the many gruelling challenges, walking thousands of miles, often through sandstorms, braving armed gangs and in overloaded trucks, as well as a sinking dinghy, and the menacing refugee camp in Calais.

His many attempts to cross the channel are frustrated by the Border force.

Can he beat the odds of getting to the UK and then, if he does, of finding the soldier. Will being a Scout help him?

This is Mo's story, his 'IMPOSSIBLE DREAM'

Vigilante Nurse

Rebecca Roberts, former army medic is usually unflappable, whether on a Middle East battlefield or the lawless streets of her hometown.

That was until she became unwittingly complicit in the death of her fiancé, Tony.

Guilt ridden by his loss she left the army and joined the NHS on the 'frontline' as an A & E nurse.

Respected for her cool head under pressure Rebecca takes the law into her own hands when she discovers her colleague, Amber, is being brutalised by her policeman husband.

Frustrated by police inaction, she metes out her own punishment to the abuser.

But the punishment goes wrong, and Rebecca is pursued by an eagle-eyed Detective Constable determined to get justice for his partner.

Nevertheless, Rebecca is undaunted; the adrenaline junkie gets her next high tackling major crimes including the drug gangs.

Despite her tough exterior she has a tender spot for the young and vulnerable and eventually even allows some romance to return to her life.

Tackling sex, drugs and violence, Rebecca is THE Vigilante Nurse.

Eddy – The Lost Years

The story is set in 1980's Australia and based at a fictional mental health hospital, '*The Imagine Mental Health Institute*' located in Manly, New South Wales,

However, the origins of Eddy's fictional story go back to the recognised failings of the Australian Mental Health environment of the 1950's.

At the time, ten-year-old Eddy was going through significant personal traumatic issues.

During the 1970's and 80's a major study was undertaken for a significant overhaul of the Australian Mental Health service, and the Richmond report was published in 1983 to identify a way ahead.

The Richmond report clearly indicated the need for additional mental health resources, which triggered a demand for more psychiatrists to achieve its deinstitutionalisation aims and the use of Private hospitals to supplement demand.

Now in his thirties Eddy is locked into a regime from which he can't escape.

Milton Keynes UK
Ingram Content Group UK Ltd.
UKHW010606080923
428287UK00001B/5